Devil Dance

ISBN: 1506011314
ISBN-13: 978-1506011318

BOOKS IN THE JADE DEL CAMERON SERIES

MARK OF THE LION

STALKING IVORY

THE SERPENT'S DAUGHTER

THE LEOPARD'S PREY

TREASURE OF THE GOLDEN CHEETAH

THE CROCODILE'S LAST EMBRACE

ACKNOWLEDGMENTS

My thanks to James Arruda for help in researching Sam's plane; to my good friend, Sandi Ault, for urging me to publish this last Jade adventure and for all the time spent listening to me read sample text; and especially to my husband, Joe, for all his support – emotional and practical. *Asante sana* to my sister, Nancy Middendorf for the gorgeous original artwork gracing the book cover and for compiling the covers. Thanks also to all those readers who have urged, begged, pleaded and waited patiently for this book. Thanks to Wooly Bear for keeping her hairballs off the keyboard.

Kifo kina milango mingi

Death has many doors

CHAPTER 1: ZANZIBAR ISLAND, May 1921

Zanzibar! To Europeans, it represents a single spice island east of Tanganyika Territory. To the native residents, the word represents a cluster of islands and, that which we call Zanzibar, is known as Unguja. Zanzibar might have come from the Persian term "Zangh Bar" or the "Black-skinned Coast."

- - The Traveler

Jade grabbed her companion's arm and yanked her out of the street. "Mother, watch out!"

The running man wearing a dingy robe missed Inez del Cameron but succeeded in tipping over a shaky table loaded with colorful fabrics. A shower of red, blue, and gold spilled onto the street where Inez del Cameron had been standing. The fabric merchant, an Indian, shook his hands and shouted at the retreating figure.

"What are you doing? Jade, unhand me this instant," demanded Inez, pushing herself away from her daughter.

She nearly stepped on the merchant who'd squatted down behind her to pick up the spilled fabrics. Jade caught her mother just in time and whisked her clear.

"Oh dear," said Inez. "Look what you made me do. You

1

made me tip over this poor man's table."

"You didn't . . ."

"You caused this, Jade. Now help him pick up his merchandise this instant."

Jade complied with her mother's edict and knelt down across from the flustered and angry merchant. *Like talking to a stone wall.*

She tried again. "You didn't do this mother." She scooped up the nearest pieces of cloth. "The man that nearly ran over you did it. As fast as he was going, he must be halfway to the mainland by now."

"What? Are you saying that . . . ooh, that's lovely." She reached for one of the pieces in Jade's hands.

Inez Maria Isabella de Vincente del Cameron, or Doña Inez as she was known back on the family ranch near Cimarron, New Mexico, was still a beautiful and imposing woman at fifty. A few strands of gray graced her black hair, but her cerulean eyes were as piercing as ever and her olive complexion, flawless. If the years had done nothing to fade her beauty, thought Jade, they'd also done little to temper her commanding presence.

Jade gave the other pieces in her hands back to the merchant and stood up, brushing off her trouser knees. "I'm saying that I grabbed you because someone came tearing down the street like a hornet-stung rodeo bull was after him."

"Ask the man how much this costs, Jade."

"Mother, are you listening to me?"

"I don't speak Arabic or whatever this man speaks. Ask him how much it costs."

Jade took a deep breath to subdue any rebellious remarks that might pop out of her mouth. With the inhalation came the pervasive scent of cloves, a reminder that she was on a spice island. The scent permeated the buildings and air so that it remained even now after the heavy rainy season several months before this year's harvest would begin.

But there was another aroma, one that she'd detected earlier and passed off as someone's perfume, a sweetly musky scent.

It had faded as they walked on. Now it was stronger.

"Very well, Mother," she said. Jade tried Swahili first since she still lacked a confident fluency in Arabic. "*Bei ganee?*"

"*Mia sita* rupees."

"What?! Six-hundred . . ." Jade took the scarf from her mother's hands and thrust it into the merchant's.

"Is that a lot of money, Jade?" asked Inez? "I want to buy something for our housekeeper. Señora Flores loves red."

"It's robbery." She took her mother's elbow and pulled her along.

"*Mia* rupees," called the Indian, knocking the price to hundred.

"Keep walking, Mother."

"*Kumi* rupee."

Jade stopped and turned. "Kumi?" She reached into her pocket for some change and gave it to the merchant. "Here, Mother," she said, handing back the scarf.

"How much did you pay him? Perhaps I should have gotten a blue one instead."

"Ten rupees. And Esperanza will have to accept this color, Mother, because if you decided to exchange it, the price will probably go up another two-hundred rupees. If you want more, there are more shopkeepers." Jade nodded down the narrow street to the line of white-washed, two-story buildings.

Unlike the souks of Marrakech, most of these shops were larger than a walk-in pantry and the street itself was not roofed in rush and reeds, allowing more sunlight to penetrate. Like the souks, the streets were laid out in no particular pattern, winding and twisting with several dead ends. As she looked down the main Bazaar Street, she spied a crowd gathering farther down the marketplace, and wondered if the runaway man had caused further commotion.

"What else did you have on your shopping list, Mother?"

"Where is Main Street, Jade? I want to find the shop of Ranti de Silva and Brothers. We still need to buy some good, hand-made lace. Your wedding is next month and ..."

"And Beverly has already purchased a very tasteful dress for me, Mother, as a wedding gift. I don't need any blasted lace."

"A lady cannot have too much lace."

Jade glared at her mother. "You may buy all the lace you want for yourself or for Esperanza, but I would prefer you did not try to decorate my dress." She looked around the crowded marketplace, tentatively sniffing.

"Are you catching a cold, Jade?"

"No, Mother. I keep catching the scent of something musky. I thought perhaps there was a booth selling perfumes nearby."

Inez tested the air. "Civet oil. I nearly purchased some earlier today. Very intoxicating."

Jade spied a cluster of three Swahili women and slipped her Kodak from her shoulder bag. As she did, a solitary woman walked in front of the group, her chin raised in a defiant manner. The trio took notice and jabbered amongst themselves. Jade took two photographs of the encounter. It would make a great addition to her article on Zanzibar. The women wore vividly colored printed fabrics wrapped around their bodies with matching swaths turbaned over their heads and draping across their shoulders.

"What interesting costumes," said Inez. "Look, Jade, there's a table of them for sale. One of those would be lovely hanging across a wall or used as a canopy outside in the courtyard."

"These are kanga, Mother." Jade followed her mother to the table and watched as she picked up a green one with pineapples printed on it. The cluster of women noticed and giggled, poking each other with their elbows and pointing to Inez. Jade edged closer to eavesdrop on their conversation.

"Um, Mother. Perhaps not that one."

"Why not? The color is stunning, and I enjoy pineapples. Look, there's something written along the border." Inez struggled with the words. "U – kila na-na-si, tunda, ling-in-e basi. What does that mean Jade?"

The three Zanzibar women nearby erupted into giggles.

"It means, Once you taste pineapple you'll never go for any other fruit," answered Jade. "But I think it means more than that based on the reaction of those women, Mother. I think it's saying that once someone . . . a man . . . has had . . . *you* . . . then --"

"Oh dear," said Inez. She dropped the fabric and picked up another, this one decorated with mangos. The women erupted into peals of laughter again.

"I think you should avoid any with fruit on them, Mother. That one says that a ripe mango has to be eaten slowly. Again I --"

Inez held up her hand, palm out. "I believe I am getting the idea, Jade. Perhaps you should ask these ladies what *they* would recommend."

Jade turned and addressed the women in Swahili. They consulted amongst themselves for a moment and then one rummaged through the piles and extracted a golden kanga with grass and lions on it.

Jade thanked them. "I think you're safe with this one, Mother. I told them that you were very brave. This one says that you fear only the lion but not a man's sharp words."

"As long as it only means the man's sharp *words*, then," said Inez as she inspected the fabric.

"Mother!" said Jade.

Inez arched her brows. "What? Do you imagine that I don't know anything about men? I'm the one who is married. Now thank those ladies for me and then help me purchase this. I'll give it to your father." She fingered one with clusters of grapes on a pale purple background. "Perhaps I should get this one as well?" She looked at the cluster of women and winked. They exploded in grins and laughter again, nodding their approval.

Jade blushed. "I refuse to translate it for you." She negotiated the transaction and, taking her mother by the elbow, ushered her down the narrow street past shops dealing in mats, shoes, and assorted curiosities. They paused to view a set of small ivory carvings, and Jade again caught the soft musky scent. A few minutes later, they reached the agitated cluster of people where Jade had noted the earlier disturbance, and again she eavesdropped on the conversations. Snippets reached her:

witchcraft, murder, vengeance.

"What are they talking about, Jade?" demanded Inez.

"Nothing good. Wait here, Mother. Pick out something nice for yourself to wear to the wedding and get two more for Beverly and Madeline," she said as she left Inez by a man selling necklaces of coral beads. She bullied her way through the throng, ignoring Inez's demands to know where she was going.

The crowd didn't part easily. Mostly Zanzibari men with a few women of a servant class, they leaned into each other, chattering and pointing. Jade jabbed several out of her way with her elbow and a few others with some well-aimed kicks at their ankle. But for every two people she moved aside, one more filled the gap.

She tried Arabic, Swahili, and English to get her point across. "*Alma'derah. Samahani nipishe.* Excuse me. Pardon me. Get out of my way, blast it!" Bit by bit she made headway until she was at the center of the throng.

Lying on the ground surrounded by onlookers was the white-robed man that had nearly knocked down her mother. Jade pushed past the last of the people and knelt beside him, feeling at his neck for a pulse. There was none. She gently turned him over and put her ear to his open mouth, feeling and listening for the faintest of breaths.

"You waste your time, lady," said one of the nearby women in Swahili. "He is dead."

She couldn't see any blood not any outward signs of a wound. The man's gaunt face and emaciated frame spoke of deprivation. "What happened?" asked Jade in the same language.

"Witchcraft," the woman replied with a shrug of her shoulders. "Perhaps this man was intended to become a witch's servant in the spirit world and he ran away." She made a "*tsking*" sound and shook her head as though at something foolish. "One cannot run from it. If a witch wishes to kill or take you, he or she will. You should leave his body alone lest the witch become upset with you and choose you instead."

Witchcraft! Jade had encountered practitioners when she first came to Nairobi. But never had she heard it spoken of with so much fear as on Zanzibar Island. It was said to be even worse on the nearby island of Pemba. It sickened her.

"His heart probably quit because he ran too far and too fast," she replied. She looked around for someone in authority to take charge of the situation. She spotted a man in a brown sporting jacket and boater hat hanging about at the opposite fringe of the crowd.

"You, sir," she called out. "Can you help me?" But the man slipped behind a row of the locals Swahili and Indians. Jade stood on tiptoe, straining to see above some of the turbaned heads. He was nowhere to be seen. She didn't even spy a boater hat. Finally she saw an officer of the King's African Rifles and hailed him. He forced his way through the crowd much more efficiently than she'd done, using a slender baton to pry a path.

"This man was running through the streets just moments ago. I can't see where he was injured, but something should be done about him. He can't just remain here."

"Don't worry, he won't." The officer ran his gaze over Jade, seemingly amused by her trousers, and boots. "Are you perhaps an American cowgirl, miss?" he asked. "That is a most quaint costume."

"Yes, I'm an American. Now about this man: what do you intend to do?"

"Fret not, miss. I'll see that he's hauled off."

"But some of the people are claiming it's a vengeance killing. Shouldn't you--"

"Any supposed infractions that deal with the native population is under the Sultan's jurisdiction, Miss. I cannot investigate. But I shouldn't pay any attention to such jabbering if I were you. Locals are all ignorant. Now, you just run along and enjoy your visit." He *shooshed* Jade out of the way as one would a pesky child.

Jade rejoined her mother, feeling more than a little riled at having been cut off twice so far today.

"What was that all about?" asked Inez.

"Dead man," said Jade. "In point of fact, the same one that was running down the street earlier and nearly ran you down. I couldn't find any marks on him. He may have had a heart attack. He certainly ran like he was scared to death of something or someone, but the people around him are whispering about murder."

"Jade, when will you stop trying to involve yourself in affairs that are not your business? I'm certain that the local authorities will handle this."

She didn't reply. Instead, she tested the air again, the musky scent was stronger. "Come along, Mother."

"Why?" exclaimed Inez. "I thought we were getting some necklaces?"

Jade took her mother's elbow again and hustled her past several shops. "Later. I think we're being followed. I keep catching the same fragrance no matter where we go. It's unmistakable."

They trotted past two more shops before Jade pulled her mother into a narrow alleyway and waited near the mouth. She slid her boot knife from its sheath and held it at the ready.

The scent became stronger and Jade heard a soft footfall hasten towards them, then slow as it reached their hiding place.

A large, dusky-complexioned man in an immaculate white robe padded past her, slowing to look over the heads of the other people as though he was searching for someone. *For them.*

In a flash, Jade threw her left arm around the man's neck, her knife point at his throat.

"Why are you following us?"

CHAPTER 2

Another possible origin for the name Zanzibar is from the Arabic language. "Zayn Z'al Barr" can translate as "the fair land" or "the green land." There is truth in both origins.
- - The Traveler

Sam Featherstone stood on the dock of Kilindi Harbor, Mombasa, and hoisted the last of his future father-in-law's baggage onto the growing pile. "Are you certain that this is everything, . . . Richard?" Even though Jade's father had insisted that they be on a first name basis, Sam still felt uncomfortable with it. Add to that, her father was an imposing man. He and Sam were matched for height, but Richard del Cameron had a presence that went beyond the rancher's bronzed hands, ropey muscles and graying brown hair. His hazel eyes looked to be a spring of experience, spilling over with tales of adventure.

"That's all of *my* gear," Richard answered, "but there appear to be some other boxes missing."

"What? Safari equipment? I thought Jade told you that we had everything arranged here including rifles. It's all up in Nairobi waiting for us."

"No. Not safari equipment."

"What then?" Sam tried to curb his impatience. It was no way to start a man-to-man safari, an excursion dreamt up by Jade so that he and her father could get to know each other.

9

Sam had found himself actually looking forward to the trip. He knew that Jade's father was no city slicker. On the contrary, Richard del Cameron was a rugged man who had a history of exploring, including an attempt at eighteen to emulate his childhood hero, John Wesley Powell, and run a boat through the Grand Canyon. Long years of ranching on an old family estate kept the man fit, and now, in his late fifties, del Cameron was as strong and agile as a mustang stallion. Presently, this mustang was acting like he'd been boxed into a canyon.

Richard paced in circles, scanning the docks for his missing boxes.

"What are we looking for?" asked Sam

"Um, some boxes that your friend Lord Dunbury wanted. I was going to see to them, personally. Get them on the train."

"They probably got put on another boat. We'll look for them when we come back to pick up Jade and Inez. Did you see them get loaded onto your ship?"

"Actually, truth be told, they were put on an *earlier* ship that should have docked two days ago." Richard fingered his chin and resumed his pacing. "All I needed to do was sign for them and get them on the train."

Sam sat on one of the larger trunks and stretched his good leg in front of him. True, he didn't really know Jade's father, but somehow he didn't seem like a man that would get into this much of a lather over a few misplaced boxes. "What's so important about these crates, Richard? What's in them?"

The older man exhaled loudly and plopped down beside Sam. "I suppose I'd better just go and tell you. It's an airplane."

Sam's eyes opened wide. "An airplane?"

Richard nodded. "The parts to build one. It's a wedding present from us and Jade and, well, everyone else. Your friends, the Bert boys, are coming on the next boat to put it together. It was supposed to be a surprise."

"An airplane!" For a moment, he was a kid again at Christmas. He grabbed Richard by the shirt. "What kind? Is it big? How many seats?"

"I'm not going to tell you that, Sam. I have to keep *some* part of this as a surprise." He grinned. "I *think* it's a pretty damn big airplane, though."

Sam scrambled to his feet and tugged on Richard's shirt. "Well come on then. We've got to find those crates."

They went first to the Customs House, then to the Port and Marine Offices where everyone seemed more interested in some upcoming yacht club race. After several hours, they were no further along at finding their boxes until a sub-assistant who'd overheard their dilemma, pulled them aside.

"You know, sirs, there is more than one harbor here. Kilindi is the newest by far but the old Mombasa Harbor on the eastern side of the island is still used. Perhaps the boxes came in there? They're probably sitting at Mombasa Harbor waiting for you."

They thanked the man, slipped him a tip, and boarded a trolley across the island.

"Once we find the crates," said Richard, "you can't let on to anyone that you know about the airplane. Jade would have my head if she found out that I told you."

"I promise." He crossed his heart. "Where should we look first?"

After getting off the trolley, they tried several places and, after several dead ends, they finally located one of the smaller boxes containing the wheels and carburetor and one square crate holding a motor. Richard stopped Sam before he could see what kind, and Sam was left wondering if it was a Hispano, a Le Rhone, or an Ox-5.

"There has to be more than this," said Richard. "I don't understand. These were big crates." He extended his arms to the sides. "Had to be to hold wings, propellers, and fuselage."

"Something that big should stick out," agreed Sam. "I wonder why they aren't listed on any manifest. Do you think someone stole them?"

"If so, then whoever did it is missing some vital parts. Why leave the motor?"

"Beats the hell out of me," murmured Sam. He looked

11

around the nearly empty harbor. Just to the south loomed the old Portuguese fortress, Fort Jesus. The jaundiced building dominated the skyline, reminding Sam that he was out of his element here, an American with no real fluency in anything besides English. He turned around and spied two dock workers, coiling rope. "Hope they speak English," muttered Sam. "Jade's been trying to teach me Swahili but I'm pretty bad at it."

"Coins often speak louder than anything else," suggested Richard.

Sam hastened over to the men as quickly as he could, reaching into his trousers for a handful of coins. He let them jingle as he approached. "Excuse me," he said, exposing the coins in his half open hand. "I am looking for my crates." He extended his arms as wide as they'd go. "Big crates."

One man shrugged. "You try Kilindi?"

"Yes, we tried Kilindi. We tried here. We found those," he said pointing to the two crates they'd found. There are many more. Long crates. Big crates."

The man's partner strolled over to the two wooden boxes and studied them, noting the labels and a painted silhouette of an airplane in black on it.

"I see that sign," he said, pointing to the logo. Very strange automobile. Only two wheels. Hard to drive."

"Where?" asked Richard and Sam simultaneously. Sam offered half of the coins in hopes of improving the man's memory.

"I think they go Port Tudor. But not much business there. Fishing." He pointed north.

"Port Tudor?" asked Richard, hoping for more information.

By now the second man had joined them. Realizing that he was missing out on a chance to earn some money, he jumped into the conversation. His English was better.

"Port Tudor, yes. A few miles north. It is not one that big ships use. Mostly local men, some small merchants that trade with Zanzibar."

"It's worth a try, Sam," said Richard.

They thanked the men and Sam divided up the remaining coins between them.

Since the trolley didn't travel to Port Tudor, they hired a rickshaw pulled by a motor bike. Whether the bike's motor was incapable of going any faster or because the driver simply didn't care to hurry, they crept along at a plodding pace. Sam felt he could have walked faster than they traveled, but since he didn't know the way and the driver did, he did his best to curb his impatience. Instead he tried to imagine the newer aircraft available and guess which one Jade had chosen for him. They *had* to find those boxes.

They felt stranded when the rickshaw driver left them in a sparsely populated area with a few huts, some small, rundown buildings and several scattered native boats called dhows. Several had nets drying nearby. The entire area smelled of fish and poverty. Most of the buildings were shaky piles of galvanized tin sheeting that looked as though they'd fall in on themselves if someone opened a door. The huts were worse, a combination of metal sheeting and wood scrounged from boxes.

He fixed his gaze on a distant, ramshackle building. "That appears to be some sort of old warehouse. Let's give it a look. Maybe someone put the other crates in there until they were claimed."

The structure had certainly seen its better days. Orphaned when Kilindi Harbor took over most of the shipping, this remnant of Mombasa harbor's busier life was not much more than a shell of rusted steel sheeting. They scouted the entire, windowless building and found the door behind a heap of old pallets.

"Someone must still use it," said Richard. "They put a good enough lock on it."

"And unlike the rest of the building, it's not rusted over," added Sam. "I think we should have a look inside. Any suggestions?"

Richard stepped around the building again and studied the walls. Sam followed. "This seam looks weak back here," he said. Maybe we can pry it apart."

Sam signaled his agreement by wrapping his right hand in a red, pocket kerchief, grabbing hold of a lose corner, and tugging hard. The lose sheeting groaned and screeched like an ill-tempered beast and peeled back. Richard wrapped one of his hands and joined his strength with Sam's. Finally the gap was wide enough for them to slip into the building.

Immediately the septic reek of ammonia, feces, and decay slapped them in the face.

"Sweet Jehoshaphat," swore Richard, fanning a hand before his face. "What a stench!" He immediately pulled off the handkerchief from his hand and held it in front of his nose and mouth.

"Does someone keep livestock in here?" asked Sam. Shafts of light fell through the numerous holes in the roofing. One shone on a long wooden structure the far end. "Over there."

He led the way to the propeller across a packed earthen floor, slippery with assorted offal. Behind the wooden blades rested long strips of spruce wood and rolls of linen canvas for wings. Long wires and struts, a rudder, and other assorted parts were heaped atop all. Sam studied the pile for a moment. "This doesn't make any sense."

"No, but at least it looks as if we found everything, Sam. Let's see if we can find someone to help us send this on the next train to Nairobi. Your friend Avery can take charge of it all."

"But, Richard, we *haven't* found everything."

"What's missing?"

Sam swung his arms towards the airplane parts. "The crates. Why would someone just take the crates?" He wondered briefly if they'd been taken as construction material for someone's hut. But it was a lot of work to bring them across the island, so that didn't seem likely.

"That is a heck of a riddle," agreed Richard. He massaged his chin as he pondered the issue. "Because of their size?" he said after a long pause. "They needed big crates to move something else big?"

"These would have been exceptionally long and large," agreed Sam. He turned around and peered into the dimly lit warehouse. "Perhaps they weren't housing animals in here."

"Then what? Are you suggesting, selling slaves?"

"Maybe," said Sam. He slowly moved around the otherwise empty building, peering into the darker corners for anything that would help shed some light on this puzzle. But beyond a lot of moldering sacks and a few mice nests, he didn't find much. Finally he noticed a nearly rectangular shape in the gloom.

"Look, one of the crates is over there. It's all busted up. Probably broke when they tried to open it so they decided to toss it."

As he approached, the scent of decay became stronger. "Damn!" swore Sam through his handkerchief. It smells like there's something dead in here." He took hold of the lone remaining board that served as a lid and flipped it aside.

"Richard. You'd better come and take a look at this."

"What is it? Part of the plane?"

"No." Sam just pointed to the crate, his jaw working as he struggled to keep his composure. He'd seen his share of horrific sights in the Great War, but that was war and to be expected. One was always prepared for it. But not today. Not while looking for airplane parts.

"Phew! You were right about smelling like something dead, Sam. I . . ." Richard bit off his words as he jerked himself back. Then he moved forward again. "Damnation. It's a man."

He was right. It was a black man, his throat cut.

CHAPTER 3

Cloves, cinnamon, nutmeg, and pepper all flourish here and bless the air with their pervasive fragrance.
- - The Traveler

Jade held the blade to the man's Adam's apple. "Why are you following us? I'm not going to ask you again."

"If it please you, most gracious lady," said the man, a coffee-colored African about Jade's height. "It is not for me to speak well with one knife at my throat and one at my heart."

Jade stole a quick glance over the man's shoulder and saw her mother pressing a stiletto dagger to the man's chest. "Mother! What in the name of St. Peter's bait bucket are you doing? Where did you get that?"

"After our time in Morocco, it seemed like a good idea to emulate you. At least in *this* regard. What do you think? Should we let him speak?"

Jade answered by releasing the man, but as she did, she positioned herself near the alley exit, her mother on their captive's other side. Escape wouldn't be easy for him. "Be on guard, Mother." She nodded to the man. "Very well. You are free of the knives for now. Speak."

"Bless you, lady. And you, as well," he added with a wary nod over his shoulder to Inez. "I am Musa. I am a Wa-Shirazi serving in the house of Ali Bin Hassan, may he be blessed. It is my duty and pleasure to protect and care for his only child, Hazar Binti Ali, a pearl of beauty and a dove in our midst, blessing us daily as the sun does the humble plants."

Jade studied him afresh, noting the Arab-style nose and eyes coupled with a skin tone that showed a blending of the ancient Shirazi Persian line with the more equatorial black-skinned peoples. His command of English, while grammatically awkward, was very good and indicated he'd had some formal training. "What is it you wish of us," she asked, adopting his more formal manner of speech.

"I seek your help. Hazar is in danger, and I have heard that Americans are a very powerful people."

"And that women generally do not hold such power. If she is in danger, you should seek the police. Surely the Sultan would protect one of his peoples."

Musa shook his head. "It is not such as that. It is her *honor* in danger.

"And how can that be, if you are her protector? Do you neglect your job? Should you be with her now?"

"No, blessed lady, I do not neglect it. And that is why I seek *your* help. Your name is known. You defend the weak."

"I'm sorry," Jade began, "but--"

"Of course we will help if a young girl is in danger," finished Inez.

"Mother!"

"Jade, at least let this man tell us his story."

"It is very short to tell," said Musa. "I have cared for Hazar since she was an infant and I had seen but thirteen long rains. She is dear to me as a little sister, and, as a little sister she has listened to me. But two years ago, my master, may he always be well, thought to pay someone to teach Hazar to read and write English and French. This man has been welcome in our household and he has never been alone with Hazar. I am always there and often Hazar's maid. And now Hazar is a budding flower of sixteen. This man, I have seen how he looks at her now. He would steal her away and dishonor her."

"Then surely your master should fire him and dismiss him from your house," said Jade.

"Alas, this man has presented my master, may he always walk in wealth, with some small jewels and blinded him to truth. But if you would speak to Hazar's mother and grandmother, they would listen. This is why I come to you, a woman. A man could not dare to speak in the master's harem."

"Why would they listen to us?" asked Inez.

"Because you are Americans. We know that Americans are to be feared and trusted. We have heard it spoken. It has been written in many newspapers. My master's mother, Nuna Binti Ramiz, has the ear of her son. She would listen to you and speak to him."

"What is this teacher's name," asked Jade.

"He is Kinahin Teasdale, my lady."

"Are you so certain that this Mr. Teasdale's intentions are dishonorable?" asked Inez? "What if he wishes to marry her?"

Musa recoiled as though the idea was an insult. "He is not fit for my Hazar," he said. His voice quavered with the force of his emotions and Jade noted his right hand clenching in a thick fist. "And there is more to tell. He lusts for more than her. He lusts for riches and power. Many times he has sailed to Pemba Island to look for treasures buried from long ago." He lowered his voice. "But there are other things to find on Pemba besides jewels. Terrible things. After his last journey, he returned changed. He brought back many small trinkets and rings, yes. But he also brought back evil."

He looked first to Jade then to Inez with an fire burning in his eyes that spoke of serious intent and deep passion. "If you will not help me, then I must get rid of him myself. I will not let harm come to Hazar."

"Of course, we'll speak to the ladies of the house," said Inez. "Won't we, Jade?"

Jade frowned, letting her unwillingness show for Musa to see. Not that he hadn't already figured out to plead his case to her mother.

And this is the woman who thinks I should mind my own business and not get involved.

But after their adventures in Morocco, Jade had already learned that her mother had become a hopeless romantic. Perhaps it had always been there, a smoldering remnant from her youth when she'd danced with gypsies in her native Spain. It had only needed the right spark to rekindle it. Jade noted that her mother had long since relaxed her vigilance and held her stiletto loosely. Jade was less trusting.

"Of course," she said. "We shall be happy to speak to the ladies of the house." Jade was careful to not say that they'd be happy to help. As far as she was concerned, it was an opportunity to see inside one of the great Arab homes on Zanzibar and nothing more. And if the older women didn't speak English and Jade had to communicate in Arabic, well, there was no reason she had to say anything about this nonsense.

"Did Mr. Teasdale come back from Pemba with malaria?" asked Inez. "We were thinking of taking a boat to Pemba to see some of the ruins there. But Hazar would not catch it from him, you know."

"It was not a sickness of the body that he returned with," said Musa. "There is evil on Pemba. From old times there are witches there, powerful men and women. But to gain power, the apprentice must kill someone close to him. Teasdale has been studying. He believes the power will help him find a great treasure. Yes, he would marry my Hazar, but only to *kill* her." He punctuated the word with a sudden twitch of his hand.

"Oh my," murmured Inez.

Jade recalled the talk of witchcraft just minutes ago in the street over the dead man. The belief was certainly prevalent here. And if Musa believed it strongly enough, he might kill Teasdale to prevent what he thought might happen to the girl, Hazar. It might do to look up this Teasdale and warn him.

Instead of voicing that idea in front of Musa, she asked for directions to the house of Ali Bin Hassan and promised to call on the ladies mid-morning tomorrow.

"That will give us time to find that lace," said Inez after

Musa left them.

"No, Mother. It will give us time to pay a call on Mr. Teasdale and warn him before Musa puts a knife in his back."

CHAPTER 4

"It might be said that, on Zanzibar and its neighboring Pemba,
money does grow on trees. Not only the spices but also the coconut palms
play a leading role in the economy.
- - The Traveler

Kinahin Teasdale lived in a two room, one bath flat above
the offices of an Indian shipping merchant. Jade tracked him
down by inquiring at the Government building. They found
him at home, maps and notes strewn across the flat board that
served as dining table and desk. A stack of ledger books stood
nearby. Jade introduced herself and her mother as Americans
visiting the island and that they had some business to discuss
with him.

"I understand that you are a teacher, Mr. Teasdale," said
Jade. She studied him as he offered them a seat on a battered
settee while he brought over a hard-backed wooden chair from
his work table. He was young and might be considered good
looking except that his hair fell to his shoulders and he wore a
long, silken scarf draped across his neck, the ends hanging
down to his waist. It was an affectation towards the defunct
poetic age of Oscar Wilde, and one for which Jade didn't care.

"I teach, but it does not pay much so I also do bookkeeping
for a few of the local planters. It takes me around the island,

especially when it is harvest time." He nodded towards the stack of ledgers. "What may I do for you ladies? Are you in need of a translator to take you around to the shops? I don't normally do that, but I assure you, unless you are in Bazaar Street, the main merchants all speak English."

"It is in your capacity as teacher that we need to speak with you," said Inez before Jade could continue. "We have recently, how shall I say it, *met* a man named Musa."

Teasdale's reaction was instantaneous. He stiffened and leaned so far back in his chair that Jade feared it would tip over.

"You don't care for him," said Jade, not bothering to form it as a question.

"How observant," said Teasdale. "To say that he is an abomination would be putting it mildly. He's a *eunuch*. He can't understand masculine love and so he misrepresents mine."

Jade didn't react. She'd suspected as much. A complete man would not be allowed to care for a girl of Hazar's age. It also explained why Hazar's father, Ali Bin Hassan, wouldn't heed Musa's argument against Teasdale. To him, Musa was probably the equivalent of a piece of livestock.

"I can't imagine he became one by choice," said Jade. "But we came here primarily to warn you that the man distrusts you and might do something, shall we say, rather drastic about it. We thought you should know."

"You are talking about my relationship with Hazar, the girl that I tutor," said Teasdale.

"Yes," chimed in Inez. "Musa feels that you have less than moral thoughts about the child."

"She's not a child," said Teasdale. "She's sixteen, and yes, I love her. I want to marry her. Is that immoral?"

"Not at all," said Inez, her tone comforting and motherly.

"But it might be imprudent," added Jade. "If this was an English girl, do you think her father would approve of you marrying her at that age?"

"You are making my point for me, Miss del Cameron" said Teasdale. "The Zanzibar Arabs often arrange a marriage for their daughters as early as fifteen. If I don't declare for her now, then she will be lost to me. There are others applying for her, but Hazar doesn't want them."

"You're certain of this, Mr. Teasdale?" asked Inez. "Have you been alone with her to allow her to speak her mind freely?"

"Please, call me Ken," said Teasdale, "But to answer your question, no. We aren't left alone. Ever. Usually Hazar has her maid with her, a Swahili girl tamed Tisha. And Musa is always there, but often Hazar orders him to stand at the end of the room. He can watch, but he cannot hear. We are free to whisper our hopes for each other." He turned to Inez. "Surely you can sympathize with our plight, Madame."

"Of course, Ken," said Inez.

"It's truthfully none of our business, Mr. Teasdale," said Jade, purposely avoiding any familiarity. "I came here to warn you of a situation that could turn ugly. In a nut shell," she ticked the points off her fingers, "Musa takes his job of protecting Hazar very seriously. Musa doesn't trust you. Musa wants you to leave Hazar alone, probably leave the household or," she held up a fourth finger, "Musa intends to take care of the problem – *you* – himself. I couldn't in good conscience let someone, anyone, unknowingly come to harm. If you feel so strongly about the girl, then apply to her father and stop this secrecy."

"I have," said Teasdale. "And I believe he likes me." He frowned. "What he does *not* like is that I am poor. But I don't intend to be for very long." He leaned forward, a fresh eagerness and passion sweeping into his voice. "There are treasures, long lost treasures on Pemba Island. Why, that island has been a stronghold for pirates and rather dubious shippers ever since people plied the seas. Imagine Chinese pottery from the Ming dynasty stored in hidden caches. The Persians used the island as a stronghold when they shipped jewels and ivory. Its coast is quite unmanageable so it's been a perfect hideaway for anyone with a lighter, more maneuverable vessel." He dropped his voice to a whisper. "It's even rumored that

Captain Kidd left treasure behind there. And I think I know how to find it."

Jade glanced to the table and the hand drawn maps scattered across it. They were held down by a box of aged wood, opened to reveal the compass nested within. *A mariner's compass.* She'd met treasure seekers before in New Mexico, mostly prospectors looking for lost gold mines. They were a curious breed, one moment anxious to tell anyone that they alone had found the secret to untold wealth, the next, clamming up tighter than a mule's backend in a dust storm. She knew that asking him for more details about his treasure would only shut him up.

"You sail, Mr. Teasdale?"

"What? Yes. I own a small dhow. Why?"

"I saw the compass, that's all. And I've heard so much talk about the Mombasa yacht club's upcoming race coming into Zanzibar port that I wondered if you were planning on entering the race yourself?"

"Me? No. My little boat isn't built for speed. But I have heard it rumored that His Highness, the Sultan is entering his yacht though I doubt he'll sail it himself."

"Do you sail to Pemba then? My mother and I were planning to go to that island soon. We hear there are some interesting old ruins to be seen there. Perhaps we could hire you to take us. Since you need the extra money, we would be doing both ourselves a favor."

"Again, no. My dhow can only accommodate one or two at most. Certainly not three people. But if you don't care to wait for the weekly steamer, I know some of the local captains. I could perhaps recommend someone to you."

"We've talked to a few of them already," said Inez. She looked at Jade quizzically, as though trying to figure out why her daughter was pretending to hire Teasdale. "What do you think of the one named Yusuf? Tall, thin man. Very dark skin. Jade, weren't you contracting with him?"

"I was considering him."

"Yusuf? He's perfectly capable, I should think. Perhaps not

the cleanest dhow." Teasdale's shoulders relaxed as the conversation moved into more harmless territory.

"Well, since you've been on Pemba so much, I imagine you've heard some of the tales about witchcraft," Jade said as a way of drawing him out. It didn't work. Teasdale immediately lowered his eyelids, looking at her with suspicion.

"What makes you ask about witchcraft," he asked. "What have you heard?"

Jade shrugged. "One can't walk in the streets without hearing the Swahili speak of it. I overheard some women talk about it just this morning. My mother and I plan to visit Pemba. I thought perhaps we might enjoy seeing some sort of ceremony. You seemed to be the person to ask since you've been to Pemba."

"I don't know any witches or practitioners." He stood, indicating the interview was over. "Now if you'll excuse me, I've been hard at work at my desk all morning but I must go out to see one of my merchant clients."

He stepped past them and opened his door and that is when Jade spied his coat and hat, hanging from a hook on the back of the door. It was a brown sporting jacket and a boater hat.

"*You* were in the bazaar this morning," said Jade. "I saw you there. I looked for you to help me but you'd slipped away."

"I . . . I don't know what you are talking about," he protested.

She pointed an accusing finger at him. "You were there when that running man died. And yet you did nothing."

CHAPTER 5

For all that, many of the plantation owners are not wealthy men.
Workers to harvest the crops demand wages. At least they do in these days
and times.

- - The Traveler

"I have no idea what you're talking about," said Teasdale. He stood by the door with his arms folded across his chest, his chin up.

"The devil you don't," retorted Jade as she reached across him and slammed the door shut. All pretenses of friendly banter were off. "You saw me examine that man to see if he was alive or not. You heard me call out to you to help. Then you disappeared like a scared rabbit."

"Mr. Teasdale," said Inez softly. "If my daughter says that she saw you, then she did. Now why don't we sit back down and clear this up."

"Because I don't see how this is any of your business," said Teasdale.

"You made it my business when you lied to me. You haven't been here hard at work all morning. In my experience, people don't lie for casual reasons. You didn't want me to know you were in the bazaar. Why? Did you know that dead man?"

"I believe he did, Jade," said Inez. "Observe how he just blinked rapidly. You did that once when you were a little girl and broke my favorite vase and tried to blame the dog."

Jade grinned. "I remember that. I couldn't sit down for a day. So you see, Mr. Teasdale, we both know you're lying. And we *both* have little tolerance for it. Now I came here in the right good spirit to warn you of physical danger to yourself, but I tell you truly with my mother as witness, if Musa doesn't thrash you, I certainly intend to." She took a step towards the slender man.

Teasdale backed up, bumping against the door. "In all my life, I've never experienced anything as outrageous as having some American . . . cowgirl threaten me."

"Very likely," agreed Jade. "But it is hardly to the point. Now sit down again and tell me if you knew this man or not and why you denied being there."

He took a seat, dabbing his forehead with his scarf. Inez sat back on the settee, but Jade remained standing, looming over him like an avenging angel.

"Yes, I was there today and, yes, I recognized that man."

"Who was he?" asked Jade.

"I don't know his name. I didn't say I *knew* him. I said I recognized him. In my business I see many people."

"Very well, where had you seen him before?"

"I'd seen him at Ali Bin Hassan's house. He ... he looked better when I saw him. He came as a representative of someone, I don't know who. Many people come to that house to see Bin Hassan. He's a prominent clove plantation owner so there are always people from the plantation or buyers doing business with him."

"How long ago was it that you last saw this man?" asked Inez.

Teasdale shrugged. "Possibly six - eight months ago. I don't really remember.

"But you never spoke with him? You don't know what his business was with Bin Hassan?" asked Jade.

"No. Why should I?"

"He's lying again, Mother. See how he keeps looking away when he's nervous?"

"Perhaps I should go and find an officer?" asked Inez. "But if I do, you must promise me, Jade, not to hurt Mr. Teasdale too badly." She shook her head and frowned. "I'm so sorry, Mr. Teasdale, but I really don't care to stay and watch." She started to rise.

"No!" cried Teasdale. "Don't leave me alone with her."

"Then stop lying to us," said Inez. "Honestly, we did come here to help you. You're the one making this very difficult. I have to say I was sympathizing with you up until now."

Jade coughed into her hand to stifle a smile.

"It is true that I do sometimes interpret for Bin Hassan, and on occasion I act as a witness and sign business papers and such."

"And did you do either of those with our dead friend?" asked Jade. "I shouldn't imagine you'd need to interpret for a non-European."

"No. But I did witness a - um – transaction involving that man. It was last month." Teasdale wrung his hands and looked at his feet. Jade sat on her heels beside him, her face inches from his.

"Mr. Teasdale," she said softly in a voice reminiscent of a lioness purring. "You must tell us everything. What was the transaction? Did this man come alone or was someone else with him? Details, please."

"He wasn't alone. There was another man, one of those black Africans that looks like they have some Arab or Persian in them. A Wa-Shirazi, I believe. I really don't know his name. Dar something or other. He came acting on behalf of his employer, a wealthy Pemba plantation man named Mubarik Bin Rafi. I remember that much because all the business was transacted using a seal belonging to Bin Rafi."

"Good. And what was the transaction?" asked Inez.

"It was a transfer of property of sorts," said Teasdale. He looked up at Jade. "The man you saw running? *He* was the property. Bin Rafi was giving him to Bin Hassan."

"But how can that be?" asked Inez. "Isn't slavery outlawed here?"

"Yes," said Jade. She stood up and paced the small room. "It has been since 1897, but that doesn't mean slaves weren't still kept." She stopped and turned towards Teasdale. "You are telling us that you witnessed a slave transfer and you never bothered to report it?"

Teasdale looked down and didn't answer.

"My concern for your safety is dropping every minute, Mr. Teasdale," said Jade. "Tell me, did you ever see that man again after that day?"

Teasdale shook his head. "No. He was probably sent to the clove plantation. But even if he were kept as a house worker, I wouldn't have seen him. I only went into a sort of parlor that Bin Hassan uses to receive people and conduct his business."

"Jade, didn't you say that this man looked emaciated and that his clothing was worn and dirty?" asked Inez.

"Yes. And his decline apparently took place within a month. What kind of master is Bin Hassan?"

Teasdale shrugged.

"Mother, don't you think that I should just save Musa the time and aggravation of pummeling Mr. Teasdale to a pulp?"

"Nonsense, Jade," said Inez. "You'd ruin your hands and just a month before your wedding. Let Mr. Musa have his fun. I'm certainly beginning to agree that this man is not fit to wed a sweet young girl. But I wonder if someone on Pemba didn't want that poor slave relinquished," said Inez. "Perhaps someone tried to reclaim him."

"Did you actually witness this man's death or merely happen upon him already in the street?" asked Jade.

Teasdale wiped his brow with the ends of the long scarf he wore draped around his shoulders. "I . . . I saw him fall. He was running and suddenly he stopped and clutched his chest. Then he fell. I swear it."

"The gossip on the street was murder by witchcraft," said Jade. "Maybe this man *thought* he was in danger either of an old adversary or from someone in his new house and escaped. He could have been living in hiding for a month. It would certainly explain his condition."

"I don't believe that Bin Hassan is guilty of trying to practice any witchcraft," said Teasdale. "For one thing, he's too indolent. He doesn't even go out to oversee his own plantation."

"I have a hard time believing that. Don't Arabs like to raise and ride horses?" asked Inez. "That's the general image, isn't it? I seem to recall reading that in Miss Hull's book *The Sheik*."

Jade arched her brows, surprised that her mother had not only read such a risqué book, but had admitted as much in front of her. "Horses don't do well on these islands, for some reason, Mother. The British and the Sultan have managed to keep some well stabled at the local polo club, but that's all."

"Bin Hassan is not a member of that club that I know of," said Teasdale.

"Then what does he do all day, Mr. Teasdale?" Inez asked.

"I can't really say," said Teasdale, "but I can tell you what he thinks about; money. You should have seen the gleam in his eyes when I gave him a carnelian ring that I'd found. He may be the owner of one of the larger clove plantations on Zanzibar but it doesn't mean that he's wealthy. From what I can see of his books, he's losing money badly and his daughter is his one asset that can net him more with the right marriage. And that's why I need to find my treasure on Pemba, and soon."

Jade stood next to Teasdale and put her hand on the back of his chair. "I should imagine any number of people have tried looking for those hidden treasures, Mr. Teasdale. You never did explain just how *you've* managed to locate any. You seem pretty certain of your information. So I'll ask you one last time, who have you talked to on Pemba?"

"Very well. I admit that I have spoken to a few people who claim to be lesser practitioners of witchcraft, but no one to be afraid of. They were all a type of healers. I only talked to them because they see so many people, people who pay them anyway that they can, sometimes with things that they've found. I pieced together what information that I could on locations and came up with a very good idea of where the major treasures could be located."

Jade stood up and offered a hand to her mother. "I don't think we'll learn anything else here, Mother. We've done what we came for, we warned Teasdale that Musa will hurt him if he persists in trying to see Hazar, and I can't see that we can learn much more about that poor dead man."

"We can pass on the man's identity, what little we know of it to the authorities, at least," said Inez. "They might be interested to know that people still holds slaves."

"I suspect they know that already, Mother. They just don't know what to do about it."

"Are we still going to see the ladies of Bin Hassan's house?" asked Inez, her voice hopeful.

"Of course," said Jade. "I told you I wanted to see what the Arab women look like here. Maybe they'll allow me to photograph them for my article." She turned to Teasdale as though she just now remembered that he was still there. "Thank you for seeing us, Mr. Teasdale." She spoke as though this had been any ordinary pleasant afternoon visit. "I believe we can see our way out."

"If you go to Bin Hassan's house," said Teasdale, "you'd do well to not interfere with Musa yourselves. He's a dangerous man. You were right about one thing. He'll stop at nothing to protect Hazar."

CHAPTER 6

*Since slavery was outlawed on the islands, plantation owners have lost
their ready source of free laborers to perform the arduous tasks of
harvesting the crops. This has markedly cut into the profits from the
plantation.*
- - The Traveler

Inspector Walsh squatted on his heels beside the body,
seemingly oblivious to the reek of decay. A middle-aged, clean-
shaven man with gray hair at the temples, he examined the
scene with an economy of motion that spoke to Sam of years
of investigations in the field. He possessed an aura of
confidence without arrogance, a man Sam decided he might
trust. "Poor chap's been dead over a day at least," Walsh said.
"Now, indulge me, gentlemen. Why again were you in here?"

Sam started to answer but Richard put out a hand as if to
stop him. Instead, Sam folded his arms and waited for Richard
to begin.

"I'd lost several important crates sent over from the States.
Two smaller ones showed up in Mombasa Harbor and we were
attempting to track down the rest. Some men at the harbor
suggested we try here for want of anyplace else to look. So we
did."

"And found the door locked," said Walsh.

"Yes," said Richard.

"So you came in through a weakness in the walls."

"Yes."

"You broke in, then."

"In a manner of speaking," said Richard. "But only to retrieve what was taken from us."

"I see. And what may I ask was in these crates?"

Sam couldn't restrain himself any longer. "My airplane." He gestured at the pile of wood and wire along one wall.

"Ah!" said Walsh. "You're a pilot. Now, would these aeroplane parts be worth killing for?" His tone suggested that Sam could have killed to get his airplane back.

Sam ignored the implication. The man was only doing his job. "If someone did," said Sam, "they missed the most important part. They left the engine back at the docks at Mombasa Harbor."

"Inspector," said Richard, "so far the only thing left that is missing from our airplane are the crates. And that man is lying in one of them."

The inspector stood and walked around the broken box. "It would appear that the man was in it when he died, not that he was dumped in it after."

Sam crowded closer, curiosity overcoming his revulsion at seeing the maggoty body a second time. "How can you tell?"

"Well, it's quite simple, actually. There are scratch marks on the interior of the box and corresponding slivers under the man's fingernails. Plus he bled out a great quantity of blood in here. The wooden bottom is rather soaked with it."

"He must have struggled a lot, even with his hands and feet bound," said Richard who held back. "Probably why the crate is broken."

"Yes, well, he was a rather large chap at that," said Walsh. "Might be a Kavirondo. Or Kikuyu. Difficult to say at this point. No kipande on him so there's probably no identifying him. The question remains, why was he killed?"

"Any ideas?" asked Richard.

Walsh shrugged, "Could be that someone has been

smuggling something, ivory perhaps. Or they could be smuggling monkeys from Pemba Island to sell in Europe. Our game laws don't have much of an impression on Pemba. Either way, maybe this man wanted a bigger cut."

"He got one all right. More than he wanted," said Sam, thinking of the gash across the man's throat.

"I may be a simple rancher," said Richard, "but it seems to me that the entire point of stealing our airplane was for the crates. And only the large ones at that. You said they might be smuggling animals or ivory?"

"Ivory would fit the bill as far as the crates, go," agreed Sam. "They could use any size for monkeys and they didn't take the smaller boxes. But we might be overlooking the obvious." He looked at each man in turn. "Humans."

"Humans!" said Richard.

"Slaves," added Sam. He turned to Walsh for his reaction.

"Slavery has been outlawed," said Walsh.

"Outlawing something doesn't necessarily end it. It only drives it underground," said Sam. "Those crates were big enough to hold two men each. That's a possible six people kidnapped and sent off to God knows where."

"It's certainly a possibility," mused Walsh. "And not one that will be easy to solve. I'm very short-handed here as it is and I've been ordered to detail more of my men to protect the crowds that will accumulate for the upcoming sailing race. The sad truth of the matter is, I can get more assistance from my betters to solve the smuggling than to solve the murder. You see, according to the ten-mile treaty, Mombasa still belongs to the Sultan of Zanzibar. It's not part of the Kenya colony but rather a part of the *Protectorate*."

"I don't understand why that should prevent you from investigating a murder," said Richard.

"I'm sure it's difficult for you Americans to understand. I'm not certain I understand it fully myself. This treaty with the Sultan was formed in 1886 and it's become a bit of a bugaboo politically. But to smooth over the difficulties, Mombasa has both British and Mohammedan law. The Wali represents the

Sultan and, nominally at least, administers justice to the Sultan's subjects, that is, to the Arabs."

"But this man wasn't an Arab," said Sam.

"No, but his *killer* might well be. It's a jurisdictional sticky wicket. But, I assure you, that smuggling comes under our tariff laws and I *can* do something about that. It's a roundabout way of doing things, but one way or another, I could bring this person to book. I do promise that I'll put some of my best men on watching this little port as well at Port Reitz. If anyone tries this again, we'll catch them."

He called for his two corporals to take the body and the broken crate away. "You chaps can take your aeroplane parts. I shan't be needing them for evidence. You might try hiring a cart to transport them to another warehouse until you can get them crated up."

It took two carts and as many trips to move the materials to Mombasa Harbor. By the time they had rounded up everything, night had fallen and nothing more could be done. They found a room at the Metropole where they contemplated what had transpired.

"It's going to take a couple of days after we hire a carpenter to get new crates made before we can send all that material to Nairobi," said Sam as he plopped down on a bed. "I think our safari plans might be derailed."

"Not to worry," said Richard. "We should be able to leave the day after tomorrow."

Sam wondered if Richard had heard back from his pilot friend, Lord Avery Dunbury, in Nairobi. Perhaps he or Neville Thompson was coming down to take possession of the parts. But any pleasant day dreams about the surprise airplane were constantly dashed by the vision of the dead man in the crate.

"Richard, the inspector said they'd keep an eye out here for anyone trying to smuggle ivory or people, but I keep thinking about those other crates. I don't believe anyone was smuggling ivory and I don't think Walsh does either. That means that there might be other people stuffed into them."

"Or something else," said Richard. "We don't know for a

fact that slaves were being smuggled, but I know what you mean. Even if the smugglers *aren't* shipping slaves, they did kill a man."

"That man was bound up in that crate," said Sam. "If he was just a smuggler intent on getting a larger share, or some poor man drafted on for muscle to move items, he wasn't simply struck down in a moment. Someone *planned* to harm him."

"Because he was tied up," said Richard as though reasoning it out aloud.

"Right. The way I picture it. This one was forced into a box, but he was too strong. Perhaps the smugglers drug the men, but his one, being larger, wasn't subdued. He fought back and in doing so, broke the crate. With no way to move him and probably no way to keep him sedated, they just cut their losses – literally – and killed him." He balled one hand into a fist and smacked it into the other. "I would love to get my hands on those bastards."

"I know what you mean, Sam. And I think the inspector would, too. But as he said, he's already short-handed and he also risks problems sending anyone off to hunt for these smugglers on the Sultan's lands. He just has to wait for them to try again."

"And by then it's too late for this last cargo of people." Sam sat up. "*We* should go look for them."

"Son, I understand how you feel. I'd like nothing more than to beat those smugglers until they swallow their own teeth, but, Sam, we don't even know where to look."

"You said yourself today that money speaks all languages. There has to be some honest fellow with a boat that saw those crates get moved. Maybe they saw them get transported out. We'll be doing the inspector a favor."

"It's worth a try. I'm game if you are."

"That's it, then. Tomorrow we'll get some carpenters hired and then we'll try to find out where those smugglers went."

"One condition. Don't tell Inez. She might not understand."

***

The next day, to Sam's delight, his American friends the Bert boys, Robert and Gilbert, disembarked at Kilindi Harbor. Sam and Richard met them and put them in charge of the airplane before they headed back to Tudor Port to pick up the smugglers' trail. But before they left, Sam unpacked his Colt revolver. If he was going after murdering slavers, he was going armed.

CHAPTER 7

Zanzibar's old city center, Stone Town, boasts many rich residences. Built of the coral limestone that abounds here, there is little carving into the stonework, but the visitor doesn't notice that omission. They are too busy looking at the elaborately carved doors.

- - The Traveler

Jade and Inez had sent a written note to the ladies of Bin Hassan's house, requesting a visit. The promptness of the reply inviting them to breakfast suggested that Musa had already described them and strongly hinted at the extreme curiosity of the bored women to meet two Americans. And while Inez put on her best dress of indigo silk along with a glittering sapphire broach, white gloves and a stylish hat, Jade wore her usual trousers, white shirt, and boots. Together they would be an intriguing blend of wealth, style and power, Inez representing the wealth and style. Jade wished she had her pet cheetah, Biscuit, with her. *He* would have made a strong impression.

They left the Hotel Africa and hired a car to take them to Ali Bin Hassan's house, arriving at the appointed time. True, the walk would not have been far but they agreed that they would make a more favorable impression on the household if they arrived driven by a chauffeur. The impression they made when they left was immaterial.

The square, two-story house did not look like anything special from the outside, but Jade knew from her experience in Morocco, that the Arab houses reserved all the beauty for the interior. Build of stone and coral plastered together with lime, the only item that marked any status on the face of the scabby white structure were several sets of beautifully arched and latticed windows on the second floor, and the massive, teak door, studded with brass spikes. The door hosted a myriad of intricate carvings including date palms and rosettes and two carved snakes faced each other across the top. Linked chains hung in short clusters of three on either side.

"The carvings depict wealth and power, Mother," said Jade, peering through the car window. "And the chains speak of security. It's a way of boasting one's status. Another, perhaps lesser Arab would be intimidated at once by this showing. Whether it's still true or not is another matter."

"One might spend all their money on such a door and have none left," said Inez who didn't look overly impressed.

"You should get out of the car first, Mother," said Jade. "Let the driver open your door and assist you. Take your time. You can be sure we are being watched from above. We want to make an impressive showing and *you* are most impressive."

Jade waited until her mother had casually turned this way and that, giving anyone inside an opportunity to observe her before she emerged from the car's other side. A woman in elegant European dress was expected. A woman in man's trousers wasn't.

"Why didn't we bring Biscuit with us to Zanzibar, mother?"

"You know very well that the poor creature would have been miserable here. But I know what you mean. One could be in rags and no one would notice with Biscuit stalking beside you."

After knocking, the door opened inward to reveal Musa. Only then did they dismiss the driver and entered the dark house. Musa wordlessly led them down a dark and narrow corridor, past a small, inviting courtyard of palms to a narrow staircase at the rear. They climbed the gloomy, twisting stairs, passing a dim recess along the way. Jade could have sworn that she heard breathing from within and wondered who watched their progress.

Eventually they reached the second floor and entered another narrow corridor. Musa took them to an elongated room, sparsely furnished with beautifully woven carpets, some velvet cushions and a few chairs; one of which was occupied by an older woman who looked to be in her sixties. Several clocks stood in high recesses along the walls. Two deep recesses broke the wall at a lower level on either side. The room smelled pleasantly sweet with the attar of roses.

Musa did not speak. He merely bowed first to the older woman and then to a slightly younger one who was seated on a cushion nearby before leaving the room. Both women wore close-fitting, colorful brocaded shirts worked in horizontal stripes and florals. These reached to their calves and a matching swath of fabric draped over their shoulders, one side tossed across the front to the back. Underneath were narrow *marinda* pants that blossomed into frills at the ankles. Innumerable anklets, bracelets and large earrings jingled and sparkled as they shifted position. Soft leather slippers graced their feet.

Jade, for once uncertain as to how to proceed, decided to speak first and introduce her mother and herself in her flawed Arabic. She translated all replies into English for Inez's sake.

"I am Jade del Cameron. This gracious lady is my honored mother, Doña Inez Maria Isabella de Vincente del Cameron." If that litany of names didn't smack of importance, nothing would.

"I am Nuna Binti Ramiz," replied the older woman. "And this is Karzida Binti Hamoud, my son's wife."

If Jade had expected to see Hazar in the group, she didn't let her surprise or disappointment show. After all, unless she was introduced, she shouldn't even know of the girl's existence. They were invited to sit on their choice of the cushions or one of the other plain chairs. Jade chose the former while her mother took a chair, assuming it as a queen would her throne.

The consummate Arab hospitality won over curiosity though Jade could see that Hazar's mother, Karzida, was itching to touch their various outer garments and inspect them. Within minutes of their arrival, three barefoot Swahili women swathed in white arrived laden with massive trays of food. Loaves of flat-bread, bowls of black and green olives, cucumber slices, assorted fruits and sugared confections, and a thick variety of yoghurt called *labneh* were spread before them. The servants offered Jade and Inez each of the dishes, allowing them to take the bread and dip chunks of it into the *labneh*.

Nuna kept pressing them to eat, ordering the servants to bring whatever dish hadn't been sampled yet to them. Neither she nor Karzida ate much beyond nibbling some of the sweet confections, as if this entire spread were only for the guests' benefit. Jade wondered if the Arab women would eat after they left.

Finally, Jade belched politely into her hand to signify that the meal was very rich and satisfying. Inez copied her and the tray was removed to be immediately followed by thick, black coffee.

After coffee, the Arab women gave into their curiosity and asked numerous questions about Inez's clothing. As Jade's vocabulary did not encompass Arabic words for gloves, shifts, and undergarments, Inez finally rose with tremendous dignity and allowed the women to finger her dress, jewelry, and hat. She drew the line at raising her skirt to expose her under things.

The two Arab women were impressed by the quality of Inez's dress and equally bewildered by Jade's seeming lack of status. Pants they seemed to understand, but not a simple shirt tucked into the waist. Jade assured them that she wore these clothes because she preferred a life of adventure. To prove it, she showed them the lion claw tattoo on her wrist, given to her by a Kikuyu shaman for killing a hyena that had terrorized their village, and lifted her short bangs to expose the stylized lion's paw tattooed in blue on her forehead by her ancestral

Berber clan. It took her nearly an hour to relate the adventures that had earned her each of these marks.

"Jade," asked Inez, "have we met enough formalities to broach the real reason for our coming?"

"Very well, mother, but I refuse to take Teasdale's side in this. I don't trust that man and the idea of him falling in love with a sixteen-year-old girl is ludicrous."

On hearing Teasdale's name, both Nuna and Karzida leaned forward.

"You know of Teasdale?" asked Nuna. The name came out as Tizdale. Clearly the older woman spoke for the pair.

"Yes," said Jade. "He told us so much of your beautiful house that we had to see it." Under her breath she said in English, "smile and nod, mother." Inez did.

"Ask them what they think of him," said Inez. "Do they like him?"

"He is a good man for your household?" asked Jade.

"He is useful," agreed Nuna. "He teaches my granddaughter English and French. She will then attract a more promising groom."

"Is your daughter here? Mother and I should like to pay our respects to her. Mr. Teasdale speaks very highly of her."

Nuna looked sharp at the latter part, and Jade feared that she'd either not translated her intent well or else the fact that Teasdale had even mentioned Hazar was bad. "He says she is a very fine student," Jade added quickly.

Karzida spoke up then. "Teasdale is a good teacher. And Hazar likes him."

That definitely drew a sharp look from Nuna, this time towards her daughter-in-law. "It is not proper for Hazar to see so much of the Englishman. Is not her maid and eunuch with her?"

"They are," said Jade. "Teasdale said they are always there. He means no disrespect to Hazar. You could ask them," she suggested. "I am sure they will tell you that he only teaches."

Nuna waved her hand dismissively. "A slave girl is not to be trusted and what would Musa know of a man's feelings for a woman? He is not a man. It will not be well if suitors hear that an Englishman has looked on their possible bride." She turned to Karzida. "I told you that Hazar must wear her *barakoa* in front of Teasdale," decreed Nuna. "I will tell her eunuch now."

"What's happening, Jade?" asked Inez. "The grandmother seems agitated.

"It seems that Teasdale should not have spoken to us of Hazar," answered Jade. "Seeing her as a little girl would have been fine, but not now. They'll make Hazar wear a face mask in front of him. Only her eyes will be exposed."

"How awful," said Inez. "This is not what we intended."

"Not what *you* intended, Mother. I just want to photograph the ladies before we go. Still, I don't want the man to lose his job."

Inez spoke up, trying to express herself using gestures with her words. "Could Teasdale marry Hazar?" she asked. She gestured with her left hand for Teasdale and the right for Hazar, joining them together.

It was at that moment that, Musa, having been summoned, entered the women's apartments. The fact that they did not bother to veil themselves spoke volumes of their opinion of him as a man or even as a human. Just as he bowed to the Arab women, Inez finished her pantomime. Jade groaned, Musa scowled and Nuna frowned thoughtfully. Of the group, only Karzida seemed intrigued by the possibility.

"It is not good for him to join with Hazar," declared Nuna, pulling her hands apart to show the idea was rejected. "He is not of our beliefs though this means less to my son than to me. A daughter is often not of such a concern to a father, but I will remind him that it should be."

"He is poor," chimed in Karzida, clearly showing where she fell on the issue of faith vs. fortune.

"He is an Englishman," argued Nuna. "And my granddaughter is now a woman." She clapped her hands twice and Musa immediately stood at her side, bowing low. "You are with Hazar when she takes her lessons. See to it that she remains veiled from now on when in his presence. Tell her slave to see to it." The older woman didn't bother to look at Musa as she issued this edict and when she'd finished, she dismissed him with a flip of her hand. Jade noticed that Musa seemed pleased with what he'd recently heard if the half smile playing on his lips was any indication. Teasdale, it seemed, didn't have a chance to win Hazar's hand. Any attempt would be squashed by the grandmother.

"My son believed that educating Hazar would make her a better match," continued Nuna with a sniff. "I will speak to my son regarding her," said Nuna. "She has learned enough. It is time she was wed. My son had doted on her long enough."

Inez acted as if she would try to speak again on Teasdale's behalf once Jade translated the most recent conversations, but Jade cautioned silence. "His job was never permanent, Mother," she said. "If we leave well enough alone, they might recommend him for some other family. If we press it, he'll never get a tutoring job in a house that has young girls."

Jade's request to meet Hazar was met with a disinterested pretense that they did not understand her. She wondered what the girl had done wrong to be banished from her mother and grandmother during an audience that could have only been a pleasant diversion for the girl.

Jade pulled her Kodak from her bag and broached photographing the women. After a brief consultation amongst themselves, they agreed, but only after they'd donned their own barakoa. Nuna wore a silken mask resembling a welder's face shield in form, but Karzida sported a small veil that covered the bridge of her nose and continued down past her throat. It was held in place in part by an ornate silver bar that passed up between her eyes to a delicate headband and also by a cord that swept around her head over her ears. The servants were ordered to pose behind their mistresses, unveiled.

Jade thanked the women and waited for someone to escort them out. That person was again Musa. She expected him to say something about the interview but the man was as silent as a mute. As they descended the dark twisting stairs, Musa suddenly stopped in front of them.

The location lent a sinister touch to Musa's action and, for a moment Jade crouched slightly, her right hand reaching down towards her boot, ready to snatch her knife. Then she caught a faint whispering. Musa resumed walking. At the base of the stairs he turned to them.

"The master wishes to meet you. You will come with me." It was a command, not a request.

Finally Jade understood the feeling that there had been some presence hidden away as they had gone up the stairs to the women's quarters. She wondered if he hadn't also been watching through one of the dark alcoves in the room, his features hidden by one of the innumerable clocks.

"Are we in trouble, Jade," whispered Inez.

Jade shrugged. "Just keep your back to a solid wall, Mother."

Musa motioned for them to enter a well-lit room off the courtyard, bowed and left. In the center of the room stood Ali Bin Hassan, resplendent in a white gown covered by a floor-length crimson jacket or *joho* which was trimmed with gold embroidery. A green silk cloth tied around his waist made a repository for the beautifully chased dagger thrust within. Yards of red and white cloth were wrapped around his head in the manner of a turban.

He had been a handsome man in his youth and traces of it remained in a pair of piercing black eyes and a stately nose under which grew a full beard, now mostly gray. But any previously active figure had swollen to a paunch around the middle. He greeted them and bade them seat themselves on several plush chairs which Jade assumed were kept for his European guests. No sooner had they sat when a white-swathed black woman brought in a tray of sweetmeats and an urn of coffee.

"Eat, eat," said Bin Hassan in broken English. "You are assuredly hungry." He motioned towards the tray and Jade noted the carnelian ring in his right index finger.

There was no escaping the hospitality. To decline would have been the height of rudeness, and Jade was glad that they'd both restricted themselves upstairs in the harem.

"I am glad you come for to visit my wife and dear mother," he said. "It is good they see how the world is become. It will give them amusement to talk of this for many days."

Jade made a slight bow to acknowledge the compliment. "It was our pleasure and honor."

"But I think you come to see my daughter? No? She is my joy, but my mother finds her tiring." He looked at Inez and winked as though conveying some private joke between parents.

"I am certain she is a delight," said Inez.

"I know as well that your friend Teasdale is in love with her," said Bin Hassan.

"He--" began Inez, but Jade placed a hand on her mother's arm to signify silence.

"I would not call him a friend," said Jade. "We do not know him well."

Bin Hassan nodded. "My esteemed mother will disapprove because he is a Christian. My wife is more practical. He is poor. He has promised to gain treasure," he added, pointing to his ring, "but I cannot wait for what may not come. It is so that I must have money now or borrow from an Indian lender. I do not wish this. Others do it. I will not."

"We understand," said Jade.

Inez kicked her softly in the foot, making it seemed like an accident as she shifted in her chair, but Jade knew that her mother didn't agree.

"Does not your plantation grow well?" asked Inez.

"It does, but now I must pay for laborers and they want very much. And so I hope to gain with a marriage for Hazar. And she will do well to marry a rich man. That is what is important. She will be well cared for with many servants."

"I thank you for honoring us with this information," said Jade. "And we wish much happiness for you and your daughter."

"My servant will show you out," said Bin Hassan. "Ah he is here now."

Musa had returned, moving as silently as an owl in flight. "A representative of Mubarik bin Rafi to see you, Master," he said in Arabic.

"Show him in, and escort the ladies out."

As Jade and her mother left, she saw Musa speak deferentially with a dark man wearing a richly embroidered vest over a long, white gown. An embroidered, pill-box sized hat called a *kofia* sat on his closely cropped black hair. Inez stepped out into the street first, but Jade lingered a moment, turning once again to watch the new visitor. What she witnessed surprised her.

Musa, motioned the man to precede him. The look Musa cast at the man's back would have blackened snow.

***

At Inez's insistence, she and Jade went straight from Bin Hassan's house to Teasdale's room, Jade reluctantly.

"Mother, didn't you tell me earlier that I should quit getting involved in things that are not my business? Why are we going to see this Teasdale again?"

"He should know that the women don't approve of him at all and that her father plans to wed her soon," said Inez. "The poor young man might wish to just find another position and avoid a complete heartbreak."

"While I'm not all sorry that he can't marry this Hazar, I'm more bothered by the fact that they're going to marry her off at sixteen to someone she's never met before," replied Jade. "It reminds me of all those suitors you used to parade into our parlor when I was seventeen."

"I didn't intend to marry you off at seventeen, Jade. I merely wanted you to learn how to socialize in polite society."

Jade replied by rolling her eyes upward.

"You were a bit of a wildcat, you know," said her mother with a smile. "Still are."

"Like mother, like daughter," said Jade as she gave her mother's hand a small squeeze. Neither of them felt particularly comfortable with overtly sentimental displays of affection, but they had grown much closer since their time together in Morocco, and Jade was grateful for it.

Teasdale was not in his rooms so Inez wrote a note, asking his landlord in the shop below to deliver it to him.

"He will not stop in here, Madam. You may take it and put it in his room yourselves. I trust you." He dropped his voice to a whisper. "His door has no lock but that of the door to my shop. All must pass by here first. You may go in."

They went upstairs and Inez opened the door.

"I don't feel right doing this, Mother," said Jade. "I wouldn't care for someone to go into our rooms without my permission."

"We're only putting a note on the table and leaving. It surely must be all right with Mr. Teasdale or he'd have said something to his landlord long before."

Jade walked in first in a natural attempt to protect her mother from anything that might harm or upset her. The small apartment held few secrets, and Jade noted an open valise on Teasdale's bed as though he'd been in the middle of packing.

"Your note of advice might be unnecessary, Mother. Looks like he getting ready to leave."

She stepped over to the table where his maps lay sprawled and studied them. One was a coastline of east Africa depicting the usual inlets and islands. What made it different was its age. The document looked as though it had been made of some sort of parchment. The other map was an equally old hand-drawn sketch of Pemba Island, marked over in ink with a series of abbreviated notations, none of which initially made any sense to Jade.

"Ch, Ph, CK, Ar," Jade read aloud. "I wonder if these stand for places where he's found coins or things or just where they're rumored to be." She looked more closely. "Ch could mean Chinese. CK might mean Captain Kidd."

Inez placed the note atop the maps. "Not our business, remember, Jade? Come along. We've done what we could."

Jade shut the door behind them, said goodbye to the landlord and strolled out into the busy street. "Where shall we go, Mother? We've seen the outside of the Sultan's palace and most of the shops."

"We still haven't purchased any--"

"Don't start, Mother."

Inez let out an exasperated sigh. "We might take that little train to Bububu and see the clove plantation there. It's only seven miles. But I don't want to walk through a plantation in my best dress. I'd like to change first."

"Good idea. And on the way we can finalize our plans to see the ruins on Pemba. Those maps of Teasdale's made me all the more anxious to visit them. There's a great deal of history on that island."

They hurried back to the Africa Hotel which was attached to the English Country Club and, technically, reserved for members. They had Avery Dunbury's membership to thank for their room. As they approached their door, Jade stopped abruptly, pushing Inez behind her.

The door was slightly ajar and a strong scent of a pleasantly musky perfume issued from the room. It reminded Jade of the scent that had been on Musa when he'd followed them.

Jade mouthed, "wait here," to Inez and then, drawing her knife, burst into the room.

"Who in the name of St. Peter's fishing pole are you?" she asked. But she knew the answer. The Arab girl seated calmly on their settee could be none other than Hazar Binti Ali.

CHAPTER 8

Clothing on Zanzibar identifies a person's social rank. As opposed to the ornate Arab dress, slaves were never allowed to veil themselves, nor did they wear shoes. Instead, they wore simple garments made of a cheap, white cloth called merikani.
- - The Traveler

"What are you doing here?" snapped Jade. As she spoke, she saw for the first time, a young, black girl standing in the corner, draped in a plain off-white garment. Her closely shaved head was uncovered. She stepped forward then hesitated, as though she'd intended to defend her mistress and thought better of it. That was when Jade saw that she was barefoot.

The Arab girl was dressed for complete concealment from her ornate face mask to the swaddling black cloth called a *shela*. But the eyes were those of youth. The figure rose with surprising grace and, in a flutter of black, she threw off the shela, revealing her colorful blue and gold shirt and marinda pants with diagonal red stripes reminiscent of those on a barber shop pole. A flowing blue veil of the sheerest silk and covered in tiny gold coins hung back from her forehead and draped nearly to the floor behind her. In her hands she held a green silk scarf that had seen much use.

It was as though a butterfly had suddenly emerged from the

homely pupa case and, along with the sudden flash of colors flew the intoxicating musky perfume, the perfume that Jade had scented on Musa. It was no wonder. Anyone associated with the girl for very long would absorb the aroma. *Civet oil.*

"I am Hazar Binti Ali," she said in English with as much pride as if she'd announced herself as the Sultan's wife. With a sense of drama one expected from H. Rider Haggard's character, Ayesha or "She," Hazar removed her mask. Unlike "She" whose fictional beauty drove men mad, Jade saw that Hazar was a pretty girl, but by no means the rare beauty she'd been made out to be. It was something about her demeanor that put Jade off, a sense of superiority on the girl's part.

"I know who you are," said Jade, putting her knife back in her boot sheath. She wondered if Musa knew where she was. She hoped not. She didn't want to face his ire. *The man's going to have kittens though when he finds out she's gone.* "And I'm not even going to ask how you got in here. I'm just going to tell you to leave."

Inez had followed quickly on Jade's heels and stood beside her daughter, a stern look on her face. "You were very foolish to come here on your own, Hazar. Your mother and grandmother will be very worried. This was most selfish and thoughtless of you."

Jade reveled in someone else finally taking the brunt of her mother's stern edicts. *Go get her, mother!*

"But I must be seeing you," said Hazar without a trace of remorse or shame crossing her face. "I know you speaked with grandmother."

"Spoke with," corrected Inez.

"Don't argue with her, Mother. Help me drag her back to her father before someone finds her here."

Inez held up a hand, cautioning Jade to stop. "I agree that she needs to go home, and we'll see to it ourselves, but first, let her tell her side of the story."

"Yes," said Hazar. "I tell you story. Then you will help me."

"Don't be too certain," growled Jade. She looked at the timid creature in white still hovering in the background. "Don't be afraid of us. Come and sit down."

Hazar frowned. "She does not sit down. She is my sl . . . my servant."

Jade noted the sudden change in wording. *So she knows that slavery is illegal. She didn't mean to let that slip.*

"In my and my mother's house, your servant is a guest," said Jade. "She will sit down if she wishes." Jade smiled at the girl and motioned to a comfortable chair apart from Hazar. The girl hesitated for a moment then hurried for the chair. Jade could only imagine how tired and sore her feet were, walking on the hot streets barefoot.

Inez slipped into an adjoining room and returned with a pitcher of cool water and two tumblers. She offered a glass first to Hazar.

"I will have tea," said Hazar.

"You will have water or nothing," said Jade. She saw Hazar recoil under the insult. In an Arab household, feeding a guest for up to three days marked a consummate hospitality. "It is all we have to offer to you, and you were not invited here. Now tell your tale."

Inez handed the other glass to the slave girl who drank it down greedily and handed back the tumbler with a broad smile.

Inez sat down but Jade decided to stay standing to make a more intimidating appearance. The girl was selfish and far too confident of her acceptance.

"You must help Kin."

"Kin? Do you mean Ken? Mr. Teasdale?" asked Jade.

"Yes. You must help him marry me."

"Do you--" began Inez.

Jade held up her hand and stopped her before she could finish the question and put ideas into the girl's head. "*Why* do you want him to marry you?" she asked instead.

"I want to be English. I want to wear dresses as you have in your room and as she wears." Hazar pointed to Inez.

"You looked through our clothes?" demanded Jade.

The girl nodded, a surprised look on her face. "You were

not here. I was bored. Do you not have nice dresses because you are not married?"

"Well if that doesn't beat everything," muttered Jade. "Can I throw her out now, Mother?"

"It is probably best that she go home sooner than later," said Inez.

"You will help me?" said Hazar. She held up the worn scarf in her hands. "Kin give this to me. It is old. I want a new one. He said he will find much gold and jewels. Kin will be rich. Then my father will let him marry me. Father needs money, and I will be English like you and live in a fine house with many dresses and hats."

"We are not English," said Inez. "We are Americans."

At that, the slave girl lifted her head higher and studied them more closely.

Hazar must have noticed the disdainful looks on their faces for she suddenly added. "And I love Kin. Truly I do."

Jade let out a derisive snort. "The little vixen is sharp, Mother," she whispered. "She's picked up that her real reason did not impress us." Jade also noticed that the slave girl watched them attentively, even more so after Inez had announced that they were Americans. She decided to try to draw her out. It would be problematic if this girl only spoke Arabic.

"You have not told us your name, miss," Jade said slowly, trying to dredge up her best Arabic. "Would you walk and speak with me?"

Hazar spoke up promptly. "She cannot go with you. I need her to take me home." She fingered the black cloak lying beside her. "It is not easy to watch steps in *this*."

"I will take you home, Hazar," said Inez. "We'll go in a carriage or perhaps you would like to ride in an automobile."

"No," declared Hazar. "Someone will see you and know I came to you. I will take a carriage to merchant and walk from store. Grandmother will think I have gone out to see shops. She will be angry but not so angry."

She stood up and immediately the slave girl reached for the

black shela and swaddled her mistress in it until not even the girl's hands were exposed. Only her black eyes pierced through as she looked first to Jade and then Inez. "You will help Kin. Tell him hurry." It was an edict made by a pampered princess used to having every command obeyed.

The two left without another word. Jade flopped into a chair across from her mother. "Well that certainly was unexpected."

"Spoiled little creature," said Inez. She rose. "If we're going to take the train to Bububu, I'd better change my dress. I hope she didn't leave all my clothes in a heap on the floor."

Jade glanced at the room clock. "It's getting too late in the day, Mother, and the train takes two hours to get there. We wouldn't have enough time to see everything. Let's have a late lunch or early dinner or whatever you want to call it. I'm famished."

Inez peered around the doorway of their bedroom. "Hungry so soon? After all that food we had at breakfast?"

"I ate one small piece of bread, some fruit and a lot of olives. It's gone by now. There's a tea room near Victoria Gardens."

"We could stroll the gardens afterwards," said Inez. "Perhaps see Mr. de Silva's shop on the way back and look for your --"

"Don't start again, Mother. No lace!"

They set out as soon as Inez had changed into simple, cool cotton dress. When they returned three hours later, they found Hazar's slave sitting outside their door, waiting for them.

CHAPTER 9

Once the slaves gained their liberty, they shed the merikani. The women flaunted their independence in colorful printed fabrics called kanga. Every kanga tells a story.
- - The Traveler

Sam stood near the shore at Port Tudor, feeling as out of place as a chicken in a church. Somehow he couldn't imagine that anyone would have any answers to their questions and wouldn't tell them if they did. But the vision of that man, bloodied and bound kept coming to the fore. He fingered a scrap of wood cut from one of the smaller crates and bearing the logo. Someone had seen the crates go into this area. Maybe someone else had seen them leave.

"I think I understand something about Jade, now," Sam said.

"Oh?" asked Richard. "Are you sure that's a good thing?" he grinned. "I quit trying to understand my Inez. I just accept her and love her all the more for it." He put a hand on Sam's shoulder. "There are some fillies you don't try to break."

Sam wasn't certain how to respond to that bit of advice. He decided to just explain his recent revelation. "What I mean to say is, Jade's always gone off on some crusade of hers, leaping into danger, and I've always felt uncomfortable with that.

Probably some Neanderthalish urge to protect her, but right now, I understand why. I keep thinking about those people kidnapped and shoved into a crate."

"We don't know for certain that people went into those other crates, Sam."

"I do. If someone wanted them to smuggle ivory, that man might have been found dead in one, but not bound up. No, he was intended for shipping out and fought back too much. And if Jade were here, she'd shoot the villains in the ass first before hauling them in."

"That sounds like our Jade, all right. Good thing she's not here. She and Inez could get into a world of trouble easily enough. They did in Morocco. Inez never did tell me everything, but something rekindled a fire in her." He grinned again, more broadly this time. "I think you know some of that story, don't you?"

"Yes, I do, and trouble doesn't begin to describe it. You're right. I was there for part of it. Did you know I had to buy your daughter from a slave market in Marrakech? Not that anyone else was bidding. Jade was too busy beating up the auctioneer's assistant." Sam had been watching several Africans working around a cluster of dhows and a few smaller outriggers a little farther up the coast. He pointed. "Over there. Maybe those men have seen something."

"Remember, Sam, we can't mention the dead man or slaves or even smuggling. For all we know, these people are involved. Say nothing until we gain their trust." He handed over a fist full of coins. "Here. Have some trust on me."

"I just hope to heavens someone speaks English," said Sam taking the coins.

It was the first question they put to the men, and to their relief, one them did. Sam began his questioning with a coin in the man's hand.

"Is this your dhow?"

"Yes. Mine. My brothers work for me." He looked Sam and Richard up and down. "If you wish to enter race. This is not so fast."

"No. We aren't interested in the race. I wouldn't think you'd want a fast dhow for fishing. Are these dhows for fishing?"

"Some, yes. Mine, yes. Others carry goods to sell. Do you wish to fish?"

"No, I want to carry boxes. Big boxes." He extended his arms. "Can these dhows take boxes far?"

"This dhow is for fishing. Others yes. Very big. Biggest not dhows, but *jahazi*. Jahazi go very far. Take goods to sell." The man had turned his back on Sam and picked up his fishing net, seeming to lose interest in someone who didn't want to hire his boat to fish.

Sam turned him back around by jiggling several more coins. "Who has a boat big enough for me? Do you know?" He put three more coins in the man's hand.

The man turned and said something in Swahili to his two companions. The men talked for a while then the first man turned back to Sam. "Ijara says the only jahazi big enough for very big boxes is not here. He says it left two nights ago."

"Does Ijara know where they went? Did they have boxes that had this mark on them?" He produced the wooden scrap and accompanied it with two more coins apiece.

Ijara took the scrap and studied it a while. Then he handed it back, nodding his head while he spoke in Swahili. The first man interpreted. "He says yes, he saw that mark. They went to Pemba. He thinks to Chake Chake."

Ijara nodded. "Chake Chake," he repeated.

Sam dumped the rest of the coins in the spokesman's hands. "I want to hire your boat to go to Chake Chake." He pointed to himself and to Richard. "No big boxes, just two men."

***

Jade and Inez nearly collided with each other as they both hastened to reach the pitiful bundle of white crouching in front of their door.

"Are you hurt?" asked Jade in Arabic. At least she hoped that's what she asked. To their surprise, the girl answered in

57

nearly flawless English.

"I am not hurt. I beg of you to help me, please."

Jade unlocked the door while Inez assisted the girl to her feet and brought her inside. Jade brought water and a tin of cookies and placed them in front of the girl.

"What is your name?" Inez asked.

"I am Tisha." She drank the water quickly and took one cookie when Inez pressed it upon her. "My mistress and I returned home and her grandmother had news for her. She is to be married very soon to a very rich man. His name is Mubarik Bin Rafi. He has a very large plantation on Pemba."

"Mother, that must have been his representative that we saw coming in this morning when we left," said Jade.

Tisha nodded, reaching for another cookie. Inez put the tin on her lap. "Yes," Tisha said. "That was him. My mistress' mother said that Bin Rafi is an old man who has had no children and his two wives have died. He hopes that my mistress, being so young, will bear him a son."

"You speak English very well, Tisha. Better than Hazar. Why didn't you speak before when you were here?"

"It would not have been allowed," she answered. "But, yes, I listened very close when Mr. Teasdale gave lessons to my mistress. And I practiced to myself every chance I got. Mr. Teasdale saw this and sometimes when my mistress was not watching, he would give me papers to read or a pencil and paper to write."

"You were a better student than she was," said Jade. Her estimation of Teasdale went up a few notches at the news of his charitable attentions to the slave. "But you said you wanted our help. Surely you don't think that we can stop this marriage. We may not approve, but it is not our business to interfere. Is this not how the Arabs make marriages? It is not for us to say otherwise."

Tisha shook her head. "I do not ask your help for my mistress. I ask it for *me*. You are *Mericans*." She tugged at her dingy white cotton shift. "I wear *merikani*."

"I don't understand," said Inez.

"I think I do," said Jade. "For years, unbleached muslin was imported into Zanzibar from the States. Merikani is a corruption of American and is the word used to mean plain cotton cloth."

"I still don't understand what this means, though." Inez turned back to Tisha. "How are we supposed to help you, Tisha?"

"I do not wish to go to Pemba. You are Mericans so I will now go with you and take care of you."

"Do you have to go to Pemba? Can't you simply go to work as a maid for another lady here in the city?" asked Inez.

"They will make me go. A slave has no choice."

"You are not a slave, Tisha," said Jade. "Slavery is against the law. It has been for many years."

Tisha's head drooped and she considered the tin of cookies in her lap. She carefully placed the tin on the nearby table and folded her hands in her lap. Jade thought she looked pitifully small sitting there barefoot in an overly large shift, her head close-cropped.

"I have heard that slavery is stopped but still my mistress and her family only give us the merikani to wear. That is the mark of a slave. And we have nowhere else to go. It is the same with Musa. He, too, is a slave though his master gives him good clothes to wear. But he will not mind to go. He loves my mistress. And he is big and strong. He will survive."

That last word, barely spoken above a whisper, stood out and screamed for attention. Jade sat next to Tisha and, tucking a finger under the girl's chin, lifted her face. "And why would you not survive?"

"Because it is Pemba. There are many witches there and many people die. If one wants to get full powers, they must kill someone in their family."

"Would a slave be considered part of a family, Tisha?" asked Inez.

Tisha thought a moment, then shook her head. "No, but there is worse for others like me. They are made to serve the witch in their spirit world. I would become as one dead but my soul must lose all hope. It is what happened to Alawi. He belonged to Bin Rafi and was given to my master. But he felt his old master's power on him, making him do his bidding. He tried to run away, to escape, but the witch cut him down in the street."

"That must be the man that fell down dead in the market street, Mother," said Jade.

Tisha looked up and nodded, her black eyes moist with tears. "One cannot escape a witch.

I think perhaps this rich plantation man is a witch. How else would he become so rich when my own master cannot make money with his plantation? My master must pay workers very much money to labor and sometimes the crops are not fully harvested. Much is lost. How does Bin Rafi pay people to harvest all his cloves and copra and still gain wealth?"

"And you think Bin Rafi would kill you?" asked Inez. "Or turn you into a spirit world slave?"

Tisha shrugged her puny shoulders. "If my mistress desires a new house, Bin Rafi will build it for her. Then I will be killed and put into the walls as a sacrifice."

"What?" exclaimed Jade.

"This time, I'm the one that understands," Inez said. She went to a dresser and picked up a volume lying on top. The cover read, *Zanzibar: The Island Metropolis of Eastern Africa* by Major Pearce. "I purchased this before I came to Africa. He spoke about this very phenomenon. It seems that, here in Zanzibar city, some of the old houses were torn down and skeletons were found associated with the foundation. Of course, the house might have been built on an old cemetery, but--"

"No," said Tisha. "It is true. That was as it was in old times. But on Pemba things do not change so much." She turned pleading black eyes on Jade. "Please, you must let me serve you. Do not let them force me to go to Pemba."

"I wonder if Musa feels this way, too," said Inez. "Perhaps he's afraid for his little Hazar."

"Musa is happy," said Tisha. "He is glad that Hazar will not marry Mr. Teasdale and instead will be a wealthy lady. She will even be a first wife as this man has no others now."

"And it's certain that he will go with her to Pemba?"

"Hazar. . ." Tisha stopped herself as if she'd spoken out of turn, saying her lady's name. "My mistress would insist on it. She is not so happy to go to a home far away from everything. She will want Musa with her. She has known him since she was a baby. There will be no one to talk to and no shops to visit."

"And no English dresses to wear," added Jade. "Tisha, you do not have to go with Hazar. You are *not* a slave. You speak English very well and, if you wish it, we will try to find you a job as a maid in an English lady's house where you would be paid. There are schools here for girls like you. You might learn more. If you like, you do not even need to return to Bin Hassan's house. You may stay here until we find a place for you."

"I would like to work in an English house, but I must go back to my old house for now to help . . . *her* prepare for leaving. I feel it a duty I must do. But if you come with me, you can tell the ladies that I am free and will not go with Hazar to Pemba."

"We will be glad to," said Inez. "I think they should owe you some back pay as well."

"And to celebrate your freedom," added Jade, "we will buy a new kanga for you to wear. No more merikani for you."

The three set back out into the afternoon heat, going first to Bazaar Street to the same pile of kanga that had attracted Inez earlier. Tisha, while able to speak, and to a lesser extent, read English, had never read Swahili.

"I speak it to the shop men when I go with my mistress to buy things, but I have never seen it as words in a book."

"When it is printed, it uses the same alphabet as English," said Jade. "Say the words out loud and you should recognize what you've heard spoken before."

Tisha did and, to her delight, quickly caught on. She pushed aside all of the cloths that contained messages about love or magic and chose a blue fabric with white birds on it. The saying on the border translated, *"I am poor. I am not debased."* She wrapped it around herself in the manner that she saw several passing Swahili women wear it and walked on, her head higher and stride stronger than before. Jade and Inez purchased a pair of soft, but sturdy sandals for her feet as well.

The women of the house were less than impressed by Tisha's new found self-worth and expression of freedom. Karzida looked bemused, Nuna pretended not to see her, but Hazar's face reddened as though it burned with anger.

"You *will* go with me to Pemba," Hazar shouted. She punctuated it with a stomp of a tiny, leather-slippered foot.

For a moment, Tisha looked as though she had been whipped. Her head drooped and her lower lip quivered, but whether out of fear of Hazar or dismay that she'd hurt the girl she'd served for so long, Jade couldn't tell. She decided to intervene before Tisha cast off the kanga and begged forgiveness.

"Tisha has every right as a free woman to make a choice," she said in Arabic for the older women's benefit. "If she chooses to go with Hazar on her marriage, then she must be paid as a servant. If she wishes to stay behind, *we* will find another place for her to work."

"Tell them that they owe her money, Jade," said Inez.

Jade repeated her mother's statement. Nuna's brows raised and her black eyes opened wide. Then she looked at her granddaughter and sighed. "We will give the girl five shilling for what is owed. She will not get so much elsewhere, I am sure. Hazar's chosen husband is a rich man. *He* will pay her in the new house. The girl will go with my granddaughter." The latter statement was an edict. Not once did Nuna deign to look at Tisha or speak to her.

"*If* Tisha agrees to go," said Jade. "She is afraid of going to Pemba. She says that it is not safe. Will it be safe for Hazar?"

Nuna made a derisive snort. "Stories made to frighten children into behaving," she said. "Mubarik Bin Rafi is an Oman Arab. He is a rich man, a Muslim as are we. What need has he of playing in devil nonsense. Tisha is a fool. If she

chooses to be so frightened, it is well she does not go with
Hazar and frighten her. Let her leave this house when Hazar
leaves. Let her know what she threw away when she hungers in
the streets."

Karzida looked less certain about her daughter's future.
"Are you frightened, my daughter?"

Hazar pouted and drooped her head to one side. "I should
be afraid all alone in a big house far away from a city on
Pemba."

Jade thought she looked less afraid and more upset that she
would not have shops and other Arab women to keep her
amused.

"Your husband will give you many servants to keep you
company," said Nuna. "And then you will have a child to take
care of."

That definitely put a frown on Hazar's pretty face.
Motherhood had not been in her immediate plan for herself, at
least not in any plan she'd revealed in their hotel room.

"Tisha," said Jade in English, mainly to confound the older
women, "you have heard the offer. What do you choose?"

"I choose to not go to Pemba," said Tisha. "But I will stay
two days to help my mistress get ready. Then I will leave this
house. I will work somewhere else."

Jade did not bother to translate for the older women. Hazar
understood. She could explain later.

"Then we shall say goodbye for now, Tisha," said Jade,
continuing to speak English. "We will not forget our promise.
We will find a position for you and let you know of it. Come to
us when you are ready. We will not leave Zanzibar for six more
days."

Jade reached into her pocket and extracted her coin purse.
"And to prove it, here is a gift from my mother and myself to
help you." She handed the entire purse containing over fifty
shillings. Tisha's dark eyes welled with tears as she accepted it.
"And Hazar's grandmother," Jade added in Arabic, "has
pledged five shillings more."

Jade and Inez turned to go and, once again, Jade had the

sense that their visit was being secretly observed. Her hunch was correct. As soon as she and Inez reached the corridor, determined to show themselves out, Musa arrived and announced that his master would speak to his daughter now. Stepping out into the corridor from some hidden recess, came Bin Hassan, resplendent in his robes, his knife glistening in his sash. Jade looked over her shoulder in time to observe Hazar's attempt to work herself into a state of terror for her father's sake. The girl slapped at her eyes to make them tear up and she pushed her lower lip out.

Bin Hassan strode past them without a second glance and enveloped his daughter in a deep embrace. "My child, if you fear this marriage, then it will not be."

Since it was evident that Jade and Inez were not included or welcome in this audience with the lord and master in his harem, they again followed a stony-faced Musa to the exit. At the outer door he gave them a look of malignant hatred.

Jade had seen that look before. It was the same look he gave to the back of Bin Rafi's envoy when he came to arrange the marriage. She wondered what she had done to anger him. Did his fury have something to do with Tisha's freedom or the end of these wedding plans for Hazar?

CHAPTER 10

The subject is not one that anyone wishes to discuss, but no one in authority truly believes that slavery is dead. Household slaves and concubines are out of sight and so also out of mind.
- - The Traveler

"I cannot take you to Pemba," said the boat's captain. "I am a fisherman. And the wind is not with me."

"Please," pleaded Sam. "I need your help, Mr. . . . . I don't know your name."

"I am Radhi."

"Ah, Radhi. It is very important for us to go to Chake Chake. We will pay what you ask."

"Is fishing that good for you that you would turn down money?" added Richard.

"We will pay," said Sam. "How much do you make selling fish?"

Radhi rubbed his jaw with one hand, the coins from Sam jingling in his other. "It is true that with the return of the *Kusi* wind, the fishing is poorer. It will be so until the *Kaskazi* monsoon returns and the winds go south again."

"And the current at least is in our favor," added Sam. "It goes south, does it not?"

Radhi nodded. "But it is far. And dangerous."

Richard reached into his pocket and drew out a leather purse. The coins inside clinked against each other. "How dangerous? Is it as dangerous if you stay close to shore as far as Dar Es Salaam and then ride the wind up to Pemba?"

"It could be done," said Radhi.

"And then you can take the wind home and fish on the way," added Sam.

"I must ask my brothers," Radhi said and turned to the two men who had been with him. They argued in Swahili for several minutes, before coming to an agreement.

"We will take you. But it will cost you twenty rupees for Sefu and Ijara and thirty for me. It is *my* dhow."

Sam took the man's hand and shook it. "Deal! When do we leave?"

***

The next morning, Jade and Inez set out after breakfast to look for a new position for Tisha.

"We might try calling on some of the English women living on Zanzibar," suggested Inez. "Perhaps someone has small children and needs a nanny. I should imagine that Tisha would be very good with children."

"That's a thought, Mother," agreed Jade, "but it would only be temporary. Once the children grow up or the woman moves back to England, Tisha would be out of a job again. I don't want to see her in just another servile position, either. No, I'd like to see her set up more independently."

"What did you have in mind?"

"She could be a teacher. Perhaps even continue studying as she teaches."

Inez reached out and stroked Jade's cheek. "What a lovely idea. Do you have a school in mind?"

Jade shrugged. "There are several schools for the non-Europeans of Zanzibar. Some for the Indian people, others for the blacks. Some are run by churches or charities, I believe, but the government also has some schools."

"Charitable ones won't pay Tisha to teach," said Inez. "We

should try the government ones first."

They decided to try the Teacher Training School first and, on announcing themselves, were shown in to see the headmistress of the girl's school, Miss Hendry. The lady wore a plain and somewhat severe brown cotton, long-sleeved dress with a button-front bodice. But her bright smile defied her clothing' austerity.

"How may I help you," she said, shaking their hands.

"We are here on behalf of a young Swahili girl," said Inez who had determined to act as spokeswoman this time. "Her name is Tisha and she has been a slave in an Arab household. We wish to free her of that."

"Of course," said Miss Hendry. "You are not English, are you?"

"We are Americans," said Inez, "here on a holiday, but this girl, on learning that we *are* Americans, sought us out for assistance. It seems that she equates us with some power."

"I understand. And how old is this girl?"

Inez looked at Jade who answered. "Fourteen perhaps. It's difficult to say. But she is very intelligent."

"She already speaks English very well," said Inez. "And she can read and write."

Miss Hendry folded her hands on the desk and leaned forward. "And how is that possible?"

"Her mistress was given an English tutor, a Mr. Teasdale," said Inez. "While the Arab girl didn't pay particularly good attention to her lessons, Tisha did."

"I have heard of Mr. Teasdale," said Miss Hendry.

Jade couldn't tell by her tone if the woman approved him or not. It's possible she saw him as competition for the school.

"We'd like for Tisha to continue to learn," said Jade, "but she also needs her independence. We don't want to see her working in servile positions. Would it be possible, do you think, for her to be given a position of teacher to some of the younger girls? Possibly a permanent position?"

"Well it would certainly depend on this young lady's aptitude," said Miss Hendry. "She might prove inspirational to the younger children at that. We will certainly do for her what we can. We can hardly allow her to continue as a slave. And she can live at the school if she has no place else to go. Her room and board would be a part of her remuneration. But I should need to see her and assess her skills before I can promise much more."

"We would be happy to bring her to you," said Inez. "Would this afternoon be agreeable?"

"Of course." The headmistress checked her appointment calendar. "Shall we say two o'clock?"

They thanked her and left.

"Looks like we won't make it to Bububu again this afternoon, Mother," said Jade. "But I know I'll enjoy the rest of our visit more once I know that Tisha is well-settled."

"Yes," agreed Inez. "She must be a remarkable girl to have learned so much on her own with hardly any assistance or encouragement." She checked the pendant watch hanging from her dress bodice. "We have several hours to kill. Perhaps we should get Tisha now? Maybe she'd like time to prepare herself."

"She won't need five hours, Mother. I thought perhaps I'd go to see Captain Yusuf and make the final arrangements to go to Pemba tomorrow."

"You're dead set on going there, aren't you, Jade. It's *why* that I can't imagine. There are ruins enough on this island. Just what are you up to?"

In truth, Jade wasn't entirely certain herself why she wanted to go to Pemba so much, but she did and she wanted to go soon. Zanzibar, with its British clubs and fancy shops seemed too tame and Jade longed for one last adventure before marriage. A day on Pemba hardly qualified but it was better than nothing. The official steamer only ran once a week and wouldn't be available for several days; days that Jade didn't intend to waste on thwarting her mother's urge to buy copious amounts of lace. If she could ensure passage for tomorrow, so much the better. If not, then they'd spend tomorrow at Bububu and go the next day.

Anything but shop for lace.

Was that it? Was it the lace or what it represented? Jade loved Sam. There was no doubt in that, and she now knew she wanted to spend the rest of her life with him. And that meant marriage. But the idea of marriage carried other baggage with it, especially as her mother viewed it. It meant an end to freedom, to adventure, to danger.

Surely it wouldn't be that way with Sam, would it? He understood her. He shared her love of adventure. He wouldn't want a demure, sit-at-home little wife. *Would he?*

Jade had always intended to see Pemba with or without her mother, but now she was doubly intrigued. She had borrowed her mother's book on Zanzibar last evening and read the chapter on the island. In it, Major Pearce gave an extensive report of the witchcraft practices on Pemba as well as hints of lost treasures. There was a time when Jade wouldn't have put any credence in tales of master-wizards but her first-hand experience with a practitioner in The British Protectorate chased that away. She still remembered the hyena that she swore she shot – the hyena that was a man. But neither Tisha nor Hazar were going to Pemba.

There was one problem with her intended expedition; her mother. Pemba didn't have motorcars for hire. Touring it for whatever purpose entailed a lot of difficult walking. The more she thought about it, the more she decided that she'd go alone, leaving her mother to shop to her heart's content. It would also mean returning to face yards of lace, but Jade was willing to make the sacrifice for her mother's safety. It would be one last fling of adventure on her own, no matter how tame an adventure it turned out to be.

And if she won't stay behind?

There was always a bored and lonesome government official in Chake Chake on Pemba that would probably enjoy hosting Inez for a day.

Jade learned that Captain Yusuf was out so she left word with one of the harbor men that she wanted to leave early in the morning tomorrow for Chake Chake. Inez, as it turned out, had no intention of letting Jade go haring off on her own, so Jade also arranged that they would come back to Zanzibar island by dusk that same day.

"Mother, the more I think on it, the more I'm convinced that you shouldn't come with me to photograph Pemba," said Jade as they strolled to Bin Hassan's house. "There are no automobiles to hire and the walking will be very strenuous."

"You are trying to get rid of me, Jade. I can tell. Why? What are you planning to do?"

"I told you, I want to photograph Pemba. And there are some ruins I'd like to try to find."

Inez shook her head and set her lips in a taut line. "And let you run off on some hare-brained scheme? You don't fool me. You either plan to look for Mr. Teasdale's lost treasures or see what sort of person this Mubarik Bin Rafi is. I cannot let you run off alone. No! I know what trouble you can get into."

"You're forgetting, Mother, that I know what trouble *you* can get into. But I can't guarantee a donkey for riding this time. If I have to hike any amount, I would worry about you."

"Do I look old to you, Jade? Let me assure you that I am very fit and strong.

Jade let the argument slide for now. If she'd learned anything after all these years it was that, once her mother had her teeth sunk into something, she never let go. For another, they'd reached Bin Hassan's house. It wouldn't do to let any of these women hear them bicker.

To Jade's surprise it wasn't Musa that opened the massive door, but another man dressed in a shift made of merikani. This painfully thin man had the downcast look of one used to constant work with never a day of relief. She made a mental note to inform someone in the government building that slavery was alive and well in this household. Jade told the man that she wished to see the women of the house. He escorted them to the stairs but did not ascend with them.

He's not a eunuch. He's not entitled to enter the women's quarters.

Nuna received them, but with much less warmth than on their first visit. They were no longer a novelty and they'd introduced dissent among one of their servants.

"We came to see Tisha, Hazar's maidservant," said Jade.

"She is not here," said Nuna. "You told her she was free."
She spread her hands out as if to express that she had no
control over the girl.

"When did she leave?"

Nuna shrugged. Her daughter-in-law Karzida was more
informative there.

"After we had broken fast," Karzida said. "She ran from the
house. We sent no one to stop her. Troublesome girl. Wanting
Hazar to look at her clothes. Why should my daughter care
what a slave wears."

Jade bit her tongue to avoid reminding the woman that
Tisha was not a slave. "And Hazar?" she asked instead.

"Hazar is not your concern," said Nuna. "She has gone just
now to be a bride for Mubarik Bin Rafi."

"Did Tisha go with her?" asked Inez. Jade translated the
question.

"She was not with her mistress. Ungrateful wretch."

"But I thought that Hazar's father had decided against the
marriage because it made Hazar unhappy," said Jade.

"A girl does not know her own happiness," said Nuna.
"And my son dotes on her too much. *I* saw to the arrangement
and saw that it was done swiftly. It is for her own good. You
know nothing of our life."

It was clear that they'd outstayed any welcome, so Jade
made their farewells and escorted her mother down the stairs
and out into the street.

"How do you like that?" said Inez once Jade had explained
everything to her.

"Where do you suppose Tisha went?" asked Inez.

"I'm hoping that she's waiting outside our door again as
before, Mother," said Jade. "We've been gone for several
hours. I wonder if --"

She had no chance to finish. Bearing down towards them
was Musa, his lips set in a grim line. He did not see them at
first. Jade wasn't certain he saw much of anything as he nearly

knocked them over, storming past.

"Musa," called Jade. "What is wrong?"

The big Wa-Shirazi stopped at hearing his name and turned. He stared at them as though he couldn't place who they were or why he knew them. Then his eyes widened for a second and his facial muscles twitched. Finally he seemed to recover himself.

"What are you doing here?"

"We came to see Tisha," said Jade. "We found a place for her to work. Do you know where she is?"

He flung his right arm out in dismissal. "Why would I care where she is?"

"We thought she would be with Hazar, but Hazar's grandmother told us that Hazar left early today for Pemba island and that Tisha did not go with her."

Musa's eyes widened and his lips pulled together so tightly as to disappear. "What are you saying? What have you done with my Hazar?"

Jade positioned herself in front of her mother. "We've done nothing with Hazar. You heard me. I last saw her yesterday when we brought back her maid, Tisha. We have not seen either of them since. I told you that she's gone to Pemba to be married. Ask her grandmother." Jade let a note skepticism creep into her voice, making it clear that she wondered what sort of bodyguard Musa if they sent her away without him.

The big man staggered and leaned against the wall to steady himself. "She is gone." His eyes grew wild. "She is my life and more than that. She is as my cherished sister. I must go to her." He clenched his massive fists. "Do you swear to me by what you hold holy that you are not lying? You did not take her or help another to take her?"

"You have our word," said Inez who stepped around from behind Jade. "We do not kidnap young girls any more than we pack them off at such a young age to be married."

"I did not think her father signed the marriage contract with Mubarik Bin Rafi," said Musa. "Hazar is his treasure and it broke his heart to see her unhappy. I will not believe he did this. The marriage was not one that Hazar liked, but my master could not send her away without me. No, Nuna is deceived. Teasdale must have stolen her away," he said with a growl. "I will crush him if he has deflowered her."

Jade grabbed at his arm, surprised to feel the power in his muscles. If she'd previously thought that eunuchs tended towards flabbiness, Musa proved her wrong. "You cannot accuse Teasdale of taking her. Not when Hazar's own grandmother says otherwise. She is the one that made the arrangements. She made them swiftly before her son intervened."

"I must go to her," he murmured. "At once."

Jade assumed that he meant go to Hazar. "We have hired a dhow to take us to Pemba tomorrow morning. It is the one belonging to Captain Yusuf. Meet us at the docks at sunrise tomorrow and come with us."

Musa nodded, but his eyes had a vacant look to them, as though his mind was elsewhere. "Captain Yusuf. Yes. I must go to my little sister." He turned away and half-ran, half stumbled to the house of Bin Hassan.

"Poor man," said Inez. "He must feel betrayed by Nuna to have not been told about Hazar. I certainly hope that is where she's gone, though. That little vixen might have slipped away from her grandmother and run to Teasdale. She might do something so rash as to try and elope with him. Perhaps that's why he'd been packing. He planned to elope with Hazar."

"Don't you start accusing him, Mother. If you want, we can pay him a call. If nothing else, someone should tell him he's out of a job. But first I want to find Tisha. We need to go to our hotel."

They hurried back to the Hotel Africa and up to their rooms. Jade's hopes fell when she didn't see Tisha waiting outside their rooms.

"Perhaps she got inside," said Inez.

Jade couldn't imagine any hotel clerk letting a Swahili girl into a set of rooms, a wealthy Arab girl, yes, but not Tisha. Still, she held onto a bit of hope as they unlocked their door.

The rooms were empty.

"We can ask if she was here," said Jade.

"Maybe she left a note for us," said Inez.

But no one at the desk remembered seeing a Swahili girl that day. "I do recall such a girl accompanying an Arab lady," said the head clerk. "But you can hardly think that we'd allow her to come in on her own."

"Where could she be?" wondered Inez. "Do you suppose she tried to reach us, but was turned away at the door?"

"It's very possible," said Jade. "But then I'd expect to find her waiting somewhere close by."

"Maybe she went to Mr. Teasdale's rooms," suggested Inez. "His landlord is Indian. He might have been more understanding and told her to go on upstairs."

"Good idea, Mother. She might have hoped that Teasdale would send word to us. But if he's not there…"

"She might at least be more apt to wait for him or for us in that neighborhood."

They set off for the shop district and the small flat rented by Teasdale. Tisha wasn't anywhere to be seen, nor did the landlord recall seeing her, but he admitted that he'd been busy and hadn't noticed if Teasdale had been at home or not either.

When no one answered at Teasdale's door, Jade opened the door. The flat was vacant. Jade looked into his bedroom and discovered that some of his clothes remained hanging in the open closet, but the valise she'd seen open on the bed during the previous visit was gone. There was something else, the faint scent of musk, the civet musk that Hazar wore. The scent clung to anyone who spent much time in the girl's presence. Perhaps Hazar had been there or Tisha. But if she had, where was she now?

One of the pillows on the bed was askew, as if hastily tossed back without thought for order. In an otherwise tidy room, it was out of place. She lifted it and saw the rip in the middle where it had been pierced through. The under portion was soaked in blood. Someone had used it as a shield to protect themselves from a bloody spatter when they stabbed at another person.

A faint breeze blew in through the partially-open window. With it came another odor; one cloyingly sweet. Jade recognized it immediately; the scent of blood, of violent death. Her attention turned to the floor, the bureau, the walls. There was a thin stain of blood on the hard floor and a trickling trail leading towards the window. She hurried to the window and leaned out over the sill.

There, in the alley below, lay a crumpled heap of scarlet red with yellow and black crouching leopards. The body in lay in an unnatural position, the head tilted at an angle that suggested it broke during the fall. Jade recognized the partially exposed face. She'd found Tisha.

Jade hurried out the building and around to the back alley, her mother hot on her heels.

"Jade, what happened?" asked Inez.

"I found Tisha. She's been murdered."

CHAPTER 11

One might wonder why the slaves don't leave their masters, but many of them are women with no education or prospects. Where would they go? And, as many of them are sequestered inside of homes, how would they even know that they are supposed to be free?
- - The Traveler

Jade crossed herself and knelt beside the pitiful little heap. A pang of sorrow and anger at the life cut short so soon after finding freedom and hope stabbed at her heart in sympathy with the deep gash that pierced Tisha's own heart. The girl had even gone so far as to buy another new kanga for herself. The words along the border translated as *"Beware one that eats."*

Beware one that eats? Jade looked again at the words. While her command of spoken Swahili was good, she knew there were nuances of which she wasn't yet a master. And, like many of those kangas her mother had looked at, many phrases had double meanings.

Had Tisha simply chosen it for the color and design as her mother had first chosen the ones with fruit, not understanding what they meant? After all, Tisha's ability to read Swahili had only just started. But Karzida had belittled Tisha's insistence that Hazar look at her clothes. Had there been a secret message intended for Hazar? A message that Tisha couldn't speak aloud in front of others in the house? Jade memorized the Swahili in case she found someone to ask about the kanga later.

"Oh, dear God," said Inez, also making the sign of the cross in prayer. "Poor child."

"She was stabbed," said Jade. "In the chest. See? Not all this red is the kanga. That darker stain on the chest is blood." If that wasn't disturbing enough, a greasy charm of finger bones lay across her throat, tied with a strip of green silk.

From Hazar's scarf? Someone wanted them to think that Teasdale was practicing witchcraft. *Or was he?*

"Those threads," said Inez. "Are they from the scarf Teasdale gave to Hazar?"

"You were reading my mind," said Jade. "But it raises more questions than it answers."

"I agree," said Inez. "Tisha was in Teasdale's rooms and her body was dumped out the window but it doesn't mean Teasdale did this. Does it?"

"It's easy enough to get into his room," said Jade. Someone could have followed her and killed her. But besides the murderer, I wonder if Hazar had also been in there with her."

"You think she got away before anyone could take her to Pemba?"

Jade shrugged. "She's a slippery little creature. She got away to come to our rooms. If she found out that she was being married off today, she might have tried to escape to Teasdale, hoping he would save her."

"If that's the case, why kill little Tisha?"

"That's what makes me think someone followed her. Perhaps this Bin Rafi's representative."

"Then why not haul Tisha off with Hazar? Why kill her?"

"Carrying off one unhappy girl would be enough trouble. Two? It would be easier to leave the servant behind. But there's another possibility. Tisha may have fought off this abductor to give Hazar a chance to escape and paid for it with her life."

"But if Hazar got away, she'd have gone home to safety,

wouldn't she?" asked Inez.

"Home isn't safe anymore."

Inez arranged Tisha's kanga to cover her exposed thigh. "You don't think it was Mr. Teasdale who did this, do you, Jade?" she asked.

"I don't know. It certainly looks bad. We need to alert the authorities." Jade wondered if this would fall in the Sultan's jurisdiction again or the British. Did both just let such deaths fall between the cracks rather than argue over them? Would they care about such a little innocuous person? "Mother, do you think you can stay here and guard her, while I hunt up a policeman?"

"I'll find someone," said Inez. "It's not too far from the Government Building. Somehow I think she's safer with *you* on guard. And I can stop quickly at our rooms to see if Hazar is there."

Jade was left with the little corpse and a mind whirling with questions. Bin Rafi's man, Darshash, would have been very displeased when Bin Hassan disagreed to the wedding. He would have been thrilled when Nuna went over her son's head to finish the arrangements. By then, he wouldn't have let anyone stand in his way of taking the girl to his master. But to resort to killing an innocent girl? Right now, Jade thought, if she had Tisha's murderer in her clutches, she'd beat the living snot out of him before turning him in.

Her mother returned in half an hour with one of the local inspectors and the news that Hazar was not in their hotel rooms. Jade related everything she knew up to the point of finding Tisha's body. And tickling at the back of Jade's mind were two unspoken questions.

Had Tisha tried to stop Hazar from running away? Had her own mistress betrayed her and killed her, leaving a sign from her own scarf tied around a filthy charm? Was Hazar a would-be practitioner?

***

There's nothing else that you could have done, Jade." Inez sat beside her daughter and placed one hand gently on Jade's shoulder.

The inspector had come and gone, someone had taken Tisha's body for burial, and Jade and her mother had informed the headmistress that Tisha had been killed. Now they sat on a bench in Victoria Gardens and Jade felt hollow and powerless. She had no further interest in Zanzibar. The veil had been ripped away from this mother/daughter excursion on an exotic island, exposing a wicked, sneering face. She longed for Sam's strong arm around her and wondered how he and her father were fairing on their safari. She imagined them happily choosing a camping spot from which they could observe Africa's myriad wildlife.

"Jade?" inquired Inez.

"She should have been out of that house sooner," Jade said. She sat with her hands clasped together, head down. "I could have insisted she stay with us."

"She was free," said Inez. "And you freed her. She chose to stay with Hazar until we found a position for her and we did, straight away. You have no cause to feel that you betrayed her in any manner. She's with God now."

"Then why *do* I feel that I *did* betray her?"

Inez pulled her arm back and sighed deeply. "I don't know. I feel that way, too. Poor child."

"But her killer is still free." Jade sat up straight and slapped a hand on her thighs. "Mother, there must be something we've overlooked, something we could turn over to the police."

"Jade, dear. I'm certainly game if you are, but what can we do? We don't even know where Mr. Teasdale is."

"We can determine if he's left Zanzibar or not. He has a dhow. He must keep it near the other boats in the harbor."

Inez sat up straighter. "Of course. We can ask at the main dock."

They went first to where the weekly steamship to Pemba Island docked and the few English owned boats were kept. No one knew Mr. Teasdale nor was anyone very interested in helping them. Everyone's focus was on the yacht race.

"Is he racing in this regatta?" one British man asked when

pressed for information. "If he is, then he would have left for Mombasa a day or two ago. The race begins there, you know."

"I don't believe he is," said Jade. "You see--"

"They leave Mombasa today and, they head straight for Chake Chake on Pemba," continued the man. "They have to stop you know and pick up an official paper proving they made it there. Then tomorrow at daybreak, they leave Pemba in the order in which they arrived, come here, turn about, and go straight back up to Mombasa."

It's very exciting," added the woman with him. "The Sultan has entered his own dhow in the race, you know. Such a beautiful boat, too."

"That's very interesting, but--" Jade tried in vain to bring the conversation back around.

"But I doubt that the Sultan is racing it himself," said the man, completely oblivious to Jade's attempts to stop him. "I believe he has a trusted and experienced captain sailing it for him."

"Thank you," Inez said. "Come, Jade, let's try somewhere else."

"There's still time to place wagers. Do you have a favorite?" asked the woman as Jade and her mother turned to leave. "Americans are so very odd," she added to her companion.

"Let's try our own captain, or if he's still away, his first mate," said Jade. "Maybe Teasdale kept his little dhow closer to the Arab boats."

They walked along the shoreline until they reached a small cluster of Arab owned dhows. Most were off shore, either for pleasure or for trade. A few sat on the shore where they were being cleaned or otherwise tended. Captain Yusuf was away but his worker, Salim was busily tending to another dhow. Jade asked if he'd seen an Englishman with long hair or if he knew the Englishman's dhow.

"I know both the dhow and the man of which you speak," said Salim with a slight bow. "He is a man of closed mouth, never speaking to the other captains. The dhow is a small one, but seaworthy."

"He is a treasure hunter," volunteered Inez. "They are a secretive type of people."

Salim bowed again, acknowledging her words. "The dhow that belongs to the Englishman with long hair is not here." He spread his hand out to encompass the entire shoreline. "I do not know when he left."

"Do you know when you last remember seeing his dhow?" asked Jade

"It was here this morning. I came not long after the muezzin called for prayers at sunrise. But I have been at work here and not watching boats like a boy," he added in a defensive tone.

"Of course," said Inez. "You are Captain Yusuf's trusted man. We are also looking for a Pemba man traveling with a young girl."

"One dhow left today. I am not certain when," said Salim. He wiped his hands on his robe. "I know the dhow. It belongs to a wealthy Pemba Arab, Mubarik Bin Rafi. It came with a big man and it took the big man and a woman. I do not know how old she was. She was swaddled in her garments as is proper." He cast a glance at Jade and Inez then looked to the horizon.

"Did they take aboard boxes or chests?" asked Inez.

Salim shook his head. "No."

"That is most curious, don't you think, Jade?" asked Inez. "I would expect that Hazar would have taken her clothes and belongings with her."

"Unless her husband promised her all new finery," said Jade. "But you're right. It is odd. I can't imagine her family sending her away without so much as a box of jewelry."

"I wonder if her father knows this," said Inez. "It was the grandmother that packed her off."

"Yes. It does make you wonder, doesn't it. Nuna Binti Ramiz didn't appear to be the most doting of grandmothers. I think she looked on a marriage with Teasdale as something that would bring shame to their house. She probably wanted Hazar out of his reach sooner than later even if it meant a hasty send off and marriage."

Jade looked at the dhow pulled onto the beach and pursed her lips. She had access to canteens and pouches of dried fruits to eat. What she didn't have and missed most of all was her trusty Winchester rifle. Leaving it behind in Nairobi was almost as hard as leaving her pet cheetah, Biscuit, but neither of them would have been proper to bring on this pleasure trip to Zanzibar.

Pleasure trip, my aunt fanny! At least I have my knife.

"I have contracted Captain Yusuf to take us to Pemba tomorrow. Do you think I could leave yet today?"

Salim shook his head vigorously. "Yusuf would be very angry if I took you. It is not my business to sail the boats. Only to clean and tend them. And he will be too tired when he returns tonight. He will take you tomorrow as you planned. And now I must return to my work. If Yusuf returns and finds that I have delayed my work to talk, it will not go well for me."

Jade thanked him and turned back to her mother.

"Mother, I think I should go alone to Pemba tomorrow and try to find Hazar. She may be able to tell me who killed Tisha. You know what the Inspector said, they would do what they could to bring Tisha's killer to justice, but they are limited by some stupid jurisdictional problems which sounds to me more like an excuse to not bother with deaths of non-English. If I can find out who, I can alert someone on Pemba to arrest the killer."

"And Teasdale and Musa?" asked Inez. "What about them?"

"I told Musa when and where to meet us. He can take me to Hazar. And if Teasdale witnessed Tisha's murder, then he might have gone on to Pemba to try to rescue Hazar. He could be putting himself in danger. If Hazar was taken by Bin Rafi and Bin Rafi marries her, there's not much I can do about that. I don't agree with it, but it's the culture in which she was raised. But if she's in danger, then I can't abide that at all." She didn't add that she half-suspected Hazar of killing her own maidservant.

"I agree with you completely, Jade," said Inez, "except for

your going alone. I intend to go with you."

Jade's brilliant green eyes opened a little wider. "Absolutely not, Mother! You stay here. I'll be back in a day or two at the most. Go . . . buy that blasted lace you want."

Inez folded her arms across her chest and tapped her foot. "You will not get rid of me so easily, Jade. I am perfectly capable of keeping up with you."

Jade knew when arguing was useless. If she tried to leave her mother back at the hotel Africa and slip off on a dhow without her, her mother would hire someone else and follow her. That would be worse. "Dad's going to have a conniption fit," she muttered.

"Oh, it would be far better all around if we don't tell your father. I don't believe he'd understand."

Jade released an exasperated sigh. "What am I going to do with you, Mother?"

"I wasn't aware that anything needed to be done. Now let us be on our way. We have some packing and planning to do."

***

The sun was an hour from setting when Radhi and his crew brought Sam and Richard to a quiet inlet a few miles north of Dar es Salaam, Tanganyika territory, on the African east coast. Radhi had followed the coast south, partially because he felt safer traveling that way, and partially because of the number of boats plying the open sea from Mombasa to Pemba in a sailing race. For a while the ocean had been thick with vessels and a few of the captains weren't above cutting out what they perceived as competition. There had been a few anxious moments in the first hour when Sam thought they'd be swimming back to shore.

"There is still light," Sam argued. "Why do we not go on to Pemba?"

"I will not sail in the dark," Radhi said emphatically. "We will sleep here and leave in the morning."

"Fine," said Richard as he eyed several large palms along the beach. "I'll sleep under one of those trees."

"No," said Radhi. "Very dangerous."

As if to emphasize his words, a huge coconut fell from one of the palms and crashed onto the beach below.

"I see what you mean," said Richard. "Okay, Sam. I'll toss you for who gets the best spot."

Sam grumbled something unintelligible and plopped down in the dhow, pulling his knees up beside him. It was going to be a long night.

CHAPTER 12

One of the archipelago's most beautiful sights is that of the graceful sailing vessels. Called "dhows" by most English-speaking peoples, that term actually refers only to the smaller of the boats. They are slender crafts with a triangular, or lateen, sail and glide as though they were born from a marriage between water and air.

- - The Traveler

"Where the hell is Musa?" It was a rhetorical question at best. Jade and Inez had waited a full hour after the muezzin had called for prayer at dawn.

"I think we must assume that he isn't coming," said Inez.

Jade turned and met her mother's eyes. "And what of his grandiose profession that he'd go to Hazar at any cost? Was all that a lie?"

"He may not be allowed to leave Bin Hassan's house."

"Or he made other arrangements and didn't tell us. Perhaps I should ask around."

She never got the chance. Captain Yusuf, who had busied himself arranging for his worker, Salim, to clean the dhow that had been out on the previous day, returned to them. He bowed deeply from the waist.

"Honored ladies, if you wish to sail to Pemba, we should leave very soon."

Inez accepted his hand and stepped onto the dhow with as much grace and dignity as a queen. Jade jumped in after her and they settled themselves onto a set of soft, worn cushions. Yusuf went in next while Salim and Yusuf's first mate, Nasur, pushed off the beach and into the waters. Nasur leaped into the boat and arranged the sail to catch the wind.

"Safe journey," said Salim with a wave. "I will have this other boat clean enough for the Sultan when you return."

"I should think that *this* dhow would suit a Sultan," said Inez as she settled herself comfortably on the plush cushion under the shade of a palm leaf canopy. "This is delightful."

Jade sat cross-legged, turned halfway so that she could see her mother and still watch the captain and his mate manipulate the dhow. Having grown up near Cimarron, New Mexico, Jade's world hadn't had much to do with the water but to quench the stock's thirst, and except for the larger steamers that plied the ocean, she hadn't been around many boats. Consequently, this was a new adventure for her. She could swim, but didn't particularly enjoy it. The dhow's nearly triangular sail fascinated her.

"I wish I'd brought my camera," Jade said. "I was going to, until this trip turned into a possible rescue mission." She looked at her mother, neatly dressed in a split skirt and riding boots, the very picture of a lady out for a day of adventure.

"When this is all done, I'm sure there will be time enough to photograph a dhow for your magazine. Now, what is our plan once we arrive?"

Jade watched the shoreline of Zanzibar recede from view as the slender boat skipped over the waves. The wind tousled her short black mane and played at teasing her mother's long hair which she'd tidily bound in a tight roll. A few wispy strands blew free. This was fun, almost as much fun as flying and with the same feeling of freedom.

Sam would like this. She wondered what he and her father were doing now. Would Sam disapprove as much as her father would of what Inez was doing? *Maybe I shouldn't tell Sam, either.* But somehow, that didn't seem to be the right way to go into a marriage.

Okay, I'll tell him after *we're married. After he's seen his new airplane.*

"Jade." Inez waved a hand in front of her daughter's face. "You've got a very faraway look in your eyes. You haven't answered me. What is our plan once we arrive?"

"Right, our plan. Make inquiries, I suppose, to see if someone came with a young girl. Ask how to get to Bin Rafi's estate. That sort of thing." She shifted on her own cushion, avoiding a wet spot.

"I assume there must be some official representative of the British government on Pemba, am I correct?" asked Inez.

Jade rearranged her position again. "What? Oh, yes. I think I saw that there's someone at Chake Chake to oversee imports or exports or some such tedious job. Mother, are you getting wet?"

"Sometimes a bit of spray hits my face. It's not unpleasant, but…" Inez paused and moved her right leg. "My leg is wet. Do you suppose these cushions were not completely dry when we got in?"

"I hope that's it," said Jade. She slid to one side and knelt next to her pillow, her knees pressing on the boards beneath her. Under her sopping pad lurked a pool of water. For some reason she couldn't have explained, she dipped her finger into the pool and tasted it.

Salty, but with a hint of sweet. Weren't some glues made of a concoction with honey added? *Glues that would dissolve in water.*

"Mother, I think we might have a bit of a problem." Then Jade felt -more than heard- something give. Immediately, sea water bubbled up into the dhow.

"Captain Yusuf!" she shouted above the wind. "We've sprung a leak!"

#

Sam leaned over the side and vomited what little breakfast he'd eaten that morning. The sea seemed choppier today to begin with, but all the traffic from the oncoming yachts had created rough waves. He was unable to anticipate which way the boat would pitch and the resulting effect was one he'd never experienced in all his years of flying. Sam vowed that he'd never set foot in a small boat again once he was safely back in Mombasa.

"What is wrong with these people?" he asked after wiping his mouth with his pocket kerchief. "Can't they see they nearly swamped us?"

"I doubt they care," said Richard. "This race is apparently a big to-do. Feel better now, Sam?"

"Not really." Sam eyed his future father-in-law. "Doesn't seem to affect you any."

"I've actually been in worse than this," Richard said. "Ever take a rather clumsy flat-keeled boat down parts of the Colorado River?"

Sam shook his head.

"Don't," advised Richard. He put a hand on Sam's shoulder and braced him. "Hang on, looks like we're about to get washed again."

"Do me a favor, Richard," said Sam as he gripped the sides of the fishing boat. "Don't tell Jade about this. I'd never live it down."

A wave hit him in the face as he leaned once more over the side.

#

"We're sinking!" shouted Jade. She used her hands to bail water over the side. The dhow had no hold and the water was rising fast.

"What happened" asked Inez as she joined Jade in her futile attempts to stem the rise.

Captain Yusuf pushed the two women to one side. "The planks have come apart in the hull," he said. "How can that be?"

"Can we stuff something between the boards?" asked Jade? The water had risen halfway up the hull, soaking her trousers as she knelt, splashing as much water over the side as possible.

Yusuf shook his head. "The coconut fibers that sit between the boards are gone. Someone has weakened my boat." He turned wide, frightened eyes on Jade and Inez. "We can swim, but what of you ladies? How will I save you?"

"We can swim, too," said Inez.

"No one can swim back to Zanzibar," said Jade. We need to roll the boat and hang onto it."

"Too dangerous," declared Yusuf. She may roll back and we are lost." He called to his Nasur. "Cut the sail!" The mate scrambled up the main mast and sawed away at the cording that held the lateen yard to the top of the main mast. When the sail and yard crashed down, Yusuf drew his knife, and the two men worked at slicing the sail free. Jade and Inez joined them, using their own knives, sawing furiously.

Jade felt her feet slip out from under her and knew that the dhow was going down. It was only a matter of seconds before it pulled the heavy, sodden cotton sail and the yard down with it.

"Watch out!" Jade yelled and pulled her mother towards her as the main mast, now free of some of its rigging, heaved to the side. The captain and his mate jumped clear as the heavy coconut wood crashed into the ocean, sending a spray of salt water that hit Jade and Inez with a vicious slap. The dhow breached the surface for a moment like a small whale. Then it gently settled, refilled with water, and sank.

If the sail wasn't free, it would go down with the dhow, pulling the lateen yard down with it. The long yard was their only hope of something to cling to.

Jade had hold of Inez in one hand and her knife in the other, both of the women now treading water. Before them, the sail splayed over the surface, held aloft at one side of its truncated triangle by a few more cords connected to the yard. Nasur was already there, attacking the wet, fibrous rope like a man possessed. The other end drifted down, pulled by the last remaining tie to the bow. Jade didn't see Yusuf.

"Help Nasur," Jade ordered. "Then hang on to the yard, Mother. I'm going to cut the sail free." She put her knife between her teeth like a pirate, took a deep breath, and dove.

Some stray pocket of air must have delayed the dhow's final

descent. It hung suspended before her, as one undecided whether to live or to die. The choice would be made soon enough, as a steady stream of bubbles drifted up from the bow. Jade never considered herself to be a good swimmer, but she kicked frog-like as her arms repeatedly pierced the water and pushed out to her sides. Before her was the captain, already at work on the last rope, bubbles rising from his nostrils.

Jade joined him, her lungs burning as she ached to take a breath and relieve what felt like a crushing pressure on her chest. Her ears rang, but she clenched her teeth against the pain and sliced her knife into the wet fibers.

The rope split, and the dhow, now deprived of a few buoyant pockets of trapped air in the sail, slipped down out of sight.

Jade surfaced with a gasp, Yusuf beside her. They studied each other for a second, then swam to the yard. The sail draped like a bride's train from one end, a train soon set free by Inez and the mate. To Jade's horror, the freed sail behaved as a thing possessed and lashed out at her mother and Nasur, lashing the man across the face and covering his stunned body like a shroud.

Before Jade could react, Inez dove and after a few seconds that seemed to last for an eternity, she rose, dragging the half-drowned mate with her. Jade and Yusuf swan to them and pulled them both to the safety of the free-floating lateen yard.

Jade grabbed hold of the yard and clung to it, gulping in the sweet air.

"Are you all right, Mother?" she asked in between breaths.

Inez nodded. "Yes, Thank heavens we *all* are."

Jade leaned to one side and slipped her knife in her boot sheath, eyeing her mother as she did so. The normally immaculate woman was a sight, her once perfect coiffure undone and streaming with water.

"You're a mess," said Jade. "Wish I had a picture of this."

"But you're glad you didn't bring your camera now, aren't you," replied Inez with a smile. The smile disappeared as quickly as a sunbeam in a rainstorm as they both looked at the captain. "Poor man lost his boat."

"It was sabotaged," said Jade. She adjusted her hold on the yard. "When I was underwater, I saw something. There was a bare spot on the hull, like where a scab has peeled away. It was fresh and I could see where the ropes that sew the hull boards together had been sliced through."

"But who would do that?"

"Only one man had access to the boat for the time it would take, and that's the captain's man back in port. But it's *who* put him up to it that has me worried. It's possible that Salim simply wanted to take over the business, but I suspect that someone didn't want us to get to Pemba."

"Captain Yusuf," Inez called down the yard. "We are sorry for your loss. I will pay for a new boat for you."

Yusuf seemed too stunned to fully comprehend her generous offer. Jade wondered if he suspected that a man he'd trusted had tried to kill him. Would it help to know that it was his passengers that had likely been marked for death? Probably not.

They bobbed like corks for nearly an hour. Jade felt her skin contract under the combined effects of sun and salt. Her lips burned and cracked and her head spun from thirst. She looked to her mother and for the first time saw the age lines. Inez's eyes were shut against the glare, but the fatigue still showed through.

A fresh fury coursed through Jade. How dare someone risk her mother's life. But anyone that would kill a helpless girl wouldn't hesitate to destroy a grown woman.

Hang on.

The thought had dual meaning; emotionally and physically. As they weakened, the mast seemed more slippery. Every wave hit with more force, battering them about like so much flotsam. She thought about singing a ditty to buoy their spirits, but her throat wouldn't allow it.

She reached out a hand and laid it atop one of her mother's and clung to her, hoping to pass some of her youth and vigor to a woman she loved desperately, but had only recently come to appreciate.

"There are sails," cried out Yusuf. "I see sails."

Everyone turned. There was a set brilliant white triangles coming in their direction. Together they called out and waved, hoping and praying that someone on this passing boat would hear or see them. They were in luck. A larger type of dhow, a sambuk, with a piercing curved bow tacked towards them. As it drew nearer, Jade could see the boat's beautifully carved and painted wood. The craft boasted two sails as well as a small cabin and a fringed canopy.

The vessel glided close them with swanlike grace coupled with the power of a whale, its narrow bow cutting the water, barely agitating the surface. Someone threw down a rope which Captain Yusuf caught. Once the mast to which they clung was pulled to the side of the vessel, a rope ladder was unrolled. Jade sent her mother up first, then, at Yusuf's insistence, went second, followed by the mate and then Yusuf.

Jade climbed on deck, dripping like the day's catch, and joined her mother. As soon as the Arab sailors had retrieved Yusuf, they all turned and bowed to the richly dressed man approaching from under the canopy. He wore an English suit and a tarboosh instead of a turban.

"You are welcome to my humble boat," the man said with a slight bow. "I am Sultan Seyyid Khalifa."

***

By the time they'd reached Pemba Island, Sam felt like something they'd hauled on board and left to die. The joint of his good leg ached from the restless night cramped on the dhow and the joint above his prosthetic leg seemed to be recalling the entire ordeal of amputation by the German prison camp doctor. He stank, too. The boat's very boards had been so immersed in fish that the smell penetrated their clothing and hair.

"I feel like a salted herring," said Sam as he tried to ease a cramp in his good leg. "This will wash off me, but my wooden leg will probably smell like fish for months. Helluva way to be for my wedding. Jade's going to notice and ask questions."

"We'll get rid of the odor one way or another, Sam," said Richard. "When we get back, we can stand downwind from the campfire and smoke ourselves. If that doesn't work, we'll find a wallow or something and roll around in it."

Sam studied the shoreline and the cluster of coral and stone buildings rising up the hillside beyond the beach. "Hadn't really thought about how we'll get back to Mombasa."

"One thing at a time, Son" said Richard. "Let's see what we can find out here about our crates."

They thanked Radhi and his crew, shaking their hands and giving them each a few additional shillings above and beyond what they'd already paid them. Sam's purpose went beyond his gratitude for a safe trip, he wanted to use them one last time to inquire about the crates for him. He posed the idea as casually as possible to Radhi, hoping that the additional coins would make the dhow captain agree either because of gratitude or because he felt he was now in debt to Sam.

Radhi, however, didn't seem to feel either of those emotions. But Sefu, a younger brother and one of his crew, had been listening and demanded to know what Sam had wanted. Radhi told him with seeming reluctance, and Sefu immediately nodded his head in agreement. He took aside Ijara and spoke with him at length. Then Sefu took the chunk of wood with the logo painted on it and, after pantomiming for Sam and Richard to stay put, set off with Ijara to gossip among the Wa-Pemba men.

"If they come back empty handed, Sam," said Richard, "then we might as well just ride back with Radhi to Mombasa. There's not much else we can do otherwise. We may not even be on the right island. For all we know, Ijara *thought* the smugglers were coming here, but maybe that's what someone told him to throw him off. There are several other smaller islands in this area and any one of them could've been the final destination."

Sam didn't answer. There was no need. Richard was right, but that didn't make it any easier to accept. The thought that anyone would put in at as public a port as Chake Chake with a load of contraband goods, whatever they were, was ludicrous. Damned thing was a wild goose chase and make no mistake about it. He kicked at a piece of weathered coral lying lose on the beach. The coral soared down the beach upsetting a sandpiper which flew up and scolded with a series of squeaking calls.

Richard, in the meantime had found a spot on a pier piling on which to sit and was looking up at the town climbing and clinging to the hills. Sam didn't believe for a moment that Jade's father was that tranquil. The man just had a quieter way of controlling the outrage that Sam knew lurked in his heart. They were two different predators: Sam pacing, ready to charge; Richard, older, more experienced, able to bide his time and wait. But when the time came, Sam knew that Richard would go on the hunt as eagerly as he.

After what seemed like an unreasonable amount of time, the two sailors strolled casually back to the dhow. Sam and Richard joined them. Once again, Radhi acted as interpreter for his younger brothers.

"A jahazi carrying such crates came here two nights ago but only stayed to pick up some food. They moved on without unloading. My brothers say that some men know this boat and see it trade with a rich Arab planter. This Arab trades more than cloves and copra. He sometimes trades very old pots with strange markings. Sometimes jewels. His fine house is on a big hill and one can see it from Chake Chake but it is very hard to get to it from Chake Chake." He pointed to a distant spec of white rising high above all other buildings.

"Do you know how we *can* get to it?" asked Sam.

"There is an inlet farther down the coast." Radhi looked to each of them as though trying to assess what to do or say next.

Richard reached into his pocket and pulled out another three shillings. "Take us to the inlet," he said, "and then go with our blessings."

Radhi studied the coins for a moment then posed something to his brothers. They shook their heads and spoke rapidly and passionately. "My brothers say it is not well to go there. There are stories of devils there. To take you there is to kill you and we will not have that on our hearts."

"We aren't afraid of devils," said Sam. "It is those very devils we are hunting."

"Why? If you wish to die, better to hunt *simba* or *tembo*. At least they will give you a fighting chance," said Radhi.

"We think these devils have taken slaves," said Richard. "They left one man dead not far from where we found you. Perhaps another time they will take you or your brothers. Will you let that happen? Or will you help us stop them?"

Radhi again translated. This time the response was immediate. Sefu, the youngest, reached for Richard's open hand and closed it around the coins in his palm.

"We will take you to this inlet," Radhi said, but will not take your money. "Then we will pray for you. This is the house of the rich Arab, but people say no one lives there but the dead."

CHAPTER 13

*Approximately thirty miles north of Unguja, or Zanzibar Island, is
Pemba Island. It is neither as accessible nor as well known as Zanzibar
proper, but it is for those very reasons that people of many cultures chose to
use it in the past.*
- - The Traveler

Jade had been in some incongruous situations before, but
none as odd as this. She sat on a low deck chair, soaked and
barefoot, her boots drying behind her in the sun. In her hand
was a delicate china cup of freshly brewed English tea. The sea
breeze rocked the anchored dhow, a two-masted beauty known
as a sambuk, and teased her drying hair into tight ebony waves
as it also dried the clothing on her body. To her right sat Inez,
her long black hair streaming in the breeze, calmly nibbling a
crumpet. Captain Yusuf's mate, Nasur, stood behind Inez like
a valet or perhaps, Jade thought, like some vassal in waiting,
intent on serving his lady. The man hadn't left Inez's side since
they'd come on board. Jade noted that her mother seemed to
be taking his dogged attention in stride.

The Sultan sat in front of them, calmly plying them with as
many foods as he did with questions. Only Captain Yusuf
seemed ill-at-ease before his sovereign. He fidgeted with his
cup and kept casting envious glances at the Sultan's crew,

96

happily lazing in the sun.

"If I understand you correctly Miss del Cameron," said the Sultan, "you and your honored mother were the intended victims of this sabotage?"

"Yes, your highness," said Jade, setting the untasted cup of tea on the little table before her. She hated tea. "I believe so."

"And do you know for certain who is at fault?"

"Immediately, the blame for sinking our Captain's dhow would most likely rest on his man in Zanzibar, Salim. He was the only one who had enough access to our boat to weaken the ropes sewing the planks together. The captain and I both witnessed that some of the coconut fibers that provide a tight fit at the seams were gone. I noticed a slightly sweet taste to the water as it first came in. If he didn't want us to sink too close to shore, he would have had to caulk his seam with something that would dissolve once we were far out to sea. Perhaps a mixture of honey and copal? The capsized outer hull showed where he'd scraped away the dhow's protective coating of lime and fats."

"But why do you feel that this man, who will be dealt with swiftly, wanted to kill you? Perhaps he only wished to remove his master so that he could take over as captain?"

"That certainly might be an extra incentive, your majesty," replied Jade, "but I would venture to say that someone knew of our reasons for going to Pemba and wanted very much to prevent us from arriving and interfering in his plans."

On request, she briefly summarized all that had happened and that they'd learned: from Teasdale's treasure seeking and his desire to marry an Arab girl, to her swift removal to Pemba and the death of her former slave. At the mention of slaves, the Sultan frowned.

"It is my hope that slavery has been abolished, but I know in my heart that some of my people still keep them. You did well to tell this girl of her freedom, I am only sad that she did not live to enjoy it. And so you seek the girl's murderer and hope to find that our Arab daughter is alive and well in her new home?"

Jade nodded.

"Captain Yusuf," said the Sultan, causing the man to jump from his seat. "From what I have been told, you behaved in a most excellent manner, risking your life to save your passengers. Such behavior is to be rewarded. I shall see to it that your dhow is replaced."

"Your majesty," Yusuf said, bowing so low that he nearly tumbled out of his chair.

"Miss del Cameron. You and your lady mother are my welcome guests on my sambuk. Please be at home as I return you to Zanzibar."

"Thank you, your majesty. But understand that we will immediately seek passage on board another dhow to Pemba. We won't be deterred."

"If that is the case, then we will turn about and take you there ourselves." He called to his own captain and issued orders, orders which clearly dismayed the captain who would not have openly voiced his opinion to his sovereign.

Jade did it for him. "Your majesty will lose the race if you turn about now. You've already risked much by halting for us."

"It is only a race. I have heard much of Americans and their determination. I know that you speak the truth when you say you will not be deterred. If so, you go with my blessings. When you have completed your task, you must send a telegram. I will send my sambuk for you to bring you back."

Before either Jade or Inez could respond, Nasur spoke up in broken English.

"My Sultan. Fear not for the ladies. I will go. I will protect."

***

"Dead people!" Sam expected to hear that the house was heavily guarded, booby trapped with primitive land mines, or even protected with wild animals lose in a compound, but occupied by the dead? "Do you mean that the house is abandoned?"

"No," said Radhi. "We have heard that a *mchawi* lives there. But you cannot see him. He keeps many servants in his spirit realm and they guard him. My brothers say that you cannot go there without first seeing a healer and getting a charm to protect you."

"Mchawi?" asked Sam.

Radhi paused to think. "A witch is what you would say."

"We do not believe in witches," said Richard. "Who is this man? What is his name?"

"He is called Mubarik Bin Rafi," said Radhi.

"And this Mubarik Bin Rafi is a, what did you call him? A mchawi?" asked Sam.

"It is his house. He is very rich," said Radhi. "Who else would be the witch but him?"

"If the man has slaves protecting him, then we will have to be more careful," said "Richard. "But if this man is a trader in jewels, then perhaps we can get past safely by pretending to be *buyers* of jewels."

Radhi shrugged like one who knew he'd lost a battle and simply gave up trying. "Maybe so. But I think it would be best not to be seen. And if you go, you will be seen. We will take you to the inlet. And because we fear God, we will wait in Chake Chake one day and then come back to look for you. But I think you will not be there."

***

Sam and Richard waved goodbye to their new found friends and watched as the men pushed off with a long pole. Radhi turned the dhow's graceful sail to catch the wind and soon their only means of leaving from this point was winding back towards Chake Chake and all that was visible was a billowing white triangle. At least the three brothers insisted on leaving them the remains of the food: several flat breads, two cakes of pressed dates, and a half-dozen dried fish, all wrapped in one cloth bundle.

Sam looked up the rugged trail disappearing up through the trees. Pemba's topography was varied with a few valleys and hills, the highest point being three hundred and ninety feet. The house they wanted to reach was probably at that elevation and the trail in front of them climbed steeply to reach it. He then turned to Richard. "Think we just did something incredibly stupid?"

"Yep," said Richard.

"Sorry we came?"

"Nope."

"Me neither," said Sam. He looked at the shadows then pulled his pocket watch. It was already nearly noon and it looked as though they had several hours of hard climbing to reach the top. It wouldn't leave them much time for searching the area if they planned to meet the dhow back here at noon tomorrow. "I hope Radhi and his brothers wait for us."

"I wonder how anyone manages to haul goods up and down this," said Richard. "There has to be an easier route of approach."

"There might be, but we're not on it so we either start walking or just make ourselves comfortable down here until tomorrow and call this a lost cause."

Richard answered by setting off up the trail.

"That's what I thought, too," said Sam and fell in step right behind him.

***

Jade spent most of the passage time talking to the sambuk's crew about Pemba Island. She asked them about the plantations, animals, stories of treasure and finally, witchcraft. What she heard didn't fill her heart with confidence. The plantations were isolated, the terrain difficult, and if half the stories of witchcraft were true, every other person on the island was either trying to learn the craft or was buying a charm to protect against it.

Inez spent most of her time trying to avoid Nasur. He clung to her less like a shadow and more like an avenging guardian angel, his scowl chasing away any man with whom she tried to converse, including Captain Yusuf. The only person to escape his protective shield was the Sultan.

By the time Jade and Inez had docked at Chake Chake, Jade had decided on a course of action that should keep her mother out of any trouble. There was just one problem with the plan – her mother.

"If you stay in Chake Chake with Nasur, Mother, you can keep an eye out for Hazar or ask about her at the British outpost. Look out for Teasdale, too, for that matter."

"You expect me to stay behind with Nasur while you traipse off into who knows where? Oh, no."

Jade grinned. "You saved his life, Mother. It's like you rescued a stray mongrel, and now he won't leave your side."

Inez shot Jade a look that would have curdled milk. "You think this is funny? The man acts as if he now *owns* me rather than owes me. I doubt he'd even let me take tea with some lonely officer in town. If anyone gets left behind, it will be him."

"He'll settle down, Mother. If anyone can make him fall in line, it's you. Besides, I really need you to stay in Chake Chake. It's called divide and conquer. I'll hunt up this Mubarik Bin Rafi and say that Hazar's mother sent me to bring something to her while you keep a watch here."

Inez folded her arms across her chest and raised a skeptical eyebrow. "And just what gift would you be bringing to Hazar? Your boots? You don't have much left." She glanced behind her at her ever-present shadow and lowered her voice. "Maybe we could give Nasur to her."

Jade looked around at the cluster of dhows in the harbor and at the rising town ahead of her. "I'll buy something. The Sultan gave us a lot of money for food and anything else we need."

She led the way up through the small clusters of Pemba residents on the narrow beach and up the inclined street into the town proper. Houses built of the local coral rock and thatched with coconut palms butted up against each other, competing for a foothold on the slope. A few children chased each other in play while mothers labored over household duties nearby. Jade saw few men as they went deeper into the town, but since most of the families made their livelihood from the sea when it wasn't time to harvest cloves, that was not a surprise.

"There's something I can buy," Jade said. "That man is

making coral necklaces." She strolled over to him and bargained for several necklaces, thinking that would look more impressive than arriving at Bin Rafi's house with only one. She saw a fourth necklace, one where the coral was chased with a silver wire and bought it as well. "For you, Mother," she said, handing over the delicately worked piece.

"Jade . . . it's lovely, but you--"

"Just say thank you, Mother. No buts." As she paid the craftsman, three women approached. Each wore their hair in a line of delicate plaits down the backs of their necks and all boasted a silver ring in the center membrane of their nose. One in particular strutted like a proud peacock, wearing one of the more suggestive kangas that Inez had previously considered. In addition to the nose ring, she had a brass stud in left nostril. Jade stopped them and greeted them in Swahili. They replied politely but with an aura of suspicion. Nasur, Jade noted, kept his distance from these local women.

"I wish to know the meaning of a kanga," Jade said. "A young friend of mine on Unguja," she continued, using the local name for Zanzibar Island, was coming to live on Pemba with her mistress. She wore a red kanga with crouching leopards."

Each of the women looked to each other, brows raised as though privately communicating some thought. Jade finished by stating the message as it was printed in Swahili.

"Your friend does not trust someone," said the saucier woman in the trio. "Someone close to her. A person that she shared food with will betray her."

"The leopard speaks of witchcraft," said a second woman. "She fears a witch."

"She should see a healer and gain a protective charm," said the third.

"I think it is too late for that," said Jade. "She is dead." The women gasped then exchanged knowing glances again. "I hope to save her mistress. She is an Arab girl. Have you seen a man bring an Arab girl to Chake Chake? She would be all in black. He would bring her to marry a wealthy planter."

None of the women had seen anyone like that. "Who is the man she marries?" asked the saucy woman who seemed to take on the role of spokesperson.

"Mubarik Bin Rafi," said Jade.

The response was instantaneous. All three women made signs as though to ward off evil. "He has a large clove plantation," said the spokeswoman. "He hires no one in the town to work for him. No one will go there. There is much evil there."

"Who harvests the cloves if he hires no one? Is there a village nearby?"

The woman shrugged but she glanced nervously over her shoulder. "He has a big man to run his plantation. Perhaps he picks them all himself."

It was clear to Jade that they didn't like to speak of Bin Rafi's manor, going so far as to avoid speaking his name or the name of his foreman. Jade wondered if that was Darshash. She asked. No one repeated his name, but neither did they deny it. It seemed that anyone associated with that plantation was tainted.

"Where is his house?" asked Jade. "I must go there to see Bin Rafi's bride and bring back word to her family that she is well."

"She will be dead," said the lead woman. "This man," she spat on the ground, "has had two other wives. They died that he would gain power in the guild. Do not go there. It will be your death, too."

"Tell me where his house is, then, so that when I walk in Pemba I am sure to stay away from it."

"It is hard to reach from Chake Chake," the woman admitted. "It is a long day's walk that way," she pointed south towards a rising cliff overlooking the sea. Jade could make out the distant glimmer of white of a fine, large house. "The road twists around many mangroves and watery land."

Jade nodded and, almost as an afterthought, asked if they had seen a young Englishman. She described Teasdale's longer hair and tendency to drape a scarf around his shoulders.

"*I* have seen this man," said the third woman, seemingly anxious to have a bigger say in this conversation. "I have seen him times before as well. He comes to dig. He asks many people in Chake what they know of things buried from long ago."

"Did he come here alone this time?" asked Jade.

The woman pondered a moment. "I think so, but I am not sure. I did not see him get off a dhow. I only saw him walking. He went the way you should not go. And he looked angry. Almost as angry as the big Wa-Shirazi ox."

"The big Wa-Shirazi ox?" She described Musa and asked if that was who the woman meant. But it was the woman in that suggestive fruit kanga that answered.

"I know that man who is not a man," she said with a scornful laugh and punctuated the statement with a chopping motion of her hands. "The first time I saw him, I thought he was . . . another man. Then I saw he was not, so I invited him to visit me and he . . ." she looked at Jade from under lowered lashes as though to gauge whether or not this white woman would understand.

Jade took the opportunity to brush back her short bangs and wipe her brow, exposing the Berber tattoo. Her wrist tattoo flashed before them at the same time. The women were impressed if widening eyes and raised brows were any indication. "I am no stranger to other cultures."

The spokeswoman nodded and smiled a Mona Lisa smile. "You are not like the English women. *You* will understand. When I invited him, I touched him. He was as an ox."

Jade nodded to signify her understanding. "And you have seen him recently?"

"Yes. He came this morning. And he was very angry."

Jade thanked them verbally, then gave each of them one of the coral necklaces which they gladly took. She was about to question them further when they quickly turned and hurried away.

"What happened?" asked Inez.

"They probably didn't want to see me," said a masculine

voice behind them.

Jade and Inez turned to see a middle-aged Englishman dressed in a lightweight suit. He extended his hand. "John Allenby at your service ladies. I'm what passes for a British presence on Pemba."

Inez took his hand. "Mr. Allenby. A pleasure to meet you. I'm Inez del Cameron. This is my daughter, Jade."

"Del Cameron," he repeated. "Spaniards?"

"Americans," said Jade. "Are the British so disliked that the local Wa-Pemba don't want to speak to you?"

"Not at all," he said. "But those women are, how shall I put this? Of questionable virtue. They know that we disapprove and they scorn *me* for it."

"Have you arrested them?" asked Inez.

"No, of course not," said Allenby. "It's out of my purview for one thing. I'm merely here to monitor exports of goods from British run plantations. And you ladies? Are you touring? Perhaps you will be so gracious as dine with me. I apologize for my forward behavior. It's just that it's rather lonely here, you see."

"Perhaps on my return through," said Jade, "although if my mother wishes to stay in Chake Chake. . ." She looked at Inez, one brow raised questioningly.

"I'm not leaving you to go traipsing off alone," said Inez.

"Where, may I ask, are you going?" asked Allenby. "Perhaps I may be of assistance."

"We're looking for the plantation and residence of Mubarik bin Rafi," answered Jade. "We have been charged by the Sultan himself to report on a young lady that has been taken to his home. Her maid was murdered just before the girl left and we're concerned for the girl's safety."

"I say," said Allenby, "on the Sultan's orders? Most remarkable. But I should advise you to not go. Bin Rafi's house is difficult to reach."

"So we have been told by those women," said Jade.

"And there are strange tales about that place."

"I've heard all about that as well," said Jade before he could continue.

"We don't believe in witches," added Inez.

"It does not matter if you do or not," said Allenby. What matters is that *they* do. If you can delay a few days, perhaps as much as a week, then I'd be able to take a few days and accompany you."

"I thank you," said Jade, "but it's not necessary. I can take care of myself and my mother. I've lived in Africa for quite a while now."

"But not on Pemba," cautioned Allenby. "I can't detain you, of course, only advise. But I will be watching for your safe return. Please stop by my office when you come back." He pointed to a distant building with the British flag flying above it, "It would greatly ease my mind."

"We shall," said Inez, taking his hand again. Then she and Jade turned away and continued their stroll up the street.

"Now you need to buy something else to bring to Hazar," said Inez. "I hope what those women told you was worth the price."

"Maybe." Jade related what she'd learned. "So both Musa and Teasdale are here, but no one has seen Hazar. Mother, I misunderstood Tisha's kanga. It didn't mean that a leopard eats you, but that someone you ate with will betray or harm you. The leopards also represent witchcraft. I truly believe that Tisha was trying to send a warning."

"A warning to Hazar?" asked Inez.

Jade shook her head. "I guess that doesn't make much sense at that. Even if she couldn't openly tell Hazar, Hazar probably wouldn't have understood the Swahili any more than her mother or grandmother did. Maybe she was trying to pass on the message to someone else."

"We found her dead outside of Teasdale's. Was she trying to warn him? Do you think she meant that Hazar would betray him?"

"That's a very interesting thought. I don't know. I do know that I need to get to Bin Rafi's house to find her. I sure wish I had my Winchester with me. Hazar might be in danger or she might be a murderess, I don't know which, but I mean to find out. Mother, are you certain that you wouldn't rather stay here and visit with Mr. Allenby?"

"I mean to go with you," said Inez.

Jade knew the look on her mother's face. It was a look that brooked no argument.

So much for her plans.

CHAPTER 14

*Imagine sleek Phoenician vessels plying the route from Madagascar,
bringing ivory, palm oil, and tortoise shell to the courts of Solomon. Think
of the Greeks sailing under orders from Xerxes. The latter, at least,
explains the odd ritualized dance with tridents performed by one group of
peoples. These islands have been visited many times over the centuries.*
- - The Traveler

Sam paused for a moment and massaged his left thigh which,
as usual, had been carrying the brunt of his weight when
climbing. They'd been at this hill for a half an hour and
something about the path struck him as all wrong.

"What is it Sam?" asked Richard. "Do you need to rest a
while?" The older man leaned against a rock and mopped his
brow. "Take all the time you need."

Sam studied Richard, looking for signs of stress in the older
man. He saw nothing more than what he felt himself. "Does
anything strike you as odd?" asked Sam.

"Besides the fact that this trail climbs straight up and seems
to choose the steepest parts of the hill?"

"Yeah, that's what I thought, too," said Sam. He took a
long pull on the canteen and offered it to Richard who
declined it and undid the cap on his own. "Why would anyone
make the only path up to their house this difficult? If this Bin

Rafi has a plantation up there, then there's got to be a better to get the cloves down to the inlet to load onto boats."

"Do you think that our friends on the boat dropped us off at the wrong spot on purpose?"

Sam shook his head. "No, I trust them. They acted to the best of their knowledge. But *they* could have been misinformed. If you're a slave smuggler, would you let everyone know how to get to your land?"

"On an island this small, I can't see how you can keep it a secret. Perhaps the best way to restrict access is to make the trail as difficult as possible."

"Maybe," said Sam but his tone betrayed his disbelief. He found a Tamarind tree that looked promising, grabbed hold of a lower limb and pulled himself up. After a few more minutes, he'd climbed close to the top, startling a pair of little blue monkeys. From his vantage point, he studied the land around them.

"There!" he exclaimed, pointing down slope. "About twenty yards down the trail I can see a break in the rest of the tree line. There's another path cutting off to the right."

He shinnied back down the tree, dropping lightly on the ground. Richard had already started backtracking. By the time Sam reached him, Richard was searching around a rock outcrop.

"Here," Richard called. "On the lower part of this outcrop. It's worn a bit smoother than the rest. As if people have climbed over it for years."

Sam asked for a leg up and scrambled over to the top. "There's a trail here." He turned and leaned over, giving a hand to Richard. In a few moments, they were on the other side.

"Stay behind me, Richard. I'll 'ride point' from now on." He drew his Colt.

***

Each time Jade thought she'd discovered a potential shortcut, an impassible ravine or a waterlogged mangrove forest blocked her path. She should have known that, had there been an easier or shorter route to Bin Rafi's high home, it would have been discovered long before. It was nearing mid-afternoon and all they'd seen were a flock of some brown-headed parrots, dramatic black and white crows, iridescently plumed sunbirds, and high in the trees, clusters of large roosting bats known as flying foxes. There'd been so sign of Teasdale or anyone else for that matter. By now it was too late to try to make it all the way to Bin Rafi's house before nightfall and it looked as though she'd need to take her mother back to Chake Chake and try again early the next morning.

If only she'd stayed behind like I'd wanted. We must be nearly to the eastern side of the island by now.

But throughout the entire hike, her mother had never once complained or begged for a rest. It would have made it easier to pack her back to Chake Chake and leave her there if she had. Of course, if she had so much as whimpered, Nasur would have been there to help. The man didn't lead, didn't try to take over Jade's position. He simply stuck close to Inez, his gaze never leaving her whether he watched her feet, face, or back.

Probably why she didn't gripe. Then she mentally corrected herself. Not only was her mother not a complainer, but she could've out walked Moses in the desert. The woman might look like a duchess, but she was made of sturdy stock. *I'll tucker out before she does.*

That's when Jade heard a crying baby. "Mother, there's a house nearby."

The threesome walked more swiftly along the trail, following the sound of the crying child. It wasn't long before they found a small village of coral stone houses thatched in palm leaves. A Wa-Pemba woman sat cradling the child to her breast, hushing it into contented coos as it nursed.

Jade barely gave the woman a second glance, her attention riveted by the event in the fenced area at the opposite end of the village. A young bull, without horns, stood bewildered in the pen while four young men raced around him, fluttering colorful cloths. One knelt in front of the bull and flicked his cloth nearly in the bull's nose.

As soon as the confused beast had had his fill of such taunting, he charged rapidly but the kneeling youth had already gotten to his feet and had leaped nimbly aside. No one had any weapons nor did it look as if anyone intended to hurt the animal. At the sidelines, the older men and the women cheered everyone, including the bull.

"Mother, it's a bull fight."

"But not like anything I ever saw in Spain," Inez said. "Surely this must be a remnant of when those infernal Portuguese lived here. You can't kick a continent that they didn't try to claim."

After a while, the bull tired of this game and knelt down as though he disdained any attempt to annoy him. The bullfighters, laughing and clapping each other on the back, climbed over the stockade to receive the accolades of the watchers. One of the village elders spied Jade and her party and, after giving some orders to another man, walked over to them with great dignity coupled with a touch of wariness. The man that had received the orders fixed a rope halter to the bull and stood waiting patiently nearby.

Jade greeted the elder respectfully in Swahili, and again in Arabic, hoping he'd respond to the former rather than the latter. He didn't. As she struggled to introduce themselves to him and to explain why they'd come to the village, the man relaxed a little and seemed particularly amused by her Arabic. Eventually, they settled on a mixture of the two languages, Jade doing better in Swahili and the man doing better in Arabic.

"I am Jabu. My wife is Kito. Come to my home and tell me what you seek. Please accept some refreshments." He issued a brief command to his wife who hurried away without speaking a word. "I will take you to my house, but first I must see to our bull." He waved to the man waiting by the bull and motioned him over. "Mahir, rub down the bull to dry him. Give him water and a handful of grain then stake him out to graze."

The man called Mahir bowed and loped back to the bull. He moved with the strength and grace of a young man though his hair held streaks of gray.

111

"Come," said Jabu. "Let us refresh ourselves."

"Thank you," Jade said after she and Inez were seated on the hard-packed floor of the house. Nasur opted to sit in the doorway facing the outside, as though to prevent anyone from harming his chosen lady. Kito served them the liquid from a green coconut as well as chunks of mango and some confections made from tamarind seed pulp. All three tasted cool and delicious after their tiring walk.

"My mother and I seek two people. One is a young Arab girl who was taken to this island to be a bride. Her father did not approve the match and wishes to know that she is safe. When this girl was taken, her maid servant was killed. The other is an Englishman with long hair. He is missing, too."

"And did this Englishman steal the girl?" asked Jabu.

"We do not know. He may have. He loves her. Or he may try to bring her back home with her honor."

"Who was the man the father did not approve to be the girl's husband?"

"His name is Mubarik Bin Rafi."

The silence that followed was so intense, it was as if all sound had been sucked from the room. Jade worried for a moment that they would be told to leave. Finally, Jabu called to his wife to bring more food and drink and urged them to eat.

"You are not English," he said after they took more refreshments. Even though it was not posed as a question, Jade knew that he wanted to know more about them.

"No. My mother and I are Americans. We are here because a young girl was killed and another is missing. We knew these girls. We cannot save the one but we can save the other."

Jabu nodded as though he approved the sentiments. "And this man who guards you like a Sultan's favorite?" He nodded to Nasur.

"Nasur served on the boat that carried us to Pemba. The boat sank and my mother saved his life. He will not leave us now." Jade knew that Nasur was listening to every word spoken. She hoped she didn't dishonor the man with her statement.

Jabu nodded again, seemingly satisfied with her reply. "I do not know Bin Rafi," he said. "I know that no one goes to his fine home. It is said to be haunted and the dwelling of many spirits. You should not go there."

"Where does Bin Rafi live then?" asked Jade.

"Perhaps he has a home in Chake Chake or in Wete to the north. His house is very lonely." He paused and rubbed his chin in contemplation. "Perhaps it is why the other man comes and goes."

"What other man?" asked Jade. "Is it his servant Darshash?"

Jabu nodded. "You know of Darshash? He sees that Bin Rafi's cloves and copra are harvested. He has been here to the village not so long ago to buy a cow and rice. Perhaps Bin Rafi will live at the house once he takes his new bride."

Jade translated all this for her mother's benefit. "Then Darshash did take Hazar," said Inez. "And now he's preparing for his master's return."

"It certainly looks that way, Mother," said Jade.

"We must go to the house and see if Hazar truly wants to stay and marry Bin Rafi," continued Inez. "If not, we must insist on bringing her back home."

"To Teasdale?" asked Jade with a frown. She didn't care for the idea of a young girl being forced into a marriage against her will, but she didn't approve of that foppish Teasdale either. Still, she wanted to find Hazar to learn what had happened to Tisha. Jade felt certain that either she or Teasdale knew something about the poor slave girl's murder. It was information Jade intended to learn if she had to drag it out of them.

"Not necessarily," said Inez. "The child should be home with her mother."

"I agree she shouldn't be in the hands of a murderer," said Jade. "It's looking more and more like Darshash killed Tisha. And since he's acting on Bin Rafi's orders, that makes Bin Rafi a murderer as far as I'm concerned."

Jade kept an eye on Jabu as they talked. He listened but

without any obvious comprehension, except when they named names.

"This Teasdale of which you speak," Jabu said in their mix of Arabic and Swahili. "This is not an Arab name. Is he the Englishman with the long hair that you seek?"

Jade nodded.

"I have seen him. He came to the village one day past and bought coconut meat and rice. He carried a shovel."

"Do you know where he went?" asked Jade.

Jabu shrugged. "Maybe." He proceeded to give a general direction in which Teasdale had last been seen. "He has been here before and asks my people what they know of jewels and coins in the ground. Some of the younger men told him tales of a magical tree that yields such wonders from time to time. I think he went to find it."

"I must go there," said Jade, "and find him, to be certain that he did not take the girl or kill her maid."

Jabu shook his head. "You must not go at night. There are many spirits abroad at night. You and your mother will stay with us, safe in our house tonight. I will find a place for your servant to sleep, too, so that you may have some peace." He winked when he said that as if to indicate that he knew they were uncomfortable with such a determined watchdog.

Jade thanked him, her mind working out a way that she could leave her mother here in safety tomorrow while she hunted for Teasdale and ultimately, for Bin Rafi. *Maybe I should ask Nasur to help keep her here.* But Jade knew if she stooped that low, there would be hell to pay later.

***

Sam stalked the trail in a slight crouch, eyes and ears wary for any sound, any sudden flush of a bird ahead of him, anything that looked like a booby trap. Everything about this trail cried out for stealth. The mere fact that it was hidden to the casual passerby was enough, and Sam doubted that there were too many casual passersby on this part of the island. Whoever had built the house originally, had planned well for defense. And if this Bin Rafi was dealing in an illegal slave trade, then he was very likely maintaining that defense.

Probably why there are stories of ghosts up there. Superstitious fear would be a prime deterrent.

Sam had never met a ghost that couldn't be shot with a Colt revolver.

He held up his left hand as a signal to stop. Neither he nor Richard said a word. Finally after five minutes, he turned to Richard and spoke in a whisper.

"We should be getting close. It's possible that this trail isn't defended because they don't expect anyone to find it that isn't supposed to know about it," said Sam.

"Or they think it's just easier to kill us when we get to the top," suggested Richard.

Sam nodded. "And someone has been on this trail in the past few days. You can see the fresh wear in spots. And they didn't drag anything."

"Which likely means that any men in those crates came out and were forced to walk up here."

"Easier than carrying them. And the need for hiding them would be over."

"I can go you one better on that, Sam," said Richard. "There are a few tracks a couple yards back that sure look like the heel was pointing up the trail. So someone returned after delivering the slaves."

"And once they were delivered, there's not as much need for a lookout on the trail? Maybe. We need to find where those slaves are kept. That's the only proof that will bring the Brits in to take charge of this."

"It will be getting dark in a few hours," said Richard. "Should we hold back and approach the house after nightfall? It should be safer to reconnoiter in the dark and if we can't find the slaves, maybe there will be a place to hide."

"I'd like to get closer to the house before dark. The understory isn't as dense up higher. Let's try the rest of the way off trail."

The two men slipped away from the path and padded up the rest of the hill moving in switchbacks, keeping to the larger trees as much as possible. Both men were experienced hunters and knew the value of stepping lightly, being certain of any dead crackling branch before putting weight on a foot. For Sam, it was an attempt at best. He's never managed to master stepping on his prosthetic leg without it coming down in a dead weight. But rainy season had just ended and the verdant lushness aided their stealth. They reached the top and viewed the large white coral limestone house before them from the safety of two burly trees.

Not a sound reached them, not even bird calls. The phrase, "quiet as the grave" came to Sam's mind. No wonder people told tales about this place. He would have considered it to be an abandoned shell of a house but for several facts: it looked in too good a repair, there had been activity on that path leading up here.

The house stood on the western edge of Pemba, overlooking the ocean. To their right, they could see the sunset through a thin line of distant clouds that marked the unseen African coast. The bottom two thirds was a ball of fiery crimson. The portion above the cloud line glimmered gold. It was as though the sun were being dipped in a bath of blood, staining the bottom.

Overhead the trees began to rustle and shake themselves awake. Sam looked up in time to see the leaves open and flex themselves before he realized that these were bats the size of cats about to take wing. They took flight, heading towards the mainland.

He and Richard exchanged glances as though to say, "Damnedest thing I've ever seen." Dusk lasted about a quarter of an hour, and then, only blackness relieved by a shining sea of stars above. No lights glowed from within the house. It could just as well have been a mausoleum.

They slipped from behind the trees and began a circuit counterclockwise around the house. True to the Arab style, the windows sat high to prevent people from looking in. These were all shuttered from the outside as well. Only to the back, facing the coast, was a shutter broken lose and dangling to one side. Sam scrambled up the rough coralline blocks to peer in. It was like peering into oblivion.

They had reached the front and tried the bolted door when an owl called from the trees to their left. The hollow-sounding, monotonal "hoos" repeated themselves for a total of four times. Sam felt his back shiver as though the owl call had startled several mice which scurried up his back.

It's just an owl. Get a grip, man!

The "hoos" stopped to be followed immediately by the snarling and snapping of large dogs.

"We need to hide," said Richard. "Those dogs sound hungry."

"Back to the back of the house," said Sam. He led the way to the broken shuttered window and yanked the other remaining shutter aside. Then, using the butt of his Colt, he smashed in the latticed screen work. This time, he boosted Richard up to the window and shoved, pushing the broad-shouldered older man through. As soon as he saw Richard's boot soles disappear into the abyss beyond, he scrambled up the outer wall and hoisted himself through. Strong hands reached for him on the other side and pulled him in. Sam fell with a "thunk" on his side.

"Are you okay?" he whispered to Richard.

"Yes," came the answering whisper. "But damn it's black in here."

"Would you rather be out there with the dogs?"

"Do you think they heard or smelled us?" asked Richard.

"Don't know. Don't think so. The barking seems to still be in those trees. Blast it. There's got to be a way to see out and look."

Sam heard a faint scrape, followed by a hiss and a sudden, small burst of light. Richard had lit a match and held it aloft. To their light-starved eyes, it was as if a flare had been lit and Sam could see that he was in what had been a beautiful room, probably designed for the women of the house. There was little furniture but he spied one small, low table in the room. He reached it just as the match went out.

It was succeeded by another. Sam watched as Richard found a clay lamp, similar in style to those he'd seen in an illustrated book of *Arabian Nights*. There must have been a little oil left in it and some sort of wick because it began to glow with a small but steady light. Sam just hoped that no one outside would see it.

Richard held the lamp so that his body shielded the light from striking an outer wall and led the way through the house towards the area closest to the snarling animals outside. Sam followed, carrying the low table. When they reached a front window near the south east corner, he set the table below a latticed window and climbed atop it. From there he could peer out through a gap in the outer shutter where the wood had warped away.

To the east, a nearly full moon rose, spilling an opalescent glow and casting shadows of the nearby trees on the open glade.

The shadows moved.

Sam motioned for Richard to join him and edged aside enough to make room for him. Together they watched as the shadows shifted and intermingled, melding with one tree and emerging from another. The shapes stayed just out of focus, hanging back at the tree line. The snarling and barking and quadruped form told Sam that these were large dogs, big enough to be wolves. The movement told him otherwise.

The actions were too planned, too much like an orchestrated dance to be canines.

These were human.

CHAPTER 15

Eleven miles west of Chake sits a small, uninhabited island known to some as Captain Kidd's Island. If the Captain had possessed half the treasure reported to be buried by him in the area, then he would have been richer than Midas.
- - The Traveler

Convincing her mother to remain at the village the next morning had not been easy. The only way Jade could finally get her to agree was to make the argument that it was crucial to keep an eye out for Teasdale should he choose to return to buy more food.

"We need eyes in two places, Mother," Jade had said. "What if I don't find this so-called magic baobab tree right away? What if he comes back here by a different route and we miss him?"

"Keep your voice down, Jade. Do you want to wake Nasur?" Inez looked over her shoulder as though expecting to see her unwelcome shadow appear. "And why do *you* get to go look for him? Why can't you stay here with Nasur and let *me* hunt for this treasure tree?"

"Because, Mother, you creak."

The look on Inez's face would have been comical in another situation. Jade hadn't seen one like it since she'd

119

announced to an assembly of her mother's art society friends that she'd rather see a man tap dance on a mule rather than help them promote a bunch of stuffy visiting artists at a soiree in Taos. It hadn't been one of the brighter moments in a rather stormy relationship with her mother. At this point in their lives, though, the look reminded Jade of a hurt puppy tied to a tree to prevent it from following its master. She immediately regretted saying it.

"What do you mean, I creak?"

"I'm sorry, Mother, but you must admit that you're not a spring chicken anymore. You're a beautiful woman, a better horseman than I'll ever be, and I'm proud of how you've handled this trip so far, but I heard your knees more than once on the walk to this village. If I can hear you, then so can someone else, and a little stealth is what's needed at this point."

Inez folded her arms across her chest, lifted her chin higher and turned away from Jade.

Jade responded by putting an arm around Inez and planting a kiss on her cheek. "Mother, I'm not trying to get rid of you," she'd said, lying as convincingly as she could. "I know what you're capable of. I've seen you in action, remember? But we have two jobs to do and I'm the best one for tracking Teasdale and you're the better choice for keeping a wary eye out for him here."

"Then take Nasur with you."

"No. He's not a landsman. He breathes too hard going across country. The man sounds like a winded horse."

"And just what am I supposed to do with Teasdale if I see him?" Inez asked, still not looking at her daughter.

"Use your imagination. Hog tie him if you like."

That had brought a smile to Inez's face and she'd finally agreed. Jade had promised to be back by mid-afternoon at the latest.

That had been over three hours ago; three hours of the most careful tracking that she'd ever done. It helped that Teasdale had quit trying to double back and disguise his tracks after a quarter mile. She found the lone baobab tree growing in a cluster of tamarind and mango trees, its size attesting to great age. Teasdale was nowhere to be seen, but it was plain that he'd been there and been busy. The red loam of the forest floor had been worked over, the resulting hole reaching deep under the baobab's roots. The edges were clean, the dirt neatly piled to the side.

A shovel did this, not some burrowing animal.

Jade examined the trunk and found the remains of a carving, so scarred over as to be nearly invisible. The marks resembled a cross. Had the person who'd buried something beneath the roots been a European, a Christian? Possibly. Then again, the shape might have been meant to represent a dagger with the point stabbing downwards as though into the earth. Perhaps it had been meant as a warning of what would befall anyone who disturbed the soil below. If so, it hadn't deterred Teasdale.

She looked back at the hole. It was nearly two foot wide, large enough to have contained a coffer of decent size. Had Teasdale found his treasure and left with it? Was he even now taking Hazar with him? They could go and good riddance but for the fact that a girl, just enjoying the taste of freedom, had been horribly murdered and one or both of them probably knew something about it. The thought of Tisha's little body lying all crumpled and bloody in her new kanga sent a fresh pulse of anger through Jade.

And it was someone close to them that betrayed her. Someone possibly involved in witchcraft, too.

She remembered that people chose the witchcraft route to seek power and sometimes wealth. Would an Englishman stoop to such a practice? Teasdale was a romantic of sorts. It was very possible that he actually believed it could help him find his treasure. But why kill little Tisha?

To silence her, his best pupil.

She stood and began a systematic search of the surrounding area, looking for any clue as to Teasdale's whereabouts. The man was certainly skilled in covering his tracks. She found one footprint and followed in that direction. It led her to an overgrown cemetery with three monuments, rising like chimneys from out of the soil. Teasdale's bedroll was tucked against the middle monument, his cooking gear beside it.

***

When Sam woke up the next morning, it was with overwhelming relief. Nothing could have induced him to go back to sleep and risk revisiting those nightmares. It was as if he'd been tossed into a circle of hell filled with writhing demons and hell-hounds, growling and snapping at his flesh. He sat up and saw Richard stretched out on the floor against the opposite wall. For a horrifying moment, Sam thought the man was dead.

"Richard, wake up," Sam whispered, shaking Jade's father by the shoulder.

Richard's eyes snapped open and he cast a wary glance around the room before he moved. When he sat up, he gripped his head in both hands and groaned softly.

"What a night," he said softly. "I don't ever want another one like that one again."

"You, too?" asked Sam. "It must have been those figures we saw outside last night that did it. I dreamt I was in Hell."

"What were those things anyway, Sam? They sounded just like big dogs, but…"

"But they weren't. Their movements were too ritualized to have been animal."

"You don't suppose this place really is haunted, do you?"

"Hell no," said Sam. Don't tell me *you* think that."

Richard ran his hand across his chin, massaging the scruffy growth that had sprouted over the past few days. "Well, no, Sam, but I've seen some odd stuff in my day and heard stranger. And that from men with sound minds. Still, I think people here are playing at some ancient ritual."

"To scare everyone else away?"

Richard shrugged. "It would do the trick, but don't discount that the participants actually believe in this ritual themselves."

"They can play devil man all they want," said Sam. "I just want to find those slaves and learn who took them."

They searched the house first and found nothing beyond a glimmering silver bangle kicked into a dark corner of what they'd assumed were once the women's quarters. From there they extended their search around the immediate vicinity, eventually moving deeper into the area where the dog dancers, as they called them, had been. Richard was the first to spot a slightly worn path through a grove of Tamarind trees. A half mile later the trail stopped.

"That makes no sense," said Sam. "There had to be a reason for the path. There's no building around here."

"Underground then," suggested Richard.

Sam nodded. "Search all around but be careful."

The surveyed the area systematically in small grids, pushing aside any debris and testing any exposed rock before moving on. On their fourth pass, Richard found something.

"Over here, Sam. This little stack of logs look out of place to you?"

"Let's move them."

They rolled the logs away and revealed an iron grating six feet by six feet. Beneath it was an equal sized pit cut into the coral limestone from which rose the stench of sweat, excrement, and fear.

And looking up at them through the grating were a dozen upturned faces.

***

Jade squatted on her heels and studied the three markers, more for curiosity than for anything else. After all, they couldn't reveal anything about where Teasdale had gone. But besides Teasdale, she felt a need to learn more about Bin Rafi. Did these stones mark his ancestors' remains? Perhaps his previous wives lay buried here. If so, was the baobab tree also part of his property?

If it were mine and someone trespassed and dug up a treasure on it, I'd sure as shooting would want it back.

Perhaps one of Bin Rafi's servants came across Teasdale as he pulled a coffer out from under the baobab. He might have demanded Teasdale come with him to his master. It could even have been Darshash who seemed to hold a position of authority for the old Arab planter. If they brought Teasdale to Bin Rafi and Teasdale admitted that he loved Hazar, what might Bin Rafi do to Teasdale? This was a remote spot. It would be so easy to get rid of a rival.

"You're letting your imagination get ahead of yourself," she murmured aloud. She had no reason to believe that anyone had found Teasdale.

So where could he be? He'd left his bedroll and his cooking gear. Was he planning to come back?

If I'd just found a treasure, would I? Or would I just get back to the old town in Zanzibar as fast as I could and claim my bride?

But Hazar wasn't there anymore. She'd been taken away from her father's house.

Did Teasdale know that? If he didn't take her, probably not. If he did take her, then where had he put her? Was she even now housed back in Chake Chake awaiting her tutor so that she could become English and wear her fine dresses?

Jade didn't care if the two eloped and ran away together. Good luck and good riddance as far as she was concerned. Teasdale was a fool and Hazar was a spoiled brat so they deserved each other. But Tisha hadn't deserved to die.

Once again she tried to focus on the carvings on the three tombs. Her spoken Arabic was passable, her ability to read it was rougher, but she at least knew the Arabic alphabet. She could try to sound these out and see if they looked to be any ancestors. A first name of Rafi would show a father to the present Mubarik Bin Rafi, or Mubarik, son of Rafi.

Two tombs had first names only and both sounded feminine, wives of whoever was in the center. Or perhaps the center tomb marked a deceased child. Bin Rafi had no living children.

She cleaned away a bit of debris from the front of the central tomb and traced the letters, reading the Arabic from right to left.

Something Rafi.

So this was a family grave site. But this was not a child. A son would have been named bin Mubarik. His father? But no, that wouldn't be right either unless *his* father was also named Rafi. Still, she was on the plantation owner's land then. She worked at tracing out the other letters with her fingers.

Mu-bar-ik. Mubarik!

The grave belonged to Mubarik Bin Rafi.

The great and wealthy Arab was dead, and by the looks of the site, had been for over a year at least.

CHAPTER 16

*Bits of ancient Chinese pottery can be seen implanted into the masonry
as decorations. Antiquity permeates the Island's fabric.*
- - The Traveler

Slaves! The word popped into Sam's mind immediately, but
he couldn't reconcile it with the horrid reality beneath him. He
wasn't sure what he'd expected to find, perhaps a rude hut with
a stone building, but not an underground pit of filth and rot.
There wasn't enough room in the pit for everyone to lie down
at the same time and for any of them to try would be to risk
being trampled on in the milling.

And those faces! The eyes staring up at them were lifeless,
devoid of hope. Sam gazed into those black orbs and felt as
though his soul were being sucked out of him.

"Do you see a way in?" asked Richard. The practical,
matter-of-fact question broke the vision's nightmarish hold on
Sam.

"What? No." Sam said. He gripped the grating and heaved
upward. It didn't budge. "Maybe if we both try on either end."

Richard moved around to the opposite side and had just
grabbed the bars when a scratch voice issued from a corner of
the hell beneath them.

"We are locked in." The voice, though weak, was clearly

English.

Sam peered into the gloom, trying to tell which one of these pitiful, half-starved un-dead creatures had spoken, but it was as if the ground had spoken instead.

Sam and Richard peeled back the vegetation from each of the edges, but found nothing, not a hinge nor a lock.

"I don't see it," said Sam. "Tell us where to look. We'll get you all out."

"It's not here," said the disembodied voice. "This is nothing more than a place to throw down food. For water, we must pray for rain and hold our mouths up to the sky."

"Who are you?" asked Richard. "How did you get in this pit if not here?"

"I'm an Englishman. My name's Teasdale. I came to Pemba to find treasure."

"You found something you didn't bargain for," said Sam. "How long have you been trapped in here?"

"A day, but it feels like a lifetime. I was--"

"Save your strength, man," said Sam. "There'll be time for explanations later. Right now, tell us how you got into this pit. Where's the entrance if not here?"

Beneath him, the standing men were being pushed and shoved as a new figure emerged from somewhere at the back. Sam saw a ragged looking young man with long hair. The man's clothes looked as though he'd crawled through a mile of muck.

"For the love of God, man," said Teasdale. "Do you have any food?"

"Yes, and you shall have it," said Richard. "Water, too. Just tell us how to get you out!"

There's a cemetery nearer the eastern side of the island. It has three monuments, with stone blocks and what looks like chimneys rising up on one side of each of the blocks. One of the blocks moves. The one most south of the three. Under it are stone steps leading down into a sort of cavern cut into the coral limestone. There's an ancient shrine there. But at one end is an iron door cut low into wall. It opens into a tunnel which finally spills out into this pit."

"Does the door lock with a key?" asked Sam. "Or is it only bolted from the outside?"

Teasdale gripped his head as though it hurt to think. "A bolt. A long bar that drops down into the stone."

"We're going find it. Rest assured. Any landmarks to help us locate this cemetery? Does it overlook the ocean on the east? Is it in a valley?"

"Not over the ocean," Teasdale said. "There's a . . . a tamarind grove, yes, that's it. And a lone baobab tree. When you find it, you're close. It's southwest of that tree, up on the top."

By now, a few of the other prisoners had stirred and showed signs of life. Sam wondered if they were the more recent arrivals, men who hadn't endured imprisonment as long as the others and hadn't lost as much of their humanity. He was counting on them to help them lead these men to safety once they had them free. Perhaps they could even tell who had kidnapped them to begin with. Their actions were infectious. One by one, the prisoners stirred, their eyes always staring upwards, but now with more focus. Hands stretched up, groping for the bars but always falling short by several inches.

The men murmured. It began as a low moan, and gained in strength as more joined in.

"*Chakula. Maji. Chakula. Maji,*" they groaned, until the words came together as a chant.

"I don't understand," said Richard. "What are they saying?"

"Food. Water," said Teasdale with a sob. "All we've had to eat are tamarind pods thrown down to us. We gnaw them open with our teeth and chew out the pulp inside. It hasn't rained in several days. Even the puddles under us are dry."

Sam grabbed his canteen and opened it. Slowly, gently, he poured a trickle of water into an open mouth below him. The men became frenzied at the sound, sight, and smell of water. They shoved each other, all vying to capture a few drops. Too much became lost, splashing over a face as one man pushed another aside.

"One at a time!" cried Sam. "One at a time."

The slaves didn't understand the words but they caught on to the idea as Richard joined Sam and together they tried their best to systematically give each man a little of their stores. One of the poor wretches grabbed a smaller man who had stepped up for his turn at the water, growling like an animal as he tried to yank the littler man away. That's when two of the less decrepit creatures took hold of the crazed slave and held him back.

All too soon the canteens were empty. Sam's had emptied out first and he immediately reached into his pack and dropped down their food stores.

"We'll get you out," said Sam repeatedly. "Teasdale, try to explain that to them. It may take a while, but we won't stop until we find that cemetery and let you all out."

"Keep them here for as long as you can," said Richard. "We'll signal you when we have the door open. Then send them down the tunnel."

"They know you are friends," said Teasdale. "I'm not sure how long I can keep them here. An hour at most."

"Do your best," said Richard. "Otherwise if the door isn't open, they'll crush each other at the other end."

Sam and Richard, after dropping the last crumbs of all their food, took their bearings and headed for the eastern side of the island. But no matter how far they went, Sam couldn't get rid of the pitiful pleading moans that kept echoing in his head.

***

"No!" Inez waved her hands like she was swatting away a swarm of annoying flies. "No, thank you," she added, ever mindful of good breeding and manners even in the face of persistent attendant. She repeated the phrase in the limited Arabic she'd learned in Morocco. "La, shukran."

Ever since Jade had left and Nasur had awoken, he'd hung at her elbow, glaring at anyone who dared look at this different woman. He tried repeatedly to usher her inside away from prying eyes, but Inez had had enough of the stuffy, dark little house. She was supposed to be outside watching for Teasdale, but she couldn't seem to make Nasur understand that. Besides she was restless. Inez's world back in New Mexico was never an idle one. She rode regularly with her husband, surveying the livestock; oversaw the household, and served on several committees for the growth and betterment of the surrounding communities from little Cimarron to the growing artist colony of Taos.

"No, Nasur. I don't care for any . . ." She hesitated. Might this be an opportunity to be rid of him for a while? "I do believe I am very thirsty. Do you think you could find a coconut and slice it for the milk?" She laid a hand on his sleeve as he turned to leave. "A *fresh* green coconut if you please."

That should keep him a little while. Maybe he'll have to climb a tree and pick one.

***

Jade could scarcely believe it. Mubarik Bin Rafi was dead! Darshash had perpetrated a ruse the entire time.

But why?

If Bin Rafi had died and Darshash was now the sole person in charge of the plantation, why couldn't he openly offer himself as a potential groom for Hazar's hand? He was rich, he was of the same faith following the teachings of Islam. If anything, he might have appealed more to Hazar as a younger, less decrepit man. Was it because he was not a pure Arab? Would that have made a difference? Or might the property have gone to some distant heir in a far off land if Bin Rafi's death became known?

Had Musa suspected? Is that why he had looked on Darshash's back with such venomous loathing? Yet he'd never actually objected to the match with Bin Rafi so he must not have known.

The thought of Musa suddenly made Jade wonder where he was. She hadn't seen or heard of him since they'd left Zanzibar for Chake Chake. Had he gone to Bin Rafi's house? Was he there even now wondering where was Bin Rafi? Had he found Hazar and already returned with her to Zanzibar? Or had he never left Zanzibar, a virtual prisoner in his own master's

130

house?

Jade sat back on her heels and pondered the situation. She hadn't found Hazar or Teasdale. She didn't know if Musa had gone on to Pemba and was even now running lose on the island looking for trouble. All she knew was that Bin Rafi was dead. That meant that Darshash was a piece of lying scum, but she was in no position to go after him without her Winchester to back her up. As much as she loathed leaving Tisha's killer go free, she needed to admit that she was in over her head here, especially with her mother in tow.

Mother! I need to go back and get her before she comes looking for me.

Jade pulled her pocket watch and stared uncomprehendingly at the face. *Three o'clock? That can't be right.* Then she realized that the watch had gotten soaked when their boat sank. She hadn't bothered to look at it since then. *Ruined.* She held it loosely in her right hand as she tried to determine the time by the sun.

She decided to get her mother and report what she knew to that British representative, Allenby, in Chake Chake. She'd convince him to take charge and continue to look for Hazar. Surely he or a superior would be interested now that she could prove that Darshash was perpetrating a fraud. And once they found Hazar, they could learn who killed Tisha.

And if Allenby's not interested, then perhaps the Sultan will be.

Jade eased to her feet, her war-injured knee twinging from squatting so long. She rubbed it with both hands, forgetting the watch as she let it slip to the ground beside her. *Blasted shrapnel.* She wondered again if there was still a fragment left behind, a speck so small that the doctors never found it. The old Berber woman in Morocco, the one that gave her the clan tattoo on her forehead, had told her that death had entered that wound and lodged with her, alerting her when he was near. She wouldn't have believed it except that her aching knee had saved her on more than one occasion.

Jade looked around her. There were very few dangerous wild animals on Pemba and she didn't see another living soul. Maybe it was warning her that her mother was in danger back in the village?

If anything, she's in danger of being overprotected by Nasur.

She retraced her steps, concentrating on how to placate her mother once she returned. Jade was sure that Nasur had been doing his utmost to attend to her every need which meant that Jade was going to be in for an earful.

Her first warning was the sound of cloth whooshing through the air. It came too late. Before she could react, the heavy bag was over her head, the heavy cloying scent of cloves nearly choking her.

She kicked out wildly, hoping to connect with someone's shins as her hands grasped at the strong hand around her throat. The blow to her head was the last thing she felt.

CHAPTER 17

If one doesn't find treasure per se, the visitor may still see the many ruins which give testimony to the Island's past visitors. Coralline limestone hardens with exposure so the ruins remain. But the unexposed limestone is soft, making it easy to cut into; perfect for passageways.
- - The Traveler

Sam and Richard followed Teasdale's directions as best they could, considering the man had been relatively incoherent from hunger and thirst. But he'd been insistent about the general direction. Sam only hoped they'd find the tamarind grove.

"Do you know what a tamarind tree looks like?" he asked Richard.

"Not a clue. But it's supposed to be a grove so we look for a lot of trees that look alike. With any luck, some of those pods will be on the ground."

"Tamarind, lone baobab, cemetery," recited Sam. "Sounds like a treasure map."

"Might explain what an Englishman was doing in the middle of this forsaken island to begin with," said Richard. "Odd-looking sort of man," he added after a reflective pause. "Reminds me of pictures of Oscar Wilde."

"My question is, was he captured because he actually found some buried treasure or did he accidentally see too much?"

"Does it matter?" asked Richard.

"Beyond giving me an extra reason to beat the snot out of this slaver? Not a damn bit."

They hiked on, pausing regularly to listen for the presence of the slaveholder and also to scan the area for anything that looked like one of the landmarks they were supposed to find. The trees grew thickly here with a substantial understory that did its best to snag their legs and impede their progress.

"You know, said Sam after another twenty minutes of silence, "if we free these slaves and that Teasdale, and report all this to the authorities, it might be hard to keep this from Jade and Mrs. del Cameron. People talk. Probably end up in the blasted newspaper."

Richard studied Sam for a few moments. "You afraid of what Jade's going to say or do?"

"Well, no," muttered Sam, "It's just that she sometimes . . . and *I've* always believed--"

"Yep," agreed Richard. "I'm scared, too. Inez'll have me strung up." He patted Sam on the back. "Welcome to life with a strong-willed woman, Son."

After an hour of fanning out to reconnoiter, backtracking, and trying again, they stumbled upon the cemetery.

"Teasdale said that the tomb on the southern end moves," said Richard. He strode past the first two and crouched down beside the third and least opulent stone marker. "Look down here. You can see where the stone beside it has been worn away."

He stood and looked around as though expecting to see Sam beside him. Instead Sam was kneeling beside the center marker. He held something metallic in his right hand."

"This is Jade's watch. I'd better my life on it."

"You're right, Sam. But then, where's Jade? And where's my wife?"

***

Inez felt like she'd cooled her heels long enough. Oh, Jade was right. Someone *did* need to stay behind at the village and keep watch for Teasdale. But she didn't believe for a moment that it needed to be her or Jade either, for that matter. Why not just order Nasur to stay? Or convince the village headman, Jabu to watch for Teasdale? After all, since he sold food to him, he'd have an easier time coming up with some pretext to detain him. All Jade had to do was ask. Jabu had seemed willing enough to assist them. True, she'd seen little enough of him this morning, but that was to be expected. A man of Islam wouldn't consider it proper to spend too much time with a woman, especially a foreign one. But he could have ordered his wife to keep an eye out. Kito was a mousy little woman. She'd do anything that her husband told her to do.

And I don't creak!

Once again, Inez wished that she spoke Arabic or even Swahili. Then *she* could propose the idea to Jabu or even to Mahir. That man seemed to be Jabu's aide de camp, or perhaps just his chief servant. At least she'd seen him come and go from the house as though he belonged there. Inez had picked up a smattering of Arabic while in Morocco but beyond saying no, please, thank you, and a few other basics, she was as good as useless.

Nasur speaks Arabic and Swahili. He could find Jabu or Mahir and ask one of them to watch for Teasdale.

But then Nasur would insist on staying with her if she walked off to find Jade. Inez never realized that saving someone's life could have such annoying consequences.

No wonder so few people do it.

So far this morning he'd fetched three coconuts and watched her drink the juice. Anymore and she'd sprout coconuts.

I could tell him I need to sleep and then slip away.

No. No, he'd see her go into the house and then he'd position himself in front of the door. She'd be imprisoned.

But maybe he didn't even need to find Jabu. Maybe just sending him off to look would give her a chance to slip away. She considered the idea. It could work.

"Nasur," she said in the same tone one used to speak to a servant. The man was instantly at her side. "I think I have had too much coconut milk." She held her stomach. "I need to . . . to walk into the forest for a while. Privately. Do you understand?" He nodded. "Good. But I'm supposed to keep watch for someone. Jabu knows this man. He could watch while I'm gone. Will you go and find Jabu for me?" She pointed to a more distant grove. "I believe he is over there somewhere."

Nasur made a brief bow and trotted out of the village.

Now to escape.

Just then Jabu emerged from somewhere nearby and joined Inez. "Nasur?" he asked, looking around.

Inez rolled her eyes and pointed to the far field. Jabu smiled and nodded as though he understood her dilemma. That's when Inez decided to try to communicate with signs. She pointed to the forest in the direction her daughter had traveled. "Jade." Then she pointed to herself and made walking motions in the same direction.

The headman cocked his head quizzically, pointed to her, and gestured to the village. It seemed he was asking why she stayed behind.

Inez pointed first to her eyes and then to the surroundings. "Teasdale," she said.

"Ah," replied Jabu with a nod. He shaped his forefingers and thumbs into a reasonable imitation of field glasses and panned the area. "Teasdale," he repeated.

Suddenly excited by her ability to communicate, Inez pointed to Jabu, made the binocular shapes and looked around. "Teasdale?" she queried. Then she pointed to herself and made walking motions with her right hand fore and middle fingers, ending with a gesture towards the distance. "Jade," she said emphatically.

Immediately, Jabu looked concerned. "Nasur?" he asked pointing first to her and then in the direction that Inez indicated.

Inez shook her head no. "Nasur, here!" she said, stabbing her forefinger to the ground.

She wasn't certain if Jabu was going to agree to this or not.

He pursed his lips as though pondering the consequences. Then he repeated her finger-walking pantomime for a long time, all the while shaking his head no. Before Inez could protest, he repeated it for a short duration and nodded yes. He seemed to be saying that she could walk a little, but shouldn't stray too far from the village.

Inez decided to agree, all the while intending to keep going until she found her daughter.

"Nasur here?" she asked, again pointing to the ground.

"Nasur here," repeated Jabu.

Inez rewarded him with a bright smile. It had occurred to her that Teasdale wouldn't come back to the village if he found anything but would skirt it. Staying behind in the village was a waste of time. Once she rejoined Jade, they could continue to search together.

***

Consciousness teased Jade. It was like trying to catch a firefly. It flashed suddenly right in front of her, then, as she struggled to grasp it, it flitted away, just out of reach, to flash again elsewhere. Every one of those brief illuminations into reality stabbed her brain with an intense pain. Finally, she caught hold long enough to sit up.

She promptly retched.

Jade wiped her mouth with her pocket kerchief and blinked. Despite the little flickering lights playing behind her eyes, she could see nothing. Beneath her knees, the ground was cool and hard, like kneeling on cement. She tentatively reached out her hand and felt a rough wall. She continued to grope upward and discovered a low ceiling of the same material. It seemed that standing was out of the question. In fact, when she tried to rise enough to sit on her heels, her head grazed the ceiling. But there was space before and behind her.

A tunnel?

She reasoned that it was carved into the island's coral - lime rock. The question was, where was she?

Jade forced herself to think despite the pain. Where had she been? What did she remember? Gradually, the bits and pieces came to her. She'd found Teasdale's treasure tree and after that, a small cemetery.

Bin Rafi is dead. Has been a long time.

After that, she'd started back to the village and her mother. *Mother!*

She could be in danger herself. At the least, she'd be frantic with worry.

She'll be mad as hell.

Jade had to find a way out. She crawled slowly ahead, letting her palms slide over the ground to avoid any potential pits. A few feet later she touched a metal door. There was no handle, no hinges, no gaps below or above to lever against. Not that she had anything to use as a lever.

There was nothing left to do but turn around and see what lay in the opposite direction.

CHAPTER 18

*In more than a few places, one might stumble upon pits dug into the
soft lime rock, pits that once held slaves. The very walls still seem to cry
out from their long anguish.*
- - The Traveler

Sam held Jade's pocket watch, his fingers caressing it as
though she'd suddenly appear like a genie from out of a lamp.
"Do you recognize it, Richard? Am I right?"

Richard nodded. "It's Jade's. I gave it to her before she
went to school in London." He rubbed his stubbled chin and
then ran the hand across his head, a mannerism that Sam had
come to recognize meant he was doing his best to cope with a
bad situation. "

"It doesn't mean that she's here now, though," continued
Sam, trying as much to convince himself as to calm Jade's
father. "She might have hiked around on the island a few days
ago, photographing ruins. Or a pickpocket could have stolen it
and then lost it here."

Richard's eyes locked onto Sam's and wouldn't let go. It
was unnerving and suddenly he understood where Jade got
that talent for staring down her opponents. "You don't really
believe that now do you, Sam? Look, there's a bedroll, and a
canteen." He shook it. "Half-full. She wouldn't leave a canteen

any more than she'd leave the watch, broken or not."

"No. I guess not. If Jade's watch had broken, she'd have kept it to get repaired and if anyone had tried to rob her, he'd have at least one broken arm by the time he was done."

Richard nodded. "So she was here, and recently, too. That watch wasn't covered with debris and it didn't sit here long enough for some monkey to see it and pick it up, either."

Sam didn't say "I'm sure she's all right," or "Inez is probably safe on Zanzibar." He knew Jade too well to believe that and his previous experience with her mother while in Morocco told him that his lovely apple hadn't fallen too far from her maternal tree. "Well, they weren't in that house last night. I'm sure of that," he said after pondering the situation.

"No, but they may be there now."

The fact that Richard said "they" meant he believed his wife was in trouble, too, even though they'd only found one bedroll.

"Then we need to go look for them. Now," said Sam.

"No." Richard took a deep breath, and Sam watched him struggle to control his fears. "First we release these slaves. We promised them. Besides, that Teasdale may have seen or heard something that would give us an idea of what else we're up against. If nothing else, he'll owe us. We can ask him to help us."

Sam nodded. "Agreed." He slipped the watch into his trouser pockets, slipped the new canteen around his shoulder and looked at the stone markers. "Did I hear you correctly a moment ago? You found the marker with the wear patterns?"

"Yes, and it looks as if it pivots to the back." Richard squatted on his heels and pressed his hands against the stone. Sam scooted beside him and put his right shoulder to the marker.

"On three," said Sam. "One, two . . ."

They pushed against the marker and felt it give way, scraping softly against the underlying stone as though it were on a pivot. A black void yawned where the marker had stood.

"Damn, I wish we had a flashlight," said Sam.

"We can make a torch," said Richard. "I've got more

matches." He patted his left trouser pocket.

"All we need is wood that's not green," said Sam. "It doesn't have to burn very long, just enough for us to find the door and open it." Looking around, he spied a coconut tree standing alone where a lone nut had been dropped and sprouted years ago. "I've got it. Wait here."

He ran with his peculiar limping jog to the tree and found remnants of some husks. Picking them up, he snapped a low-lying branch from another tree and brought them back to Richard. "The fibers in this husk will burn well and we can shred and twist enough to make some twine to tie it to this green branch."

Richard patted Sam on the back and pulled his pocket knife. Together, they scraped off a growing pile of fibers. "I'll make the rope," said Richard. "You loosen up the rest of the hull so that it burns steadily."

Sam scraped and sliced into the hull, fanning it out. As he did, he spared a glance at Richard's work. The man's fingers worked adroitly, twisting the fibers into a thin but ever-lengthening strand.

"This should do it," Richard said when he had nearly three feet of length. "If the husk doesn't burn too fast, maybe the rope won't catch too soon."

"I left a thick chunk at the base," said Sam. That should resist long enough for us to do the job." He took Richard's cording and bound the frayed husk to the branch. When he was satisfied with the job, he held it out for Richard to light.

The loosened fibers caught immediately. Sam held the torch into the hole and gave a quick look. Then he stepped back. "The door is in that far wall," he said pointing. "There's a set of steps carved into this rock. I'll go down and open the door. You stay up here to help the men up. They may be too weak to climb on their own."

"I'm going, too," Richard said. "If Inez and Jade are down there, I need to know."

Sam nodded. He knew he wouldn't have agreed to stay behind either so there was no point in arguing. What he'd dreaded the most, Jade's lifeless body lying broken in this pit, had not been revealed when he'd passed the torch into the hole. So if she was here, then chances were that she was alive.

He carefully stepped down the steep flight, worn down in spots by years of use. The air was cool but dank, as if he were in a living cave. Once he hit the bottom, Sam held the torch aloft to light the way for Richard. But his focus wasn't on his companion or even on the small iron door in near wall. It was on the shrine rising up in front of him.

Carved from the same soft limestone was a statue that seemed to be a composite of every night creature imaginable: bat, owl, leopard, and dog; all melded into one monstrous form. In front of it was a low rock table, stained with dark splotches that could only be blood.

"What in the name of . . .?"

"If there was ever anything unholy in the world," said Richard, "it's that. Come on, let's get this door open and get out of here."

"I don't know whether to hope that our women are in there or not," said Sam.

"I'd rather they were in there and unharmed. Then we'll have them."

Sam knew he was right. As much as he dreaded knowing that Jade had suffered any harm or fright, not knowing where she was would be worse. But if she and her mother weren't here, he'd tear the damned island apart until he found them. He handed the torch to Richard, seized the iron bar that held the door shut, and raised it.

The heavy door swung partly open with a dull creak. How many countless souls had been pushed in here, Sam wondered, losing all hope of ever gaining their freedom. How many had become slaves, and how many had been sacrificed to that monstrous stone figure or whatever it represented?

"Jade?" Sam called into the black tunnel beyond. There was no answer. "Teasdale, send the men down." He paced in a tight circle. "I expected to see Teasdale and those men here by now. It's been nearly two hours since we left them. I don't like this."

"Maybe they can't see to find their way out. We might have to go in part way with the torch to light the way."

"Then you stay here," ordered Sam. "Keep that door open."

He crouched down until he was on all fours and, taking the torch again, inched his way inside.

***

Jade crept along the tunnel, groping every step of the way. Her fingers traced the ground, her shoulders brushed the walls. As she went further, the air became more stale, more pungent. It didn't bode well for what she might find at the other end.

A scuffling noise echoed down the passage towards her and she froze. Something was at the other end. But what? She reached down to her right boot, her fingers searching for her knife. It wasn't there. She had nothing with which to defend herself except her bare hands and her teeth. And while she could put up a good scrap when she needed to, the confines of this tunnel didn't allow for swinging a solid punch. At least whatever was at the far end wouldn't be in much better odds.

Unless it's not human.

Was it coming towards her? She couldn't tell.

She thought about backing up, then remembered that there was no place to go. Instead, she twisted around until she was sitting on the ground. With her boots on, she could at least give one swift kick before anything got hold of her.

"Who's there?" she called into the darkness.

The scuffling stopped. The silence scared her more than the noise. It meant that whatever was at the other end knew she was there and was listening, deliberating, waiting.

Waiting for what?

"Who's there?" she repeated with more force in her voice.

"Lady del Cameron? Is that you?"

"Musa?" Jade could hardly believe her ears. For a brief moment she felt a wave of relief, then squelched it. She still had serious doubts about his role in Tisha's death.

"You are captured?" he asked from the far darkness.

His voice sounded clearer, as though he had moved a little closer towards her

"Yes," she replied. "Someone hit me. I woke up trapped in this . . . this maze."

"Come to me," he said. "There is room here."

She still wasn't sure she could trust him, but under the circumstances there was little choice. She certainly couldn't stay cramped up on her hands and knees in the tunnel.

"It is not far," Musa added as though to reassure her. "There are no traps. I have been through."

Jade resumed her methodical crawl, still trusting her hands to protect her from a sudden, hidden pit rather than Musa's words. The tunnel angled to the left and, once she made the turn, saw a faint glimmer of light ahead. It was enough to illuminate the floor in front of her. The last half of her crawl took her only a moment to finish.

She entered a small, square room with one high and very small window. It was more of a vertical slit than anything else and would only illumine the room for a short time each day. If there was going to be any chance of escape, it wouldn't be through there. A stout door with no interior handle was the only other break in the white walls. The rest of the room was bare but for one large jug in the far corner. Judging by the odor in the room, Musa had used it for his more personal needs.

"Where are we?" she asked as she stood and dusted off her trousers.

Musa leaned against the wall and waved a languid hand towards the walls. "In the house of Bin Rafi. This room is under the ground."

Jade studied his actions, noting how slowly he moved and spoke. *Drugged?*

"How long have you been here?" she asked.

Musa shrugged. "The window has gone dark once. Long enough for my throat to grow parched."

At least one day, she reasoned. "Did you find Hazar? Is she alive?"

His brow furrowed and his lips grew taut. "I have not

found my little sister. But I heard her voice. She was here, in this house." His scratchy dry voice intensified as he related his search and his eyes glowed with an inner fire. "I called to her and she cried for me to come. I followed her voice. It led me down a dark stairs to this place. I knew that she was in here, but when I came into this room I found nothing." Musa stared at Jade as though to see if she understood his horror.

"The room was empty?" she said, prompting him. "And then?"

"Before I could turn, the door shut behind me. I heard the bar fall and I was trapped. There is no food. No water." He sank to the floor.

That explained his languor. The big man was dehydrated.

"Have you heard Hazar's voice since then?"

Musa shook his head. "No. Perhaps I did not hear it at all. It was witchcraft. We will die now."

Jade resisted the urge to slap the man into action. "If you want to die here, then that's your choice. I don't intend to. So help me find a way out."

"There *is* no way out!" Musa's shoulders slumped and he covered his face with his hands. A faint sob escaped his lips. "He will kill Hazar. It is how he will gain power. The practitioner must sacrifice someone close to fully enter the guild."

"Who? Bin Rafi? He's dead. I've seen his grave."

"No. Darshash. *He* will wed Hazar. And then he will sacrifice her."

Jade wasn't sure what disgusted her the most; the idea that someone would kill a young girl in a bid for some pretext at power or this man conceding defeat so easily.

"And what will he plan for you? Will he sacrifice you, too?"

Musa looked up sharply, his eyes half-lidded. "What would he gain sacrificing me? Am I even a full man? No. He will simply let me die of thirst in this room. It will be better that way. Better than if he turns me into his spirit world slave.

His head drooped again and Jade saw her opportunity. Unlike herself, Darshash had not had an opportunity to disarm

Musa. She'd seen his blade glint from its hiding place in his waist sash, just under a plain white robe. She lunged towards him and snatched it before he could react. She held it in front of her, ready to defend herself if need be from this volatile man. He started to his feet, then sank back down and laughed mirthlessly. It echoed in the empty room as a hollow laugh, the sound of a man devoid of hope.

"It will not aid you," he said. "No one will come and open the door. That is why there is a tunnel. If food and water is to be had, it is left at the mouth where it is hard for a man to rush out and overpower the captor. He only opened it to deposit you. I know. I heard the door and crawled to it like an animal to see, hoping for water. There was only *you*." He nearly spat out the last word. "I could not see in the dark, but you did not have Hazar's scent. I knew it was not her so I crawled back here."

"And you left me there?" Jade repaid the scorn and spat at his feet. "Then you are worse than him. *I* came here to help your Hazar." She purposely omitted telling her other motive, to find who killed little Tisha. It would mean nothing to this man. His world, his life revolved only around the girl he'd cared for since her birth.

"You can still be a man," she said. "Help me escape and we will find Hazar. We can still save her."

"Woman, have you not heard? There is no way out!"

Jade jerked the knife towards the door. "There's a door. Doors open."

"But it is barred from without."

"Then we will raise the bar." She held the knife aloft. "With this."

***

"Stay back, Richard," said Sam as he crawled into the dank tunnel. "This torch smokes something fierce."

"Do you see anyone?" asked Richard. His voice rang close and Sam knew that the man was speaking directly into the tunnel mouth despite Sam's caution.

"Not yet. I thought they'd be waiting by the door."

"You don't suppose there's some pit in the way, something to keep them on the other side?"

"Could be. Maybe there's another door. I'll continue on and try to draw them out."

"Careful, Sam."

Sam thrust the torch forward. The creamy white rock immediately around him reflected the light, but the black void beyond drank it in so that he could only see an arm's length ahead at a time. If that was the case, the men at the other end wouldn't see him either. He called out again, but not too loudly. If the slaver was still around, it wouldn't do to alert him.

Crawling with one hand wasn't easy but Sam pushed forward, his heavy prosthetic leg dragging against the stone floor. The foul air reeked of years of human excrement and fear. When he'd gone forward nearly ten feet, he stopped to catch his breath and to listen.

Somewhere in front of him men were jabbering softly. Someone yelped as though another had trodden on his hand, trying to get through.

"Hello?" called Sam. "Teasdale?"

"We're coming," called the Englishman. "The men . . . are like beasts. Everyone . . ." Sam heard a smack and a grunt. "Get back there. One at a time. My stars! It's like some sort of stampede."

"Are there two women with you? Have you seen them?" asked Sam.

"What?" exclaimed Teasdale, his voice inching closer. "Women?"

Sam felt his heart sink into his stomach. As much as dreaded finding Jade and Inez in this pit, it was better than the horrific uncertainty that loomed before him. Where could they be? What had happened?"

"I'm going to start backing out," said Sam. "Just follow the torch and I'll explain everything once you're out."

He inched backwards, anxious to get out and continue his search for Jade. The narrow tunnel made him feel a little claustrophobic and the thought of those panicked men hurrying towards him didn't help.

"Coming out, Richard. Our women aren't here, though."

Instead of an answer, he heard an soft thump and an "*oof.*" It was immediately followed by a hard thud and the sound of a heavy door slamming shut. The reverberation echoed along the tunnel.

Sam looked over his shoulder and saw Richard lying in a heap behind him, their exit shut. In front of him glowed the widened eyes of frightened men, crawling in a maddened rush.

CHAPTER 19

Arabs and Persians have made these islands their home, driving out the Portuguese and leaving behind many unique structures and graceful mosques.
- - The Traveler

Jade tried to visualize the door's exterior. It would have some sort of handle to grip the door to open it, but with nothing corresponding inside, it was only a grip and not a knob. That meant the door was barred from the other side rather than locked. There were too possibilities: one was a bolt that shot across the gap, the other was a bar that dropped across it. She prayed it was the latter.

"What do you mean to do?" asked Musa. Jade noted a little more life in his voice this time.

She'd found a thin crack between the door's wooden slats and peered through. There was daylight in most spots but in the center, the light was blocked. That boded well for a cross bar. "When you came into this room, Musa, did you have to raise a beam?"

"The door was open a small ways," he said. "My mind does not remember anything but hearing my Hazar."

"What side was open?"

He glared at her. "Fool of a woman. What does it matter

when we cannot open it?"

"What side was open?" she repeated. "If my questions annoy you, then answer them so I do not have to repeat them."

He pointed to the right side. "There. That side was open."

"Good. Now then, after you went in, when the door shut, what did you hear then?"

"I do not know."

"Think!" she ordered. "What did you hear?"

The big man closed his eyes. A moment later he opened them. "Something fell across."

"Excellent!" exclaimed Jade. "That's what I was hoping for. The door's barred by a drop beam. We have to raise it."

"How?" Musa got to his feet. "We cannot lift what we cannot touch."

"We use a knife," she said. As she spoke, she demonstrated and jimmied the blade into the slit on the right side underneath where the beam sat. It was tight, but it fit. "If we can slide this knife up, we can push up the bar. It only has to go high enough to clear whatever holds it in place."

"I will raise the bar," said Musa.

"We will do it together. The door will still be heavy and will stick. Once we have raised the bar, I will hold it up. We will need your strength to push the door open." She knew that, once Musa knew what to do, he could probably open the door himself, but there was no way in hell that she'd let him loose with his knife. She had no proof that he killed Tisha but she didn't want to end up like her anyway.

"The knife sticks," she said after trying to slide it up. "I need to widen the gap."

She sawed back at forth, slicing away at a knot. Her position was awkward and it put a strain on her upper arms until she felt them cramp. But she also could feel that she was making headway in the door and kept at it, unwilling to relinquish the knife. Finally, the blade slipped through and she heard it strike the bar. She extracted the knife and reinserted it, the dull side facing up.

"Okay, Musa, take hold of my hands in yours and together we push up." She moved to the left, squatting down while making room for him on the right. "Squat down. We have more strength pushing up with our legs and arms." She waited for him to get into position and wrap his large hands around hers. "Now! Up!"

His big hands nearly crushed her fingers in his tight grip. But the surge of force worked. The bar moved higher and higher as they rose to a nearly standing position. Surely the bar had cleared its case by now. "Press your body against the door, Musa. See if it opens."

He slammed against the wood and the door flew open. Musa tumbled out, spilling onto the floor as she'd hoped. Jade retained her grip of the knife handle and used it to balance herself. Before Musa could recover, she extracted the blade and slipped it into her boot sheath, shoving it down out of sight.

"We're free!" She held out a hand to the eunuch and helped him to his feet.

"I must find Hazar," said Musa. "I must not let him sacrifice her."

"We don't know where she is," said Jade. "Do you know *when* Darshash would kill her? Or where?"

"He will kill her when the moon is full. Tonight."

"That doesn't leave us much time. Where will it happen, Musa? Do you know? Would it be at this house?"

Musa shook his head. "Houses, even this one, are for the living. He will choose openness. A place for other witches to witness. He would choose a place of death."

"A cemetery?" asked Jade.

Musa nodded. "I think, yes."

"Then I think I might know where to look."

***

Inez had walked briskly to the south west. Jade had gone that way, so she'd probably return that way, too. Inez intended to track her and managed to follow her tracks through a mango grove. Then the impressions became harder to locate. It seemed that Jade had gone off trail and Inez was admittedly not the tracker her husband and daughter were. What she needed was some high ground.

She considered shinnying up a tree, then decided that her shinnying days, if they ever existed, were long past. Instead, Inez found an exposed outcrop to sit on and rest. From here she could see any traffic coming, going, or avoiding the village. If Teasdale came anywhere within the area, she'd see him. More importantly, she could spot Jade.

She found Darshash.

Inez wasn't certain where he'd come from, but he looked to be heading towards the village. She recognized him from a brief, near-encounter when leaving Hazar's home. Here was an opportunity! Even if she couldn't speak Arabic, he would recognize the girl's name and her questioning tone. After all, she reasoned, she'd become adept at getting her point across with gestures and a few words.

"Darshash," she called as she rose gracefully from her rock. It wouldn't do to appear too undignified, she reasoned. Not if she was supposed to be an emissary from Hazar's mother and grandmother. Luckily, she had the coral and silver necklace in her pocket that Jade had given her. She could pretend it was for Hazar.

Darshash turned to her at the sound of his name, his face registering nothing including surprise. He looked the part of the perfect overseer for a wealthy plantation owner, one used to anything, disturbed by nothing.

"I am looking for Hazar Binti Ali." She waited while Darshash approached. When he stood immediately before her, Inez held out her hand with the necklace. "For Hazar from her grandmother Nuna Binti Ramiz." If the man took the necklace, it would mean acknowledging that he had Hazar. Inez took a chance that he spoke some English. After all, such an overseer surely had to deal with British people, too.

"I was asked to give this to her and to see her so that I can send word back to her grandmother and mother that she is well and happy."

Darshash spared a glance at the necklace and bowed deeply to Inez. "Then come with me. I will take you to her."

***

"Richard! Richard!" Sam pivoted and scooted on his knees to Jade's father, holding the torch as high as the low ceiling permitted. The man had plopped in a crumpled heap just inside the door, a trickle of blood staining the back of his head. Sam jammed his torch branch into a corner crevice and leaned over Jade's father, his fingers feeling for a pulse.

It was there, and still beating strongly. Sam sat on his heels and cradled Richard's head in his arms. "Richard. Stay with me."

He saw that Richard still had his canteen slung around his shoulders. Sam gently slipped it over his head and opened it. "Drink this," he said, forgetting that they'd given away their own water earlier. Only a thin trickle dripped onto Richard's lips. Sam slipped off the canteen they'd just found and dribbled a bit of water onto his pocket kerchief and dabbed the man's head wound.

Richard groaned and tried to open his eyes.

"Stay still," Sam commanded. "You've been hit and hard. Here, drink something." He held the fresh canteen to Richard's lips and doled out some of their precious water

Richard pushed aside the canteen. "Save it. We'll need it. We're trapped."

And soon to be overrun by half-crazed men expecting their freedom. Sam shifted to position himself between the slaves and Richard.

"I didn't even hear anyone coming," said Richard. "He didn't make a sound."

"Don't blame yourself," said Sam. "I left you nearly in the dark."

"There was a little light coming down. I could have seen a shadow. He was like . . . a ghost."

Sam felt his future father-in-law shudder and quickly tried to rally him. Anything that could frighten a man like Richard del Cameron was doubly unnerving. "Now don't start speaking nonsense, Richard. It was no ghost. Just someone who knows these pits better than we do."

He offered the canteen again, but Richard pushed it away. "No. Sounds like we have company."

The excited chattering and slapping of palms on stone grew louder as the slaves and Teasdale approached. Sam propped Richard against the big door and turned to face the mob, pulling his colt. He didn't want to shoot anyone, but these men were desperate and there was no telling what they'd do when they found out they were still trapped. In the flickering torchlight, Sam spotted a long-haired man in European dress less than ten yards away.

"Teasdale?"

"Thank God you came for us," said the Englishman. "We were beyond hope." Then the man's gaze noted the closed door and, for a fleeting second, a feral look flashed across his face.

"Stay calm," ordered Sam. "We're all trapped, but we're going to find a way out. And even if we can't, I have my revolver. Someone has to come to either feed us or haul us out eventually, and when they do . . ." He let the result hang unspoken.

"What if we're just left here to rot?" wailed Teasdale.

"Quiet, man!" ordered Sam. "You're going to panic the others. They may or may not understand English, but they damn well will understand your tone."

"It's too late to stop a stampede," said Richard. "They've seen the shut door."

The slaves closest to the front had seen that the way out was shut and were pressing forward, pushing Teasdale into Sam. Sam knew he needed to do something soon or these poor souls would trample them on hands and knees in their mad drive to escape. In their half-starved state, they were like beasts herded into a chute for butchering. They knew no other way than forward.

"Stop!" he ordered.

But it was too late. The swarm kept coming, an

overpowering wave of delirious bodies.

**

Inez fell in step behind the big Wa-Pemba man, her gaze taking in his powerful build and his self-assured stride. It wasn't easy to keep up with him. He walked fast and his legs were long. It was almost as if he didn't care that she was an older woman and might tire easily. This was not a man to tamper with. Still, it was her opportunity to locate Hazar and, once and for all, decide if the girl was safe.

"Thank you for taking me to her," Inez said. "I'm afraid I was getting lost trying to find your master's house."

"My master will be pleased to see you. He would not want his bride's family to worry."

The words were spoken politely, methodically, as though the man were practiced in diplomatic pleasantries. Inez knew the type. After all, she'd served on social committees with enough people to recognize a phony answer when she heard one. It told her that Bin Rafi may well have made this marriage to benefit both Hazar's father and himself, but that he did not intend to deepen any family relationship. He was a man that liked his isolation, not even deigning to haggle for his prospective bride himself, but instead delegating that to a servant.

She instantly imagined Bin Rafi as an indolent man, pampered and privileged. Darshash, on the other hand, acted like a man that had been in charge for so long that he had taken on an air of superiority. She wondered if he secretly controlled Bin Rafi by manipulating him. Pampered men often succumbed to false flattery. It wouldn't be hard for Darshash to get his way.

What's his game? Is he hoping to eventually control all of Ali Bin Hassan's lands on Zanzibar?

They passed through the forest on a nearly imperceptible path, skirting thin streams lower lying mudded areas. Inez looked everywhere, trying her best to remember landmarks, but it was difficult to concentrate at this pace. She needed to make him slow down.

"When is the wedding?" she asked as she paused to take a long drink from her nearly empty canteen.

"Very soon." He kept walking, not bothering to look back at her.

"I should like to stay and see it. Then I will have the best news to take back to Hazar's parents."

Darshash turned his head just enough to glance at Inez. His full lips curled up. "She will welcome you, I am certain."

Inez tried one last play to get the man to speak freely. People often slowed down when they talked. "Are there many ladies in the harem for Hazar to spend her days with? Will she have many maid-servants or will her maid, Tisha, be the only one?"

"The maid Tisha will not allow any other to serve her mistress."

Immediately Inez knew that all was not right. Even if Darshash had nothing to do with Tisha's death, he would at least know that she hadn't come with Hazar to Pemba. He was keeping secrets and possibly toying with her. It was time to cut loose and go back to the village and find Jade.

Or had Jade already met with this man? If that was the case, her daughter could be in terrible danger. Perhaps she could slip away and just follow him unseen. *Long enough to know if Jade's safe.*

They rounded a bend and Inez saw that they'd reached a summit. In the distance on the left, the ocean sprawled as a silken fabric, rippling gently in the breeze. To her right was a pond, murky as a dark tea from rotted leaves and distinctly uninviting. She felt exposed and halted.

"I need to rest," she said. "Go on. I'll follow in a moment." She finished the water in her canteen and recapped it.

Darshash turned back for her. "Yes, it is time for you to rest."

Every muscle in his body announced his intent to kill her. She saw his shoulders flex under his robe, saw the fleeting sneer on his face. There would be no outrunning him either. She had two choices, be struck down and fall to her death into the ocean or risk drowning in the foul waters on her right. Would he follow her in to make certain she was dead?

He left her little time to reflect, but Inez had long ago learned to act on instinct. *He's right handed.* She shifted inland a few steps so she'd fall to the stagnant pond.

The blow came faster than she'd predicted, forcing a sharp cry of pain. Within seconds she was flying through the air towards the pond. She smacked into it with tremendous force and felt the water resist, striking back at her entire body. Then it wrapped dank, putrid, watery arms around her, a stagnant lover swaddling her with the scent of corruption. For a brief moment she flailed, her left hand reaching above the water, grasping at nothing. Then she sank.

A moment later she floated face down, bobbing like a cork, her hair undone and streaming wet behind her.

CHAPTER 20

The People of Pemba, or Wa-pemba, claim to be descended from the Shirazi Persians. They are an energetic, proud, high-spirited people.
- - The Traveler

Sam needed to act and act fast. The panicked men up front saw nothing but a torch light and wouldn't stop until they reached the door, while those in the rear pressed forward relentlessly. He and Richard would soon be overwhelmed and crushed.

He drew his Colt and studied the wall. In a heartbeat, every engineering and mathematics course he'd ever taken, every pool game he'd ever played, all swirled in his mind as he calculated the angles and risks. A corner would be optimum, but this tunnel's corners were too rounded for a bullet to stick.

He fired.

The Colt's *boom* reverberated in the confined chamber, so loud that Sam swore he could see the sound.

The bullet struck the coral limestone floor at a nearly forty-five degree angle, ricocheting up to the side wall. With each strike, the softer rock absorbed some of the force, lessening the bullet's momentum. If it managed to come back towards the floor, it would hit with less of an impact, but it would still do damage. His hope was that the reverberating sound from the gunshot would startle the men and drive them back, halting the stampede while keeping them out of the trajectory.

He held less hope for himself.

The ceiling had not been worn down or chiseled as smoothly as the floor and side walls and the bullet hit a slight protuberance, altering its course. Sam threw himself onto Richard, using his back to shield him.

The bullet struck with a solid "*thunk*," directly in his prosthetic leg, a thunk which Sam felt rather than heard.

"Not again!"

Sam released Jade's dad and turned to face the hoard. The shot had done the trick. The men had halted in their tracks, a confused and frightened murmur rippling down the ranks. Their voices reached Sam as though from a distance, his ears still ringing.

"Teasdale," he shouted, hoping the man could hear him since he hadn't been as close to the blast as Sam. "You speak their language. Explain that the door is shut. We're all trapped. They need to move back and give us room to try to find a way to open the door."

"There's no way--"

"You're going to have to speak up," shouted Sam. "I can hardly hear you."

"There's no way to open the door from in here," wailed Teasdale. "It's iron. You can't even shoot into it."

"Then we'll just have to get out through that grating back where we found you."

"It's impossible!" Teasdale exclaimed as he pushed past two men and crawled closer to Sam and Richard.

"Not if we hold someone up on our shoulders and give them a tool to dig with," said Richard. "It may take some time, but we could worry away the ground around the grating and get at least one man out. That man could come back and reopen the door."

"Oh, like you did?"

Sam's right fist shot out and smacked into Teasdale's jaw. The Englishman plowed backwards onto his heels, colliding

159

with another man behind him.

"Do you have a better idea?" Sam said with a snarl. "If not, shut up!" He flexed his aching fingers and massaged his knuckles. "Now tell those men to go back."

Teasdale spoke to the slaves who responded with agonized moans. Then, like a freight train that begins moving car by car until the last is tugged down the line, the mass of men returned down the dark tunnel.

Richard tugged on Sam's shoulder. "Do you really think your plan will work?"

"Hell, no. But we've got to try."

***

Nasur had refused any offer of food or drink in the village, demanding instead to know what had become of the lady Inez, the woman he had sworn to protect. Finally, Jabu's wife whispered that the lady had walked into the forest to be alone.

And that was what she should not be. He had heard too many stories of Pemba. Every one born and raised on Zanzibar island knew these tales, knew of the dangers on Pemba. The lady Inez and her daughter were very brave, it was true, but foolish in thinking that they would be safe from the witchcraft of this island simply because they were of the Merikas.

He had to find them, but first the lady Inez. She had saved his life and he had sworn an oath to his Sultan to protect her.

Nasur was a man of the sea, not of land. He knew how to find a path by the stars and how to read the currents and swells of the ocean, not the tracks left on the ground. But he put his mind to it.

If she walked, light and delicate though she was, the lady would leave a mark. And she would not push through where the trees reached out to cling and tear at her clothes and hair. No woman, however brave would do that.

He first followed the visible path, hoping to find Inez at every turn. She was nowhere to be seen. Then, a cry reached his ears, a sharp sound riddled with betrayal and pain. A woman's voice.

He ran only to find the forest impeding his pursuit as if the very trees were bedeviled. They probably were, he reasoned. Everything on this island was either in league with witchcraft or in fear of it.

By the time he broke free of the last grasping branch, it was too late. His lady lay face down in a filthy pond, her wondrous black hair undone and sodden around her. He would come back for her later. If he could.

Now, he needed to find who committed this horrid deed and kill him.

***

Musa insisted on going first out the open door. Jade didn't argue. If someone planned on attacking them, the strongly muscled Musa stood a better chance of disarming a foe than she did.

At least now she had a knife. She had slipped Musa's blade into her boot sheath, hoping he'd forgotten about it. The handle at least was not overly ornate and the dirty bronze blended more or less with her brown boots. Perhaps he wouldn't notice it there.

The short corridor was empty. So it seemed were the stairs leading up.

"You said you thought you knew where to look for Hazar. Where should we go?"

"We?" Musa's tone was derisive.

"I got us out, didn't I? Otherwise you'd still be rotting in that cell. So, yes, *we!*"

Musa looked her over briefly then shrugged. "There are other hidden rooms in this house. We must search for them. Look everywhere. Perhaps even in a place hidden in the forest nearby."

Jade nodded. "We'll go together then. Watch each other's backs."

The man did not reply. Jade followed him down the corridor. If this house was built on the plan of many Arab homes, then there should be a central courtyard. So far, that did not seem to be the case. Instead, the corridors meandered,

161

sometimes rising up a few steps, sometimes going back down. It reminder her a little of the kasbah she and her mother had been in back in the Atlas mountains.

She dropped her voice to a whisper. "If we do not find her here, then we must wait to try to free her on the eve of the ceremony."

"Very dangerous," said Musa. "Darshash will not come alone. The guild will witness."

The guild. Jade wondered how many that meant. Would there be time to go all the way back to Chake Chake and inform Mr. Allenby? But what could he do alone? *He could provide me with a gun. Surely he had some rifles around.*

She stalked the edges of every room they entered, tapping and listening for the sound of a hollow space on the other side or perhaps the sound of a young girl crying, alone with her fears.

She also studied the walls for any tell-tale gaps or lines which looked like breaks in an otherwise seamless wall. So far they'd found nothing. She let Musa enter each room first, mostly because she didn't trust him fully. She didn't intend to get shut into another room.

The eunuch had gone into another room while Jade examined the walls of the corridor. Once again, there was no sign of any hidden doors. She wondered if they should go back and check all of the floors. She'd seen a woman's wrist bangle in one back room, a room with a broken lattice, but no hidden doors. It might have been one of Hazar's bracelets, or it could have belonged to a long dead wife.

"Musa?" she called. After searching for over an half an hour, it had become obvious that the house was deserted and the need for silence was gone. If anything, letting Hazar hear their voices might induce her to cry out or, if gagged, make some noise.

"Musa! What in the name of Millard Fillmore's bathtub is that man doing?" she muttered. But when she walked into the room, it was empty.

For a moment, Jade couldn't believe her eyes. The man

must be around somewhere, but after another quick scan of the room, she forced herself to admit the truth. He'd disappeared. The question was, did he leave willingly or not?

She hadn't heard any sounds except for Musa sliding some furniture out of the way. Except that this room, like most of the others, was completely bare except for one large urn sitting to the right of the door. So it wasn't furniture that he'd moved.

He found a wall panel.

"Son of a biscuit!"

Before she completely entered the room, she reached around and grabbed hold of the heavy urn. Bracing herself against the doorframe, she dragged the urn towards her and jammed it against the door. There was no way in hell she was going to risk getting shut in the room. Even if someone tried to move the urn, she'd hear them and be on the attack before they could lock her in.

Slowly she padded around the perimeter, searching for a break in the wall or floor.

She found it, not by seeing a gap, but by noticing where the floor dust had been scraped aside by Musa's slippered feet. But how did it open?

She pulled her newly found knife, ready to slip it into a crack and force open a wider gap. Then she saw the tiny pin wedged into the corner of the floor against the wall. She squatted down to look more closely. Someone, probably Musa, had brushed their hand against the floor here. The pin must be the trigger to open a panel.

Jade pushed first, but the pin didn't budge. Next she pulled and the pin slid out a half an inch. That's when the wall swung back and another black hole yawned before her.

Terrific, still more darkness and no torch or flashlight.

At least there were no immediate drops. Instead, the floor just inside looked level. She went in. Three steps in, the panel closed behind her, engulfing her in a dark void.

She waited a minute, allowing her pupils to dilate. Sure enough, there was a faint light. It seeped in from a few cracks in the roof, another indication of how long the house had gone without any care. The space to her left was open. Ahead was wall.

Jade turned and stepped slowly, letting her feet and hands slide across their surfaces. About forty yards in, the tunnel turned left ninety degrees. She paused and listened again, expecting to hear Musa's breathing or footsteps in front of her. There was no sound. Either the man was lying in wait for her or he knew the tunnel well and made it out quickly.

At least she had a knife now. She held it ready, the blade's tip facing her elbow, sharp edge out. Once again she padded along, feeling her way with her hands and feet. At the end would be some sort of door, possibly triggered like the one leading from the room. Or perhaps, she'd already passed the door on the outside wall and this led into a blind alleyway or a trap.

She paused again to consider. Even someone familiar with the tunnel would need a light to see a hidden side door or would need some sort of cue that the door was near. Something to touch? So far she had only felt smooth wall. Had she missed something? Should she go back?

On what side of the house am I?

It stood to reason that an escape door would go out the back. Despite the pervasive darkness, Jade closed her eyes to form an image of the house as far as she'd seen. That last room, the one in which Musa disappeared, it sat on the right side of the house as one looked at the front. The passage had followed the outermost right side and went towards the back. She opened her eyes to the gloom and continued.

Again, after several minutes, she hit wall and again the passage made a ninety degree turn left.

Now I'm on the back wall.

Jade proceeded more cautiously, feeling with her feet for a pin or lever along the edge. Her hands caressed the wall high and low, searching for a notch or projection to let her know that a door was near.

She nearly tripped over the pointer, a rock set in the path. On the other side, the passage continued, perhaps to wrap itself around more of the house or possibly to end abruptly in another doorway to another room. Jade didn't bother to investigate. Instead, she felt along the right-hand wall for a doorway. It wasn't hard to find, nor was it difficult to open. A small latch lifted up and served as a handle to push the door open. It swiveled easily on well-oiled pins and opened into the sunlight and a view of the expansive ocean beyond.

The door must have been counter-levered for it swung shut behind her. When she tried to find it again, she saw that the stone work blended so well as to be nearly impossible. Clearly it was a door intended for escape, not for re-entry. And judging from the window with a broken shutter just five feet beyond, the tunnel must not have gone much farther. She wondered briefly why the window had been broken from without. A few pieces of broken coral stone lay on the ground beneath it, where someone had possibly climbed the wall to gain entrance through the window.

Someone had gone inside. Someone who didn't belong. Perhaps a very brave thief? Or had Teasdale risked all to get to Hazar. Was she already safely away from here?

As intriguing as it all looked, Jade had no time to look further. She needed to get back to her mother in the village. She took her bearings and guessed the direction. There was still no sign of Musa. The man had simply disappeared.

Good luck finding Hazar. May you get to her in time.

Jade set off at a loping trot northeast in an effort to intercept the cemetery. From there she could retrace her steps to the village. She hadn't gone more than a hundred yards when she ran into Nasur. His clothes were disheveled from where branches had snatched at them and his face was dirty and streaked with tears. She felt her heart sink to the pit of her stomach.

."Nasur! What has happened? My mother?"

"Lady Jade," he said, his voice catching, "your mother is dead."

CHAPTER 21

Along with the Shirazi blood is a blend of former mainland African tribes. Initially brought to Pemba as slaves, many married in or were united with as concubines.
- - The Traveler

The man spoke nonsense. Why would he ever dream of saying something so foul? He might well have said, "Your mother is on the moon."

"Nasur, why aren't you at the village with my mother?" Jade demanded. "You swore an oath to your Sultan to guard her." She took a step past him. "I'm going there now. Come along if you want."

He put his hands out to stop her. "You must listen to me. Your lady mother is dead. She has gone to God."

"No! She's in the village." This time the words were meant to convince herself. Jade heard the earnest sympathy in Nasur's voice, felt the gentle pressure of his palms on her shoulders, watched a single tear roll down his cheek.

Was it her heart? Did she fall? How could it happen? A part of her mind refused to believe it, told her repeatedly that it was all a lie, a bad joke.

"She's not dead!" Jade snapped. "She can't be dead. She wouldn't allow it."

"Please," coaxed Nasur. "Please sit. There is much to tell. It will be hard to hear."

Jade remained standing, her muscles tensing as she gripped Nasur's arms "What happened?"

"Your lady mother sent me to look for Jabu, the headman. I did as she commanded me. I was foolish. She only did so to escape my watchful eyes. I think she went to find you."

Jade felt a cold chill creep into her innards. This was no joke. This was real. Something had happened.

"Jabu, he had his wife offer me many refreshments. Told me that the lady Inez was only sitting at the edge of the village, keeping watch. That she wished to be alone to think. But how could I eat and drink knowing I should guard her? And when she did not return, I went to look for her. I found a path and followed it."

The cold chill spread up into Jade's heart. She felt a choking weight on her chest, making it difficult to breath. She resisted the urge to throttle Nasur and shake the rest of his story out of him.

"I heard an outcry. A woman's cry. When I came to her, she was floating as a lily in a pool. Her face was in the water."

Jade gasped and sank to her knees, her fingers clutching Nasur's robe and dragging him down with her.

Once again she was in the strangling depths of the ocean, the water's crushing strength forcing her under, wave after wave slapping her down. This time she didn't want to rise to the surface. She didn't want to face the blinding truth beating on the waters. She made one attempt to lessen the horror.

"She fell?"

Nasur knelt beside her, cradling her as gently as if she were a fragile baby. "No, my lady, Jade. I fear she was struck down."

The horror washed over her again and, this time, Jade succumbed to it and went down into the depths.

***

Sam studied the grating high above him, searching for a week spot. He didn't find one. This idea was looking more like a fool's errand minute by minute. Unfortunately, there was no other option.

"I think you should try for that side," said Richard as he pointed to one corner. "I think I see a little bit of metal through all the rock."

Sam nodded. "I still think *you* should be the one doing the digging, Richard."

Richard put a fatherly hand on Sam's shoulder. "Sam, don't be an idiot. You and I are the only ones out of this group that haven't been half-starved and of the two of us, I weigh the most. I don't think you'd be able to support me on your shoulders for very long." He slapped Sam on the back. "Hell, after that bullet walloped your leg, it'll probably crack in two under the strain."

"It didn't do much damage," said Sam. "Turned oak is hard to split. And it adds a lot more weight than you might imagine. If I could sit on your shoulders I'd take the leg off. But I would have to reach farther and couldn't put as much into my chiseling. I'm going to have to stand."

"I know. And we're burning daylight, so let's get a move on."

Teasdale held his hands like a stirrup and Sam scrambled up onto Richard's shoulders, doing his best to distribute his weight evenly as Jade's father gripped him by the ankles for stability.

"You let me know when this gets to be too much for you," Sam ordered. "We can do this in spells."

"If I buckle under, you'll be the first to know. Your clue will be when you hit the ground."

Sam took hold of one of the iron bars to both steady himself and to remove a little of his weight from Richard's shoulders. Then he attacked the ancient coral surrounding the metal, praying that his plan would work. His mind played out various scenarios for where Jade could be, but the hideous image of that shrine statue kept rising before him.

***

"Lady Jade. Lady Jade, You must rise."

The relentless voice droned in Jade's ears, buzzing like a

mosquito. She ignored it.

Mother is dead. Through my fault. Through my fault. Through my most grievous fault.

Could any absolution cleanse her of this guilt?

Dad! Dear God, what can I tell him? How can I face him? How can I face anyone?

Jade struggled to picture her mother's face. All she saw was a black void. She longed for that void to swallow her whole, and drown her in blessed oblivion. Anything than face a future without her brave, maddening, clever, beautiful mother. Jade couldn't recall a time when the woman hadn't driven her to distraction. She couldn't think of a time when she didn't love her mother intensely.

Mother is dead. Struck down. I brought her here. She just wanted to buy lace for me.

There would be no lace. There could be no wedding. People who ripped the loving, devoted spouse away from another as she had from her father didn't deserve a marriage of their own.

Why didn't she stay in the village? Why didn't I stay in Zanzibar?

The answer came quickly. *Because poor little Tisha was murdered. Because mother feared for Hazar's safety. Because, like me, mother couldn't abide by evil winning. She loathed the thought of someone harming an innocent.*

Well, mother was innocent, too, in her own way. And someone had killed her for it.

And now he's going to die for it if it's the last thing I do.

Jade raised her head. How long had she lain collapsed this way? She reached for her pocket watch. Gone. When had she lost it? It was as if the watch was a metaphor for this horror, her tangible connections with her father disappearing one by one, his gift, his wife.

My mother.

"Lady Jade. It is well that you have returned. I must take you to safety."

Jade looked at the shadows, noting how they'd begun to lengthen.

Early to mid-afternoon?

"Do you hear me?" pleaded Nasur. "I swore an oath and failed your mother. I must not fail you."

"It wasn't your fault, Nasur. It was mine for bringing her here."

"No, my lady. It was the fault of the demon that killed her. But he must not kill you. Come."

"I'm not going back." Her voice came out flat and matter-of-fact. There could be no going back for her. She accepted that. Embraced it. She would kill Darshash, for surely it was he that killed her mother. Jabu had been in the village coaxing Nasur with food. Teasdale wasn't strong enough. No, it was Darshash. He was the only one left.

"You must go back, Nasur. Go and collect my mother's body and take it to Chake Chake. Find Mr. Allenby and tell him what happened. He can deliver my mother safely to Mombasa and to my father."

"But you must come, too," pleaded Nasur.

Jade shook her head slowly and drew Musa's knife. "No. Tonight Darshash will be at the cemetery. And tonight he will die."

"But the other witches," pleaded Nasur, "they will kill you."

"So be it."

CHAPTER 22

Once the Portuguese left, the Wa-Pemba remained isolated from
Europeans for nearly a century, more than enough time to ingrain their
own traditional beliefs.
- - The Traveler

Screeches, warbling songs, chatters; all reduced to a
whisper, faded like fabric too long in the light. Lukewarm
water below, cool chill above as the damp clothing sun-dried.

Neither life nor death.

Limbo.

A tadpole wriggled closer, grazing on bits of algae clinging
to the woman's cheek. It swam too close to her ear canal and
the woman twitched, at first almost imperceptibly, and then
more boldly.

She rose gasping above the dank water, an aging Aphrodite
from an old sea of muck. A coughing fit quickly followed the
initial intake of air, and she spat out the taste of fetid water.

Inez had always believed in carrying more than enough
water. Now she was doubly grateful for canteen's volume. The
pond's murk had served to hide her frantic movements as
she'd rapidly unscrewed the cap and sucked on the precious air
she'd trapped inside moments before being struck down. It
bought her the time she needed to convince her attacker that

he'd killed her.

And Jade? Did he capture or kill her, too?

She pulled back her sopping hair, wringing out most of the water. The loosened hair clips probably sank to the bottom of the pond. In any event, looking for them was a waste of precious time. Inez snapped a green twig, took her knife from her pocket, and scraped one end to a point as if sharpening a pencil. Then she twisted her hair into a roll and jammed the twig through the mass, securing the bulk of it. Next she removed her boots and drained them, all the while scanning the area for any sign of movement.

Jade probably followed the trail, but then so did Darshash. It wouldn't do to run into him again. Inez kept her knife in her right hand, holding it with the point towards her elbow and the flattened edge against her arm as she'd seen her daughter do. Then she stepped into the forest and paralleled the path as best she could.

***

"I must not leave you," pleaded Nasur. He knelt beside Jade, imploring her. "You must come with me. Together we will take your dear mother's body, may her soul be at peace, back to Chake Chake. The Sultan will send his fine boat for you.

"No. I told you I'm going to kill Darshash." Her voice sounded cold, lifeless.

"Please. Your lady mother will understand her death. But her soul will haunt me if I let ill come to you, her only daughter. I beg of you to come with me."

"NO!" Jade turned to Nasur, seeing him for the first time since she heard his dreadful news. "I promise you on her very soul that my mother will not haunt you. We cannot leave her body to rot here. You must see that she gets to Mombasa and to my father. Swear to me that you will do this."

"But--"

"Swear to me!"

"I swear it."

Jade nodded. "Good. Now go." She spoke calmly now, her

decision made and accepted. "I'm going to wait here until late afternoon. Then I will go back to that cemetery I found. He will be there tonight and, when he comes, I will kill him. Tell my father that. Let him know that his wife was avenged."

"What will you do all alone here?"

Jade examined Musa's knife. "Sharpen this. The blade is dull."

"Is there anything else, my lady?" he asked.

"Yes. There is one more thing, Nasur. Find Sam Featherstone in Nairobi. Tell him that I love him. Tell him that I always will."

***

"How are you doing, Sam? Any progress?"

Sam heard the strain in Richard's voice and knew that the man wouldn't hold much longer.

"It's slow. The rock's been weather hardened and my arm is getting tired. I need to rest it a while. Coming down."

Sam hung from the bars until Richard moved away. He intended to dropped to the ground, but was instead gently lowered by a half-dozen hands. The slaves looked at him with touching hope in their eyes. Sam smiled and nodded, allowing them to believe in a progressing bid for freedom.

He sat down and Richard joined him.

"You weren't kidding about that fake leg of yours," Richard said, rubbing his shoulders. "Tell me the truth. Do we have a chance?"

"It's the only chance we've got," said Sam. "But it's going to take several hours and you aren't going to manage it. Maybe I can hold up Teasdale. He looks pretty light."

"I doubt his arms would last ten minutes against that rock before they cramped up," said Richard. "He doesn't look very strong to begin with and his imprisonment has weakened him further. Is your arm that sore?"

Sam rubbed his right shoulder. "No. Not so bad. I was more concerned for you. Thought you needed a break."

"I wish I could say that you were wrong, my boy. Maybe if I had some more padding for under your feet?"

"We could fold up my shirt and use it under my wooden leg," said Sam. He began to unbutton his shirt when a dark-skinned hand stopped him. He looked up to see one of the slaves, a sturdy man with sinewy arms. He didn't have the same time-worn appearance of the others and Sam wondered if he were one of the ones that had arrived in that last shipment of crates.

"Teasdale," Sam said, "ask this man his name and how long he's been in here?" To his surprise, the man answered on his own in English.

"My name is Thomas," he said, putting the accent on the second syllable. "I was taught by a mission school. I have been in this pit of hell for four days." He cupped his hands in front of Sam. "Come. I will hold you up."

Sam scrambled to his feet and slapped the man on the back. "Very well, Thomas. I'm ready when you are."

***

Inez did her best to follow the trail without actually walking on it, but if it led to Bin Rafi's big house, then there was no sign of it yet. She wondered if she'd strayed too far from it when she had to circumvent another ravine farther back. And worse yet, she hadn't seen hide nor hair of Jade.

She resisted the urge to call out for Jade. If Darshash still lurked nearby, she didn't want to alert him. Better that he thought her dead.

I'm thirsty! Helluva time to have an empty canteen.

Inez scanned the surrounding trees and spied a grove of coconut palms. One tree, shorter than the others, looked possible. She couldn't climb it, but she could certainly lob a few stones at the fruit. She picked up several chunks of loose coral stone and hurled one at the lowest cluster of coconuts.

She missed.

The next attempts hit the mark, but the nuts refused to fall. *Blast! I'm out of rocks.*

Inez widened her search for more projectiles when she spied a green coconut lying on the ground beneath one of the taller trees. Using her knife, she attacked the husk, stripped it, then sliced into the green seed.

The milk flowed rich and cool down her throat, invigorating her.

Get moving. Jade would tell me that I'm burning daylight.

She dropped the drained coconut beside the husk and continued on. Something about the distant trees and shrubs looked artificial. If her tired eyes didn't deceive her, she'd spied some man-made structures in the distance.

***

"I can see part of the iron on the sides," called Sam. "I've broken through."

"Fantastic!" said Richard. "Can you shift it?"

Sam gripped the grating and heaved upward. Nothing. Not so much as a jiggle. "No, sorry." He heard a collective moan from the men. They might not understand English, but they caught the word "no" easily enough. He tried to sound more positive. "But I think it's coming more easily now. The stone breaks along the iron. It's softer underneath once I get past that outer layer. Maybe it will send a fracture along the length and, after a little more pecking away, an entire section may break free."

"That's good, Sam. How's your arm holding up?"

"Fine."

"Thomas," said Richard. "You've help him up long enough. It is my turn again."

Thomas must have shaken his head vigorously because Sam felt the man's shoulders move. "Hey, hold still down there."

He tilted his head down to see Richard. "If Thomas is willing to hold me up, then don't stop him and for heaven's sake, don't make him move.

He looked back up at the grating only to stare straight into a living Medusa with scraggles of algae-matted hair flailing about a mud-encrusted face.

"Aaaah!" he yelped and dropped his knife.

"Hello, Sam. I didn't expect to see you down there. I was looking for Jade. I don't suppose my husband is with you, is he?"

CHAPTER 23

*Many customs and practices seem strange or exotic to the non-African
eye from the clothing and the hair styling to the dances. Some people find
these customs simply curious, some amusing, some bewildering.*
- - The Traveler

Nasur stumbled through the brush and over rocks, trying to
retrace his steps back to that dreaded pond. Every noise made
him look over his shoulder, which only increased his clumsy
steps. And every step closer to Inez's corpse filled him with
more remorse. He prayed for forgiveness and courage. He
would gather up the fallen lady. He would carry her down to
Chake Chake and look for the Englishman, Allenby. Perhaps
this Allenby would send help to the lady Jade in time to save
her. He prayed that the man would be receptive to his plea.

He would, in time, go to the mainland and seek out this
Featherstone of which Jade spoke. He would deliver the fateful
message. It was a task he dreaded with all his heart. For if this
man truly loved the lady Jade, then he would be delivering a
deathblow to yet another human's heart.

The pond appeared sooner than he'd anticipated and he
hastened towards it. If he needed, he would swim in the foul
pool to fetch the brave lady. She was slight of build. He knew
he could carry her if he prayed for strength. He would carry

her as a loving father carried a treasured child.

The lady was not there.

Had she sunk?

He picked up a long stick and waded into the water, probing the depths.

Shallow! Somehow that made it worse. If the lady Inez had not been struck down, she could have stood and climbed out. She need not have perished.

Back and forth he waded, poking and prodding with the stick, expecting at any moment to trip over her body. Each time he crossed from side to side, he came out without encountering her.

The lady had gone. The witch had returned for her corpse to perform unspeakable desecrations. Possibly he planned to make her his spirit slave. He would have to return and tell Jade.

***

"Inez! What the hell are you doing here?" scolded Richard. "You're supposed to be on Zanzibar staying out of trouble."

"I might ask the same thing about you, my dear," said Inez. "I cannot let you out of my sight, it seems."

"Enough," shouted Sam who now stood on the ground. "Get us out of here. Please."

Inez grabbed the bars and pulled. "I don't believe I can, Sam. The bars seem to be held fast in the rock."

"We know that," explained Sam. "There's a door. You have to find a cemetery first."

"I did. I passed it not a half of an hour ago."

"Wonderful," interjected Richard. "Go back there and slide the tomb marker. You should see the skid marks. It opens up a shaft but for heaven's sake be careful. We went in trying to free these men and got trapped in here ourselves."

They explained as briefly as they could how to find the iron door and open it. "Once you have the door opened, just get away and hide somewhere until we come out," ordered Richard.

As soon as Inez left, Sam took charge. "Richard, take my Colt and lead the men down the tunnel. Go as quickly as you can. No dawdling. I'll bring up the rear."

"No, Sam. You should lead. I--"

"Dammit, man. Just do it!"

This time, Thomas explained the plan to the other slaves who quickly took fresh hope at this new opportunity, talking excitedly. Sam asked him what the men said.

"They say that this woman has the appearance of a demon so she will be able to do what you could not. Even the witch master would not oppose her."

Despite the men's eagerness, they progressed slowly down the pitch black passageway. This time nothing lit the way. Sam could only pray that Inez had managed to move the stone marker and open the door.

And where the hell is Jade?

What did it take to keep that maddening woman out of danger? Why in the name of all that is holy did she go haring off on some wild escapade?

Why did you?

He ignored his own question. Men did that sort of thing. It was different. Maybe.

Joyful exclamations in front of him broke his reverie and informed him that Inez found success and they had found freedom. He crawled out the door, struggled to his feet, and trotted up the stairs, trying not to see that hideous statue in the shrine.

Sunlight and fresh air never felt so good.

Richard shoved the Colt back into Sam's hands and raced for the tree line and Inez who ran to meet him.

"Inez! My Darling!"

"Oh, Richard! Dearest husband!"

Sam watched as Richard wrapped his arms around Inez and hoisted her off her feet, swinging her in a full circle.

For a moment, neither of them spoke as they kissed with a passion that Sam found amazing for a couple married so long. He couldn't recall his own, more staid parents ever being that demonstrative.

He looked away. Thomas and the other freed slaves did

not. They seemed to find amusement in the demon woman and her mate.

"Oh, Richard, I am so glad to see you. You cannot imagine."

"Inez. Sweetheart, How can I thank you for saving us?"

"I was looking for Jade. What are you doing here? You're supposed to be on safari."

"What am *I* doing here? What the hell are *you* doing here? What happened to you? You look like something Jade's dog drug home."

"How dare you! I'll have you know that I've just had someone try to kill me."

"Oh? And that's supposed to fill me with relief? Can't I leave you alone with Jade just once without worrying about you?"

"Me? And I suppose I'm supposed to feel nothing but joy at finding my husband trapped in some dungeon pit? Why aren't you on safari?"

"We got sidetracked. For your information, Inez, *we're* trying to stop a murdering slave dealer."

"Of course. You big strong men are allowed to run off and put yourself in danger whenever you please and you expect us poor little defenseless females to pant over you and admire you for it? We have noble intention, too, I'll have you know."

"And what does it earn for you? You taste like fermented seaweed, Inez."

"Richard, Inez," interjected Sam. "I hate to break this up but--"

"You stay out of it," they shouted.

Sam gritted his teeth and counted to ten. Then he roared at them.

"Shut up both of you!"

Richard and Inez stared at him as though slapped. Then they looked at each other and embraced again.

"Oh, darling. Someone tried to kill you."

"My own sweet, brave husband. You could have been killed."

Sam took a deep breath as, this time, spoke as calmly and quietly as his now panicking nerves would allow.

"Inez. If you don't mind my interruption. *Where* is my intended bride?"

Richard released his wife and motioned for everyone to move into the forest and out of plain view. Once they had put distance between themselves and the cemetery, he sat everyone down.

"Okay Inez. From the beginning. Tell us everything."

***

Jade never found wishing very useful. It led to regrets and regrets led to time wasted. She'd always believed in doing, in taking action. Until now. Now regret filled her, spilled from her marrow.

She regretted bringing her mother here, regretted coming to Zanzibar instead of taking her mother on their own safari. But more than anything, she regretted not having said "yes" to Sam sooner. They'd be married now, off together filming Africa from the air, exploring its pristine skies together.

She regretted not having any paper or pencil with her to write one last note to him, to tell him how much she hungered for him. She longed to tell him that she'd loved him since they met on Mount Marsabit, that the night they spent in one hammock, huddled against the mountain's chill had haunted her every night since, keeping her warm against the coldest air. She closed her eyes and hugged herself, remembering Sam's warmth and his scent.

Fresh air and leather.

She regretted not having her blasted Winchester rifle with her.

One good shot and Darshash could join his unholy demons in Hell.

She took a deep, shuddering breath, honed the knife a few more times, swiping it on a nearby stone.

"Forgive me, Father, for what I am about to do."

Then she stood, gave one parting look towards the unseen African mainland and Sam, and started for the cemetery.

***

Inez finished her tale, the telling hindered by her husband's attentions and ministrations. They'd given all the rest of the fresh canteen's water, limited though it was, to the freed slaves, so with no other available, he'd insisted on spitting on his pocket kerchief and washing her face.

"Stop it, Richard," Inez said as she swatted his hands away. "You're taking the skin off of me." At least they had some measure of privacy now. Richard had sent Teasdale and Thomas off to find some green coconuts for them all. She wondered if she should tell Teasdale that his Hazar was now another man's wife.

Better he wait to find out later, when they were safely back at Chake Chake or, better yet, on Zanzibar.

"Your mouth is still dirty," Richard said. "And when I kiss you again, I don't want to taste slime and tadpoles."

"It appears that we're all looking for the same scoundrel," said Sam. He paced back and forth, his concern for Jade pushing him to the breaking point. "You think she went to Bin Rafi's house, then?"

"She didn't say as much when she left, only that she was going to scout for Teasdale. But it's where we planned to go together." Inez took the kerchief from her husband's hands and patted her lips with it.

"We were there, Sam," said Richard. "It was an empty place. Whoever this Bin Rafi is, he doesn't live there."

"No, but that Darshash fellow might spend time there," said Sam. "Richard, you take Inez and Teasdale and the men down to Chake Chake. Wait for me there. I'll get Jade and join you."

"Shouldn't we stay together?" said Inez.

Sam shook his head. "These men need immediate help, and Richard needs to send a telegram to Inspector Walsh telling him that we found them. I'll be faster without all of you. Now get moving."

He looked around to gain his bearings back to the house. As he did he overheard Inez's protest and Richard's response.

"If anyone can handle our Jade, it's Sam."

***

Nasur ran with the slightly bow-legged style of many seafaring men. He focused on the path before him, not only to prevent getting lost, but to avoid the horrid mental images popping into his head. He possessed no actual first-hand knowledge of witchcraft, only the tales related to him as a child or heard from other sailors coming from Pemba. These tales, enhanced by a vivid imagination, terrified him. Witches perpetrated horrid enough acts on the living. What would they do to the dead?

One of the more lurid images forced its way to his consciousness. He stopped and shut his eyes against it, forcing visions of the sea and sails into his mind instead.

It was why he never saw the figure approaching him from the side.

***

Sam didn't know whether to laugh or to cry. Being freed by Inez should have resulted in an indescribable joy and relief. One problem; Jade wasn't with her mother. What had she gotten into now?

Same thing as you.

But, Sam reminded himself, *he* hadn't gone off alone. Jade had.

Just wait until I get my hands on that little Varmint.

A more stimulating thought battled with images of Jade wounded, captured, tortured, murdered. That Darshash person did his best to kill Inez. What had he done to Jade? Surely Jade didn't let herself get captured.

She's been captured before and had enough people try to kill her. Why would this time be any different?

Jade was nick-named Simba-Jike, the lioness. Did lionesses, like housecats, get nine lives? If so, Jade was running out of them.

Sam sped up his pace. Twenty minutes later he heard determined footfalls approaching with the assurance of one familiar to this island.

Darshash!

Sam moved off the narrow path and hid behind a broad-trunked tree. He'd let Darshash move past him, then come from behind with his Colt drawn. He'd force the man at gunpoint to take him to Jade.

Then I'll shoot him in the leg to hold him until the authorities arrive.
He barely made it behind the trunk without being seen.

***

Hide near the cemetery. Cut branches. Bind them around me to blend in with the surroundings. Wait until moonrise for Darshash. Kill him!

Jade rehearsed the plan over and over. It grew into a type of cadence.

Hide. Blend. Wait. Kill.

She marched to it, picturing the kill spots on the human body. Her safest bet? Strike from behind. Jade didn't like that scenario. A back-stabber was euphemistic for the quintessential coward. And Jade wanted to see the pain rip across his face.

Hide. Blend. Wait. Kill.

A new voice forced its way into her consciousness, a masculine voice. Nairobi big-game hunter, Harry Hascombe, stopping her on Mount Marsabit. *"Jade. You're not a killer."*

Today she'd prove Hascombe wrong.

Hide. Blend. Wait. Kill.

She felt a hand on her left shoulder and she reeled, her knife ready.

CHAPTER 24

But some of the Pemba practices are far more disturbing.
- - The Traveler

The glint of light off the blade provided Sam with the only clue to danger. It came sweeping up from low to the side, ready to slash at his arm. He twisted aside as his right arm shot forward, gripping his assailant's forearm.

The knife twisted, seeking the vein pulsing just under his wrist.

He tightened his grip, at the same time dodging a fist to his diaphragm. It caught him a glancing blow.

"Jade." The knife scratched his forearm.

"Jade!" He danced aside, avoiding a boot stomp to his instep.

"JADE!"

His assailant froze. Her eyes stared at him; dead, uncomprehending."

"Jade, it's me, Sam."

"Sam?" The word eeked out, her voice breaking, child-like. "My Sam?"

She fell into his arms, and Sam folded her close to him.

"Hush, Hey. It's all right. I'm here."

She sobbed uncontrollably. This was not the Jade he'd ever

known before, vulnerable, despairing. *What the hell happened here?*

"Shush, now. You're safe." He stroked her hair.

"No. Sam. Mother's dead."

"What? No! No she's not. I just saw her. Granted she looks like hell on a cracker, but she's fine. Feisty as ever. Took all your father's strength to drag her off to Chake Chake while I came looking for you?"

"What? What are you saying? She's not dead? She's not dead!"

Sam led her aside and found a log. He pulled her down gently, avoiding the exposed blade still in her hands. "Let's put that away, shall we?"

"What? Oh!" Jade shoved the blade into her boot sheath.

"Where did you get that? It's not your knife."

"Long story," said Jade. "Mother's really not dead? You've actually seen her?"

Sam stroked Jade's cheek with the palm of one hand. "Yes. Good thing, too. Your dad and I were in a pit and . . . . anyway, she said someone named Darshash tried to kill her, but she faked her own drowning until he left. Are you all right?"

Jade nodded and swiped at her eyes and nose with her pocket kerchief.

"You're certain that you're all right now?" asked Sam, his voice gentle as though speaking to a frightened child.

"Yes. I'm fine. I'm--"

"Then what in the name of hell are you doing here!" he roared. "You nearly killed me. Your own mother almost drowned. Can't I leave you alone for a moment?"

"Me?" Jade pulled back and stood, her fists clenched at her side. "What are *you* doing here?"

"I'm not talking about that now," Sam said, raising his voice as he stood. "I'm talking about you and your dag-blasted attempts to get yourself killed. I want to know--"

"What gives you the right to tell me what to do? We're not married yet, Sam Featherstone. And if you think . . . Wait a minute, did you say that you and Dad were in a pit? And just what in the name of St. Peter's bait bucket were you two doing in a pit on Pemba?"

Sam knew he'd lost the argument. He did the only thing he could do at that point, and to be honest with himself, it was the only thing he wanted to do. He grabbed Jade in a tight embrace and welded his lips against hers.

"Sam," she mumbled, straining for a moment against his embrace. And then he felt her melt into it and meet it, her arms wrapping around his shoulders as her lips searched his. She tasted faintly of dust but underlying that was the sweet taste of Jade. *His* Jade. Safe and in his arms.

"Sam," she said in a soft, subdued voice as she pulled away. For some reason, the tone filled his with dread.

"Yes, Darling?"

"Just what were you and my father doing in a *pit* on Pemba?"

"I'll, uh, let your dad tell you about it. If we hurry, we can catch up to them."

"I'm not going anywhere until I kill Darshash," she said as calmly as if she were announcing dinner. "He tried to kill my mother. He killed a helpless little slave girl on Zanzibar, and if he has his way, he plans to kill another girl tonight in some ceremony from Hell."

Sam sat back down on the log, an image of the hideous shrine rising before him in his mind. "Your mother told me some of this already. Maybe it's time for both of us to compare notes." He proceeded to describe his own adventure, omitting only the part about finding the surprise airplane.

When they'd both finished relating all their details, they reached an agreement. Darshash needed to be stopped before he could kill anyone else. It was up to the two of them.

***

Inez slowed her pace, feigning fatigue. "Richard, I need to rest." She recognized the spot and for good reason. She'd spent enough time there that morning, waiting for Jade.

"Are you tired, my love?" asked Richard. "Should I carry you?"

"Certainly not, my darling. You have had a difficult time, too."

"There's a village not far from here, Mrs. del Cameron," said Teasdale. "I've purchased food here before."

"Yes, I'm familiar with the village," said Inez. She smoothed back her wild, algae-laden wisps of hair, conscious of how crazed she must look.

"Can you make it that far?" asked Richard. "They would have water there. You could wash if you liked."

Her womanly vanity rose to the fore, but her motherly concern for Jade won out. "No. Teasdale can take the men on, though. Let them eat and drink before going on to Chake Chake." Inez looked up at Teasdale. "Could you do that, Mr. Teasdale? Take the men to Chake Chake alone?"

"But--" Teasdale began.

Richard patted one of Inez's knee. "I believe I understand, Mr. Teasdale. My impulsive wife is having second thoughts about leaving Sam and Jade behind. Isn't that right, my dear? Truth be told, the same idea's been hammering away in my head, too."

"Oh, Richard," Inez said, clutching at his sleeve. "Please don't make me stay here again, waiting. I won't you know." She set her lips, tilted her chin up, and folded her arms across her chest.

Richard laughed and kissed her on the cheek, making a sour face after he did. "We do need to clean you up, my dear."

"Oh, there's no time. Besides, these men think I resemble some she-demon. So much the better. Perhaps I can frighten Darshash into thinking I've come back to haunt him."

Richard took a deep breath and exhaled slowly. "I don't suppose there is any use in my ordering you to stay, Inez, any more than my ordering you to go on to Chake Chake."

Inez smiled and shook her head.

"In that case, then, I'd be foolish not to take you with me," he said. "Otherwise, I'd be too distracted, wondering what trouble you'd gotten into on your own."

"Then it is settled," said Inez. "Mr. Teasdale, you will take these poor men to Chake Chake and contact Mr. Allenby. Oh, and you should stop by the village and pick up a man named Nasur. He'll be worried sick about me by now. Tell him I'm perfectly fine and in the safe company of my husband."

***

Teasdale watched the older couple disappear into the forest. Strange couple. That woman, Inez, would not explain why she was here. He supposed, that she had traveled to the island to see some ruins. Her overbearing cowgirl daughter had told him as much in his flat just before she threatened to pummel him. Silly American women, they certainly found more than they'd bargained for, falling into muck and swamps. Still, he had to admit his gratitude for her timely rescue.

Teasdale had found the man's story very interesting. Those two American cowboys, as he'd come to think of them, had actually come alone to catch a slaver. Teasdale wondered at the brass and daring involved in such an adventure. The men certainly appeared to be well matched with their women.

He wondered if such devoted happiness existed in his future. Possibly. After all, he found his treasure and reburied it where only he could find it. And he knew something that the Americans didn't know. He could read Arabic. When he'd recently discovered the cemetery, he read the name "Bin Rafi" on the center tombstone with surprise and some alarm. That scoundrel Darshash had played with them all pretending to be Bin Rafi's emissary. The scoundrel probably knew that Hazar's father wouldn't give his only child in marriage to a Wa-Shirazi man, no matter if he ran the plantation now or not. And Darshash must have known that or else why perpetrate such an elaborate fraud to gain a wife?

Darshash had nearly killed him then and there when Teasdale ran across him the cemetery. But for some reason that Teasdale didn't wish to dwell on, Darshash had instead chosen to lock him up. Being a slaver wouldn't bother Bin Hassan, but being a fraud?

But now Teasdale had his treasure. He would see these men safely to Chake Chake, then come back for it. He'd take it to

Bin Hassan, reveal what he knew, and be given Hazar as his own. The next time Darshash came, pretending to deal on Bin Rafi's behalf, he'd earn himself a severe beating for it. The thought made Teasdale smile.

But why wait to come back for it? Why not fetch it now? Did he really need to go with these men to the coast? Couldn't Thomas, the newest addition to the slave pit, do just as well? He spoke English. He could tell this Allenby fellow what had happened.

His plan formed quickly, and Teasdale felt the better for it. He'd direct Thomas and the others as far as the village and then turn back. Anyone could follow the path from the village to the coast. They didn't need him.

But Hazar did. He thought of her, waiting for him back in Stone Town, impatient for a lesson. She loved seeing the British newspapers, especially the society pages and the pictures of the ladies in their fancy gowns. The very thought made him tingle all over.

There was no time to waste. Darkness would come soon, and Teasdale knew that it often brought Death with it. He didn't want to be in the forest then.

CHAPTER 25

Blood-curdling, horrifying practices. They begin with an owl call.
- - The Traveler

Visibility diminished as if the lights were lowered for a play. On cue the nocturnal noises began. A staccato *chuttering* followed by several barks erupted from the trees. Underlying those cries issued a monotonous *hoo hoo hoo*. From somewhere to Jade's left came a plaintive mewing quickly followed by a *chirrup*.

Jade was no stranger to nocturnal sounds but on an island where the largest predators were a small civet and the little mongoose, it struck her as strange that all these calls sounded fearful. Perhaps she was only projecting her own emotions, but even the air carried a stench of terror. She felt even more grateful for Sam's close presence.

They hid in the brush with a full view of the cemetery. Beyond the stones to the left and obscured by the dark, stretched the path from Bin Rafi's house. To the right the path continued on its winding way to the village. And behind them rose the full moon. Jade suddenly felt very exposed. The owl hooted again, this time from in front of them.

A shadow seemed to rise from the ground in front of them, and with it, a flickering fire.

More shapes appeared on all sides.

Where did they come from? She hadn't heard footsteps. Surely they didn't simply materialize. Get a hold of yourself.

The shapes remained hunched over, scrambling about on all fours. They snarled, barked, growled, and snapped at each other, a pack of monstrous dogs. Some wore short robes, others appeared to be naked.

"I've seen and heard this before, back at the main house," whispered Sam.

The second glow accompanied the small fire. This time, the light appeared to come from inside the earth.

"Someone's in that shrine room," whispered Jade.

The barking and howling intensified as did the gyrations, taking on a grotesque and chaotic choreography that somehow carried an underlying pattern. That more than anything else, told Jade that these were humans, not wild animals.

As the underground light grew, it illuminated a small figure lying in a heap a foot from the smaller fire. A slight breeze stirred and carried a faint whisper of perfume.

Civet musk. Hazar's scent.

Jade nudged Sam and pointed. "Hazar," she whispered. Sam nodded. He made a small, sweeping gesture with his palm and followed it with a shrug as though to ask if she recognized anyone else in that macabre group. Jade shook her head. Nothing resembling Darshash. None of the other shapes even appeared large enough to be a man of his size.

Jade wrestled with her own desires. As much as her very marrow longed to see Darshash die, she knew that Hazar's safety was preeminent. "We have to get her away from here, Sam."

Sam raised his Colt. "I'll move around to the other side and create a diversion. Free Hazar and get back into hiding. Run for the house. You should be able to find a defensible place there. I'll join you as soon as I can."

"But…" Jade didn't get any farther than that before Sam had slipped away. The questions poured into her head.

Run for the house? Is he serious?

Hazar didn't appear to be in any position to run, and Jade didn't know how long she could carry the girl. And what if she *could* get the girl to the house? Where could they hide? Most of the rooms bolted from the outside. And what if that entire mob went after Sam? He only had a limited number of bullets.

She simply had to trust in all that was holy to protect them. She pulled her knife, ready to cut any bindings on Hazar. The girl would be too terrified or perhaps too drugged to move on her own. She'd have to carry the poor thing. Jade wondered if her parents had made it to Chake Chake yet. It was unlikely but it gave her some comfort to know that the two were safe and re-united.

Jade shifted position, ready to spring forward as soon as Sam drew the pack away. A noise to her right distracted her. Was Sam coming back?

She peered into the trees and saw a man approach, slipping from trunk to trunk. He wore a brown shooting jacket, belted at the waist and long trousers tucked into boots.

Allenby! Her parents must have met him somewhere on the way down, and he hurried up to find her. Jade motioned for him to join her and put a finger to her lips to caution silence. He hurried to her side and squatted beside her. She longed to ask him a number of questions: how he located her, when did he see her parents, were the slaves being cared for? Jade stifled all of them, focusing on the business at hand.

"I'm going to slip in and free that girl lying by the fire," she whispered as she struggled to rise. Her left knee, injured by shrapnel during the Great War, ached from squatting too long.

Or is it from something else? As inexplicable as it sounded to modern ears, that knee always ached when danger loomed close by. An old Berber woman in the Atlas Mountains once told her that Death had entered the wound and lived there. He became excited when danger loomed close. Well, there was certainly enough danger to go around tonight.

"Not a very good idea," Allenby whispered back.

Before she could reply, she felt the cold ring of a gun's nozzle on her neck.

"You should not interfere in things about which you know nothing."

***

Inez stumbled over a root and pitched forward, landing against her husband's broad back.

"So sorry, darling," she said as he turned and took her by the shoulders.

"Are you all right, Inez?"

She nodded then, realizing that he might not have seen that in the deepening gloom, added, "Yes, I'm fine. I just tripped."

She heard him exhale hard and could almost feel his frown. She knew his every mood and senses that he disapproved of her being in trouble on this accursed island. She'd be in for a stern scolding when they finally got back to the mainland. It was nothing she couldn't handle, especially since she also knew that deep down inside he was proud of her. He hadn't married a tame wife, and after her adventure in Morocco, he got his original wild Spaniard back.

Inez smiled. *Just wait until we get back.* Just as quickly, she shoved the thought back. They weren't back yet, and there was still the fate of those two poor girls to contend with. Tisha was past saving, but they could bring her killer to justice. The other spoiled little creature deserved better than to be forced into a marriage with some old man on a dismal plantation with his maniacal manservant. She might yet be helped.

"Are you ready to go on?" asked Richard. "Do you need more time to rest?"

"I'm not in any need of rest, Richard. And there is no time to waste."

They took a few more steps when they heard someone approach from behind. Richard took Inez by an arm and pulled her off the path and deeper into the shadows. A torch floated up the trail towards them, carried by someone sure footed. Others, less certain of the way followed.

At first Inez thought that Teasdale had brought help from the village, that people had come to assist them. But judging by the scraping, muffled mumbles, and sounds of shoving, at least one travelled against his will.

Inez didn't need Richard's firm hand on her shoulder to remind her of the need for silence. This was no search party.

She pulled back then froze. As the torch came nearer, she glimpsed the torchbearer's face. All the others were obscured by the shadows around them, but Inez had seen enough.

She prayed that Teasdale and the men hadn't stopped at the village.

***

Sam wended his way around the cemetery, sticking to the trees. When he reached the opposite side, he squatted down to re-evaluate the situation. No change. The hunched figures still loped about on all fours like a pack of dogs, barking and snarling at one another. From time to time, one of them would raise his or her head to howl, an action swiftly followed by the rest of the pack. The revolting scene would have been comedic if not for that pitiful heap lying by the fire.

So create the diversion and let Jade free Hazar.

He reached for his Colt and stopped once his hand rested on the handle.

And then what? I can't shoot all of them, there are too many. I've only got five shots. There's no good place to hide. And what if they don't all run after me? They'll be on Jade in an instant. She'd never make it to the house with her burden.

The solution came to him. *Then you'll just have to make sure they all run after you and that you make every shot count.*

He looked past the fire to the other side, taking care not to stare into its glow and ruin his night vision. It took him a few moments to find Jade, a testimony to how well she'd hidden herself.

Sam looked again. Someone knelt beside her. His breath caught in his throat until he realized the person's face looked pale enough to be British rather than Arab or black African.

Re-enforcements! This might work after all.

Sam raised his Colt and studied the howling mob, looking for a sure target. He'd shoot for the hips, a crippling shot.

He chose his target, a near naked man squatting on this side of the fire. Before he could shoot, another man enters the clearing with an accomplice, dragging two prisoners with them. Both staggered as though they'd been beaten within an inch of their lives. Dirty rags spilled from their mouths, reducing their outcries to heart-rending moans. One wore sandals and a torn robe girded up to his bare knees. The other wore European trousers, shirt and boots.

Sam couldn't see the second man's face, but the shoulder-length hair identified him.

Teasdale.

***

Jade remained as motionless as any of the neighboring trees. Allenby's breathing sounded in her ears. She heard his regular intake and exhalations. They spoke of his assurance that all would go as he wished, that she was of no consequence and would remain compliant.

Well, let him think that. Arrogant overconfidence has been the downfall of others. It will be his, too.

Once she'd detected the slightest relaxation on his part, she'd act. She only hoped it was not too late to save Hazar.

Does he know about Sam?

She heard no noise from that quarter, so presumably no one was trying to take him prisoner. Good. Sam's distraction would startle Allenby along with the others and that would be her moment to strike.

"You'll regret this," she whispered.

"Quite the contrary, Miss. I find it particularly fascinating."

"Oh? Don't tell me you're one of them."

He chuckled softly. "Don't be preposterous. The very idea is ludicrous. No, my interest in strictly monetary. Certain parties wish me to turn a blind eye to various . . . *imports* as it were. And I do. In return, they pay me very handsomely. It is immaterial to me if they like to pretend at witchery."

"Then why are you here?"

"Because of you. After you left, I began to make inquiries about you. It appears that you have quite a reputation. *Simba Jike*, indeed. The famed white lioness of Kenya Colony. I didn't believe half of the tales I heard but even half was enough to know that you were persistent, especially when you felt you were defending some helpless person or noble cause. And when you and your mother didn't return, I worried that you might be gumming up the works here. I couldn't have that."

"So you plan to kill me?"

He didn't answer for a moment. "It remains to be seen. I shouldn't like to, you understand, but I can't allow you to spoil my arrangements."

New noises grabbed her attention and she stiffened.

"Relax, Miss del Cameron. You should find this most interesting. I understand that you write about Africa. It should make quite a story. *If* you get a chance to tell it."

A moment of panic seized her, and she felt her knees quiver momentarily. Had someone found Sam after all?

Four living shadows emerged from the opposite side, two unwillingly. As the leader of the new arrivals entered the clearing, his face caught the moon's light.

Mahir! So the village man that had taken care of the bull is part of this demonic charade. But where is Darshash?

Jade didn't recognize Mahir's confederate, but she stifled a gasp when the two prisoners were pushed closer to the monuments and the firelight.

Nasur! And Teasdale! The panic threatened to grip her again. Had her parents escaped? Or were they lying dead in the village? Allenby hadn't mentioned her father at all, so chances are he didn't know about him. And that meant he also hadn't seen her mother recently. But Mahir's presence didn't bode well.

Her right hand trembled and she fought to calm herself.

"You know these people?" asked Allenby? "I think you recognize Mr. Teasdale at least. Bloody fool. I told him that looking for treasure here was not safe." He made a few "*tsks.*" "Some people simply do not listen to reason."

Jade took a deep breath and let her fears and hatred brew deep inside, using them as fuel for her upcoming actions.

Come on, Sam, shoot!

A deep voice rumbled from the bowels of the shrine, speaking in Swahili.

"Kill the ones you brought. Then bring down my bride to me."

Mahir slipped a knife from his waistband and raised it aloft, its blade glinting in the moonlight.

CHAPTER 26

Practices only spoken of in hushed whispers.
- - The Traveler

The voice from beneath the tombs sounded like Satan himself calling up from Hades. Except Sam didn't think that Satan spoke Swahili, not that he really gave much thought to what language the Devil preferred.

Sam's fluency in the language didn't extend much beyond hello, goodbye, please, and thank you so he had no idea what the disembodied voice was saying, but judging by the new man's reaction, he'd just heard a command to kill.

The hell with that. He quickly changed his choice of target to the new arrival. Sam aimed at the man's right shoulder as he held the knife aloft. The shot, while not immediately fatal, would certainly stop him and drop him.

Boom.

Mahir's scream ripped the air, the knife dropping before it could do the same to Teasdale. The man clawed at his clavicle as he fell beside his knife.

Teasdale spun around on his knees, his eyes wild with frantic fear. Most of the participants that Sam could see bolted into the protective cover of the dark forest.

Sam waited for Jade to run in and release Hazar and the

others, but she didn't move.

Something's wrong. He started for the clearing, keeping his Colt handy.

A well-bred English voice sang out across the cemetery. "Cease fire immediately or Miss del Cameron dies."

***

"Kill the ones you brought. Then bring down my bride to me."

The sepulchral command was answered by Sam's Colt. At that point, Jade should have made her move. She didn't.

Her decision to stay put didn't stem from cowardice, or even from a lack of feeling for poor Teasdale. It was a matter of survival. Allenby never relaxed his vigilance, even when Mahir's right shoulder blossomed into a spray of gore.

He would have killed her if she'd so much as twitched.

And I still haven't killed Darshash. Surely it was his voice she'd heard belch from the shrine.

Granted, he hadn't actually killed her mother, but he'd tried, and Heaven knew how many others had fallen victim to his delusional beliefs.

"Cease fire immediately or Miss del Cameron dies," shouted Allenby. He pressed his lips against Jade's ear and spoke his next words with a growl. "Who's out there?" he demanded.

"Hell if I know," Jade said. "I thought he belonged to you."

He rewarded her with a rap of his gun barrel against her ear.

"Who is out there? Tell me or I'll shoot off your ear."

"It's an American. Sam Featherstone."

"What's he doing here?"

"Sport shooting?"

He struck her again, harder.

"You are trying my patience."

Jade tensed. *He's predictable.* As long as he was swinging the gun, he wasn't aiming to fire it. She'd goad him one more time, but this time she'd be ready for him.

***

Blast and damn! Sam couldn't believe it. An Englishman had just ordered him to stop shooting or risk Jade's life. This wasn't an officer or constable. He pulled back farther into the trees. If the man demanded that he come out and drop the gun, then there was nothing to stop any of these crazed creatures from killing both of them. That wasn't an option.

He'd retrace his steps back to Jade, circling wide enough to come up on this jackass from behind.

***

"Tell him to come out. Do it!" commanded Allenby.

Jade moaned and let her head droop a little, feigning disorientation from that last blow. It didn't take much pretense either. The second strike had cut her. She felt a trickle of warm blood dribble down her scalp.

"Tell him!" He shook her arm.

"Go take a long hike off a short cliff," she said.

She heard his sudden intake of breath, felt the gun's muzzle shift up from her head preparatory to another blow.

NOW!

Jade spun on her knees, her left arm slamming up into Allenby's as it descended with the gun. At the same time, her right fist shot straight out, aiming for Allenby's chin. He pulled his head back in surprise and her punch struck him a glancing blow in the throat instead.

He muttered "You dirty b--" which ended in a choked gurgle. But the strike didn't hit dead on, and he recovered in an instant. His left hand grasped her right arm in a vise-like grip, preventing a repeat blow to his face.

Allenby, despite his quiet demeanor back at Chake Chake, was no milquetoast. His arms displayed considerable strength and he had no apparent compunction against using his power against a woman. It didn't help that Jade had been on her aching knee and partly twisted around. She struggled to keep him at bay while she regained her full balance.

"Damned hell cat!" swore Allenby. He pushed forward, throwing her onto her back.

Jade didn't reply, saving her breath for the fight.

Then, from behind her in the cemetery came a blood-thirsty scream that spewed hate and anger into the night.

"Who dares desecrate these rites?" shouted the voice, speaking Swahili. "Who will pay with their own blood for killing my servant? You will all die!"

A second, ear-splitting bellow followed these invectives.

The outcry or perhaps the promise of a horrific death startled Allenby, giving Jade the moment she'd waited for.

She slammed her head up and forward, butting him in the chest.

"Ooof!"

As he exhaled, the grip on her arms relaxed and she heaved upwards, rolling him to his side. At the same time, she jerked her knee up, striking him in the groin. "You call me a hell cat? I'm worse than that. I'm Simba Jike, remember?"

"Aaaah!" moaned Allenby.

Jade believed in her heart that the voice from the shrine belonged to Darshash. Who else could it be? He'd risen from the earth like some Mephistopheles up from the damned after hearing Sam's gunshot and, with as much noise and she and Allenby were making, would be on them in a flash. She didn't intend to let him kill her. Not, at least, until she'd done him the favor of putting her knife through his demonic heart.

"You can go to hell, Allenby," she muttered as she pushed her way clear of him. As she struggled to her knees, she looked for his fallen weapon, hoping to arm herself with it. The gun had flown backwards, and to reach it, she'd have to expose herself to the furious high priest.

Even now, the man from the shrine looked up from where Mahir lay writhing in pain and glanced in their direction, attracted by the noise. But before coming their way, he pulled his knife and, dropping to his knees, plunged it into Mahir's back.

Mahir's sharp scream died quickly into a wheezing moan.

"You failed me. You pay the price," the high priest swore.

Then he turned his face fully towards Jade and Allenby and into the moonlight. She knew this face, had seen its festering hatred before.

Musa!

CHAPTER 27

*Many mainland African tribes have people who claim to possess
magical, supernatural powers but most of these powers are parlor tricks.
Not so on Pemba.*
- - The Traveler

Sam heard the struggle before he saw it. He pressed harder
through the underbrush, no longer concerned about secrecy.
Fear for Jade's safety fueled his legs, made him impervious to
scratching vines and stubborn branches.

The shrine had belched out some new monstrosity, most
likely the man called Darshash; the one Jade was gunning for.
Sam initially expected just another delusional man, scampering
about on all fours, barking like the others. Clearly this man
exceeded that nonsense. Through the intervening brush and
trunks, Sam eyed the new threat. His bulk exceeded any of the
other scrawnier practitioners, and his outcry possessed more
violence and power than Sam had heard since the war.

Such a man could be counted on to control his minions
with fear, a fear that would soon bring them back from where
ever they'd scattered. He wouldn't go down easily and Sam was
in no position to shoot the man now.

For a split second, he considered pushing his way into the
clearing and shooting this demon. Then he heard thrashing

bodies and knew it would have to wait. Jade was in trouble and Sam needed to reach her first. He only hoped he wasn't too late already.

Sam's first clear view of the struggle came when the Englishman's gun flew out of his grip and landed six feet to the man's left. He saw Jade look for it as well as her realization that she'd expose herself to this wrathful high priest.

A short-lived, high-pitched scream sent icy shivers through his blood, but it didn't come from Jade or her attacker. It came from the cemetery.

Sam witnessed the priest plunge a knife into the man that he'd previously wounded. He saw the effect it had on Jade. She'd frozen instantly.

The Englishman must have noted that, too, because he took that opportunity to roll over and scramble for his fallen gun.

Sam pushed through the last brush and reached it just as the Englishman did. The man's fingers were already pawing for the handle, trying to drag it into his grasp. Sam lashed out with his foot and kicked the man in the face. Blood spurted from the man's nose as Sam lunged for the gun. He didn't even bother to examine it, he still held his preferred Colt, the model 1917 issued to him as a pilot in the war. It had taken down six Germans before the rest had captured him after his plane crash. It would take down this man.

"Don't kill him, Sam," shouted Jade. "We need Allenby alive."

"Fine," said Sam. He turned to the man, his Colt trained on his knee. "Allenby, is it? Well, Allenby, if you try to run away, I'll shoot you in the leg," Sam said.

"Don't leave me here," whimpered the Englishman, as he pinched shut his bloody nose. "He'll kill me." He nodded to the high priest who'd retrieved his knife and eyed them from the clearing.

"Is that Darshash?" asked Sam.

"Yes, no," said Jade. "I don't know. I've only seen him from the back but it's his build. But his face... Sam when the moonlight hit it before I could have sworn it was Musa, Hazar's bodyguard. But that can't be."

"And you planned to kill him yourself?" asked Sam. "With only a knife? Woman, do you have a death wish?"

"I did."

The admission stunned Sam momentarily. "Then change your plans, Jade. *That* monster will take both of us to dispatch. I'll provide the cover shots and you free the captives. I'll carry the girl, Hazar. I just pray that Teasdale and that other man will be able to follow on their own."

"I didn't get a good look but I think the other man is Nasur. He's the sailor that my mother rescued when our dhow sank."

Sam turned to Allenby who sat nursing a bloody and possibly broken nose. "Stay there. We'll deal with you later."

He looked at Jade who was studying the high priest.

"What the...? He has my knife," exclaimed Jade. "That's my knife! Shoot him, Sam," she said. "And make it count. Quick before he has a chance to kill Hazar or the others. Before it's too late."

Too late, indeed. The priest flashed a malevolent grin at Sam before the man strode as calmly as he pleased towards the little heap that was Hazar. The man did nothing to protect himself as though he dared Sam to shoot.

"Bastard acts like he wants to be shot," said Sam. He took quick but careful aim at the man's broad chest, accounted for the distance and fired.

Nothing.

"You're out of ammunition?" asked Jade.

"No. I can't be," said Sam. He aimed and fired again with the same result.

The brute stood towering over Hazar, his feet apart and his hands on his hips. He laughed over the little creature who responded with a piteous whimper.

"Use Allenby's gun."

Sam shoved his Colt in his holster, raised the other, and squeezed the trigger only to hear an empty click.

"NO!" he shouted.

The high priest laughed at him. Then he bent down and grabbed the girl by an arm and hoisted her to her feet.

"Your bullets have no harm to me," shouted the high priest in English. "My power is strong."

He shook Hazar. "And soon it will be even stronger."

CHAPTER 28

*Pemba claims three classes of magic practitioners. The lowest grade
consists of practitioners of white magic, the "medicine men."*
- - The Traveler

Jade had seen her share of inexplicable events in Africa,
from a hyena that was a man to seeing a magnificent cheetah
disappear into a lost King's tomb. But despite witnessing all of
these phenomena she'd always maintained a cool disbelief, a
grasp on reality.

Sam's revolver is useless against the priest's power.

It made no sense. It couldn't be. Sam must have been out
of bullets. But Allenby's gun, too?

"We'll have to charge him, Sam," said Jade. She'd retrieved
Musa's knife from Allenby's foot and brandished it. "He won't
be impervious to a blade."

"Are you sure?" asked Sam.

She shrugged. "The witch he stabbed wasn't. Why should
he be different?"

Sam nodded and the two pushed forward, leaving Allenby
behind.

The brush that previously served to conceal them now
fought against them as though it, too, defended the high priest.
The harder Jade pushed, the more the branches seemed to

shove back and the low grasses and stones tried to trip her feet. As they struggled, the high priest pulled Hazar along with him towards the maw that led to the underground shrine. He seemed unperturbed, even amused by their efforts to reach him. At times he stopped and watched their progress as though goading them on.

"Sam, as soon as you get a chance, get him. Don't let him go into the shrine."

She redoubled her efforts, but before they could break out and into the clear, another bulky figure entered the clearing from the opposite side.

The newcomer wore the clothes that Jade had seen on Musa when they were trapped in the house together.

So the high priest is *Darshash.*

Darshash reached the first step into the shrine and stopped to pick up Hazar.

"Come, my bride."

The girl seemed to have enough will to resist but certainly not the strength and she beat on the man's chest with her tiny fists. Darshash laughed, but cut his laugh short when he saw Musa. He tossed Hazar into the pit as easily as if she were a toy and turned to face his attacker, his knife, Jade's knife, gleaming in the firelight. Musa didn't appear to be armed, and Jade suddenly regretted taking the man's knife for herself.

Sam and Jade halted at the edge of the clearing and stared as the two men grappled with each other by the monuments. The combatants appeared evenly matched in size and in ferocity, neither one gaining any advantage over the other, their feet splayed wide for balance, hands gripping forearms, head against head. If one pushed forwards five paces, the other quickly pushed back. To and fro they struggled, sometimes pivoting until they'd trampled out a small circle.

A strangled cry reached Jade's ears. The battling bulls had trodden on one of the prisoners, Nasur judging by the voice. It didn't stop them however. By now they seemed to have forgotten anything else around them. Darshash, pushed back against the small fire, didn't even notice that his robe had caught and that the flame was climbing up his back.

A branch snapped behind her, but before Jade could react she felt her knees buckle beneath her. A sharp pain blossomed up the back of her thighs and she hit the ground, kneeling.

She twisted around in time to see Allenby haul back his thick branch, preparatory to striking Sam.

"Look out, Sam!"

He didn't need her warning. He was already facing Allenby.

Allenby took too long to manhandle the stout branch. It gave Sam the chance to duck and dodge the blow aimed at his head. The swinging, heavy log threw Allenby off balance. Sam rose up in front of him and jammed his fist into the man's stomach, knocking the wind out of him.

Allenby doubled forward, gagging and wheezing. Sam waited, apparently with some misguided sense of fair play until the man had regained his breath before punching him again.

"What are you waiting for?" Jade yelled. "Hit him again. Knock him out."

Allenby didn't seem to carry that burden of fair play. While he was doubled over, he reached for the gun that Sam had recently taken from him. Just as his fingers brushed the grip, the Englishman screamed as Jade drove her borrowed knife into Allenby's foot. He jerked his leg up, pulling his foot free of the ground, the knife still pinned in it.

Despite the pain or because of it, Allenby renewed his attempt at regaining his gun, lunging forward at Sam, screaming as he moved. Jade tried to retrieve the knife, but Allenby had shifted out of her reach and her knees refused to carry her weight.

"Sam!"

Sam quickly aimed his Colt and fired into the man's right shoulder.

Allenby fell back with a moan. Sam jerked the knife free and handed it, blade first to Jade.

"Can you stand?" he asked.

"I think so. Nothing's broken." She held up her left hand. "Help me up."

He pulled her to her feet, and she stood for a moment braced against him, letting her legs recover their strength.

"Your gun worked against Allenby all right."

"You noticed that, did you?"

She didn't answer but nodded instead to the battling men. By now their hands were both wrapped around each other's thick necks.

"Come on," she said, "while those two are occupied, let's get in there and free the others."

Jade and Sam broke free of the last bit of tangling cover and raced for the monuments. Before them loomed the two combatants, now locked as one. Fire flashed across the back of one side of them, framing him as in tongues of licking blood. Musa shoved his opponent against the edge of the stone marker and the pair tumbled. The battle continued on the ground as they rolled, half-ablaze, the fire diminishing each time Darshash rolled to the top.

Closer and closer they came to the opening into the shrine.

"*Al mawtu alaikum!*" shrieked Darshash, raising one hand and the knife with it.

Death be upon you!

Musa gave a titanic heave. "*Al mawtu alaikum, Akhee!*" he yelled.

Teasdale gasped as the two opponents tumbled over the edge and into the shrine.

CHAPTER 29

Such a person can make charms to bring love or to cast out a thief. Or they might be hired to make a charm to render a thief invisible. They'll work both sides of the law for a price.
- - The Traveler

"Hazar is in there!" said Jade. "Those two will crush her." She noted that someone else had the same concern. Teasdale, his hands still bound in front of him, struggled on his knees to reach the stairs into the pit.

"Hazar!" he shouted. "Can you hear me? I'm coming."

"Untie them," ordered Sam as he dashed into the hole.

Jade used Musa's knife and sliced through Teasdale's bonds. Then she freed Nasur. The sailor moaned, and Jade gently prodded his hands and forearm to see if they'd been broken when Musa and Darshash had stomped on them.

"Teasdale, help this man away from here. Hide before anyone else comes back."

"No. I must help Hazar."

"Sam'll take care of her. Trust me." She hurriedly examined Mahir, feeling at his neck for a pulse. The man still lived, Darshash's knife blade having grazed or possibly pierced his right lung.

Sam emerged from the shrine pit with Hazar in his arms.

"Over here, Sam." Jade motioned to the trees where Sam had previously waited before shooting Mahir. "How is she?"

"I think all right," he answered. "She was huddled flat up against the near side. Good thing, too. Otherwise she would have been crushed but as it was, those two must have rolled right over the top of her. I left them down there still struggling."

Sam handed over Hazar to an insistent Teasdale then joined Jade in assisting Nasur to his feet to follow.

"Get under cover," Jade ordered. "Hide yourselves in case any of those other people come back."

"What will *you* do?" asked Nasur. "Please, you must come away from this evil place."

"Nasur," said Jade, gently gripping the man by his shoulders. "My mother is alive. But I must stop the evil before it strikes again."

"Alive? The lady Inez lives? Truly? Then God is good and I must help you."

"No, Nasur. You must rest here so that we can all leave together."

She didn't wait for his compliance. Instead she joined Sam as he headed back for the shrine.

"Get behind me," Sam ordered. He held his Colt in front of him.

"What if it still doesn't fire?"

"Then I'll use it as a club."

They kept close to one wall as they descended the steps and entered the shrine. A fire burned in an earthen bowl below the altar, backlighting the titanic struggle before them. Sam had said there that was a bizarre sort of altar down below. Jade had not known what to expect but nothing in her wildest imagination prepared her for the hideous statue that gloated over the battle in front of it.

An owl's body gave rise to bat wings and its talons rested on what appeared to be a dog which grew out of the same twisted hindquarters as did a leopard. Each animal appeared to be in a death struggle and, behind them all was a gaping maw with human teeth, seemingly devouring them. The flickering fire only enhanced the horrific vision, making the limbs twitch and the wings beat. Worst of all, she heard a rasping breath issuing from that mouth. It sounded as if the human portion was softly laughing.

The two men shifted their struggle from the opposite wall to just before the low, stone altar, blocking Jade's view of the shrine. They stepped in and out of the fire bowl, indifferent to its flames on their sandaled feet. Darshash still held her knife, and with his hands wrapped around Musa's thick neck, he twisted the blade so that it sliced across Musa's shoulders. Already Musa's robe was shredded to ribbons.

"What should we do?" Jade whispered to Sam. "Can you get a clear shot on Darshash?"

Sam shook his head. "In here I can't tell who's who."

"Darshash is on the left," Jade said. "I can tell by the burnt robe. And he's the one with my knife."

"I'll aim for the dirt in front of them. That should startle them enough to separate. Then I'll be able to get Darshash without hitting the other fellow."

Jade held her borrowed knife at the ready. If Sam's Colt refused to fire, she planned to jump in and help Musa.

"Cover your ears," Sam said.

She didn't. The *bang* exploded in the room and in her head. The roars of Darshash and Musa continued unabated but now sounded as if she were underwater. The bullet struck the shallow dirt in front of their feet, hitting rock beneath it. It ricocheted at a low angle between the men's legs and into the fire bowl, shattering it. Charcoaled wood spilled out across the floor, each glowing red like some demon's eye. From there the bullet struck the statue.

Through it all, Darshash and Musa continued their battle.
Enough is enough.

Jade darted forward and made a low swipe with her blade into Darshash's right hamstring. Blood spurted out, hitting a coal with an evil sizzle, filling the air with its hot, sickly sweet scent.

It gave Musa the edge he needed to finish the job. The big eunuch heaved Darshash backwards and rammed the back of his opponent's skull on the stone altar.

Jade's hearing was returning and she heard Darshash cry out in pain, his eyes wide with hatred laced with a newfound terror.

Darshash's grip on Musa lessened. Musa held Darshash down with his left hand and, with his right, grasped the knife that has worried his back for so long.

Then in one slicing motion, Darshash lay dead against the altar, his throat gashed.

Musa tilted his head back and released a victorious roar.

Once again, Jade could have sworn she heard the hellish statue laugh softly.

CHAPTER 30

The next grade consists of the Mchawi, the wizards. They utilize corpses to make poison charms and thrive on fear and the night.
- - The Traveler

Jade didn't wait to congratulate Musa on his victory. She only wanted to get out of that hell hole as quickly as possible, knowing that what she'd seen and had imagined hearing would haunt her dreams for years to come. She didn't even care to retrieve her own knife. There was no way she could ever carry that one again after it been party to that sacrifice.

She stumbled up the stairs and into the cool night air, her legs twinging with pain. Sam followed close behind, his hand warm and supportive on her back. And then it was his arm around her, leading her away from the opening and towards the trees.

She didn't make it that far. Six steps from the entrance, her legs buckled under her and she stumbled. Sam sat her down on the ground, her back against one of the lesser stone monuments.

"It's over, now," he said softly.

"Is it?" Jade looked around, expecting to see a hoard of dog-people charge them. Quiet ruled. Only Mahir's labored, wheezing breaths broke the stillness.

Sam sat down beside her. "Darshash is dead. We have that Allenby fellow, too." He looked around at the still cemetery. "Yep. It's all over except to haul Allenby back to Chake Chake."

Jade struggled to get up and reached down for Sam's hand. "I'm worried about Mother and Dad. We sent them back with Teasdale and somehow, Teasdale ended up a captive. And that man lying over there," she pointed to Mahir, "The one you shot. He's from the nearest village. If they stopped there, he might have taken them." She shuddered. "They might be dead. We need to get back to the village and find them."

"First we need to have a word with your Mr. Teasdale." Sam started to stand up, groaned, and sat back against the stone. "Hell, I hurt all over. Teasdale!" he called. "It's safe now. You can come out."

Teasdale emerged a moment later from the trees holding hands with a trembling Hazar. Nasur followed half behind her, lending support when her slippered feet stumbled.

"What happened, Teasdale?" asked Sam. "We sent you back to Chake Chake. Where are the freed slaves? Where are Jade's parents?"

"I . . . I left them or rather they left me." He pulled himself up straighter and peered down his nose at Sam. "Miss del Cameron's parents decided that they should come back to assist you and left me to take the men to Chake Chake."

"But you didn't," said Sam, rising to his feet. He stood four inches taller than Teasdale and lorded every inch of it over him. "So I'll ask you again, what happened?"

"I sent the men to Chake Chake with Thomas. I decided to return for my hard fought treasure so that I can marry Hazar."

"You let my parents come back on their own?" Jade grabbed Teasdale by the collar and shook him like a rag doll. "Where are they? Why haven't we seen them yet?"

"How did you get captured?" asked Sam.

"I'll tell you if you get your she-cat under control."

"No, I don't think I will," said Sam. "Because she's all that stands between you and me. Now answer my question."

"I stopped at the village to get some food and water. Mahir took me prisoner. I didn't know that he was one of them. The other men wouldn't stop. Now I know why."

Hazar moaned and swayed, slipping to the ground in a faint. Teasdale instantly knelt beside her, patting her hand.

"Poor kid," said Sam. "She's had a terrible ordeal."

Jade looked over her shoulder to the opening to the shrine and shuddered. "Where's Musa? He vowed he'd save his little Hazar and bring her home. He should have come up by now."

"Maybe he was injured more than we knew," suggested Sam. "I'll go down and look."

"Not alone you won't," said Jade. "That place gives me the shivers and I'm not letting you out of my sight down there." She flinched with pain as she took a step.

"Nasur can come with me, right Nasur?" asked Sam.

Nasur took a wary step back, his eyes darting from Jade to Sam.

"No," argued Jade, but the remainder of her words were cut short when Musa rose like Lazarus from the tomb. He clutched the bloody knife that had slain Darshash and his own ripped robe was dashed with blood which looked like wet black smears in the dim firelight. Only when he turned into the full moonlight did the crimson splash reveal its true origins. His black eyes stared in a haunted way, past them, through them and his steps were labored and sluggish.

"Musa," said Jade. "You did it. You saved Hazar from Darshash.

At Hazar's name, a spark of awareness came to Musa's eyes. He turned to Jade.

"That spawn of hell was wed to my little sister. He planned to sacrifice her to join the guild."

"I know," said Jade in a soothing voice. "But her suffering is over now. You can return her safely to her father to await a better suitor, a real suitor." She avoided looking at Teasdale, afraid that Musa would turn his rage on the Englishman.

As though he could read her mind, Musa's gaze shot around towards Teasdale as he knelt beside Hazar's still little body. He took one menacing step forward and Teasdale immediately scrambled back, putting distance between himself and his beloved.

"He meant her no harm," said Jade, trying to step between them. "He was tending to her. He knows what she suffered."

Musa's head dropped so that his chin touched his thick chest. Suddenly he threw his head back and, gripping his robe, ripped the front as his throat erupted in an anguished cry.

"It is not enough!" he shouted. "It is not enough!"

And from the distant trees came a howl, followed by the barking of dogs.

CHAPTER 31

Their night rituals begin with the call of an owl. And fearsome as these wizards are, they still do not possess the highest power.
- - The Traveler

"They're coming back, Sam. They're coming back. We need to leave now and find my parents."

"What about Allenby?" Sam asked.

"Leave him. He's hidden. We'll report him when we get to Chake Chake."

"I'd like to shove him in that slave pit and hold him there until the authorities arrive," said Sam. "Give him a taste of his own medicine."

Another howl, less faint than before cut through the night.

Jade shook her head. "No time." She turned to Musa. "Musa, can you carry Hazar?"

The big man didn't respond. His eyes had a distant look to them, his head turned towards the location of the last howl.

"Musa!" said Jade. She shook his arm. "Musa we need you. Hazar needs you."

He glanced at Hazar, lying on the ground in a dead faint then turned his hollow gaze to Jade. "It was not enough."

"I know," said Jade. "Darshash didn't deserve such a quick death for what he did to Hazar. But he's dead now. He can't hurt her. Not anymore." She jerked her thumb towards the forest and the barking. Jade thought she detected at least three different voices in the now-diminished pack, but wondered if more would come once they regained their courage. "But *they* can. We need to leave. You need to carry her."

"My Hazar," he murmured. "My dear little sister." He stooped and picked up the girl as easily as if she were a doll.

Jade took a step and winced, her left knee throbbing. As she rubbed her knee, she saw Musa cradle the spoiled little Hazar to his exposed chest and felt another pang, this time in her throat.

And who ever cared for little Tisha? Who was there to protect and cradle her?

She thought about Tisha's brightly colored new kanga, the one with the leopards on it. What had the women in Chake Chake told her? The leopards represented witchcraft. So Tisha had somehow guessed or found out that Darshash meant to sacrifice the girl after marrying her. She wore the kanga to warn Hazar.

But would Hazar have even recognized that coded message? Perhaps the message had been meant for Musa's eyes. He went out into the streets. He's seen women wearing khanga. He surely would have understood the underlying warning.

Darshash must have seen it first. He, too, would have known the message. Tisha paid the price of loyalty with her life.

Darshash's death didn't bring back Tisha so perhaps, as Musa exclaimed, it *hadn't* been enough.

The next dog-like howl sounded closer. The opportunity to leave unnoticed had rapidly dwindled to nearly no time. Jade fingered her borrowed knife. The pack head lay dead. *Time to finish the rest of the pack. Then it might be enough.* Somehow Jade doubted it.

"Can we make it, Sam?" she asked.

"Possibly, if you run for the house."

His pronoun choice wasn't lost on Jade. "While you hold them off alone? No. But Musa could take Hazar there. I think I hear three voices, maybe four. The two of us can take them."

"Obedience isn't your strong suit, is it dear?"

Jade grinned. "Are you just now learning that?"

Sam planted a quick kiss on her cheek and handed her Allenby's gun.

"All right then. The two of us." He turned towards Musa. "Quickly, take the girl to safety at the house. Lead these two men as well," he added pointing to Nasur and Teasdale. "They are unarmed and cannot help us fight."

Musa raised his head as the barking grew louder but he didn't move. Then he half-turned and looked back at the gaping hole leading into the shrine.

"Hurry, man!" shouted Sam.

Teasdale's eyes grew wide with a look of panic. "The slave pit!" he exclaimed. "We could hide in there. If we're very still, they won't know we're in there."

"You want us to lock you in there again?" asked Sam.

"You could shut the door on us but leave it unbarred," said Teasdale. "In case . . . well in case you . . ."

"You mean in case they kill us?" asked Jade, "So you can still get out later?"

"Right," said Teasdale.

Another howl followed by several snarls. This time the noises sounded no closer but, instead, seemed to be moving around the periphery. Jade tried to count the voices. "They're trying to flank us."

"Come on," urged Teasdale. "All of us. Miss del Cameron and Mr. Featherstone can take cover behind that statue and shoot anyone that comes in."

Teasdale ran towards the stairs, waving Musa to follow him with Hazar. Nasur hung back, clearly uncertain about going into the pit. Jade understood his hesitation.

"Sam and I are not going to stay down there and let these monsters shut us all in by sliding back the monument over the pit. If you want to take cover behind that statue from hell, do so. Make up your mind, the pit or run for the house, but do it now!"

As Teasdale hurried towards the pit, a horrid thought jumped into Jade's mind. The kanga's written message meant that someone who had shared a meal with Hazar was an enemy. Teasdale had been served refreshments with Hazar during his teaching sessions. He'd lived on the island long enough that he probably knew about kanga. He was ambitious.

And now he's anxious to take Hazar into the shrine! It can't be true, can it?

But there he was, next to the pit, encouraging Musa to hand Hazar to him. Musa, however, was having none of it. He took two steps down, turning Hazar's face away from her erstwhile suitor.

That's when Hazar regained consciousness and, seeing either the horrific statue below or Darshash's bloody body, screamed. She clawed at Musa, struggling to be free. Teasdale saw his advantage and grabbed for her.

In the distraction, no one saw Mahir struggle to his knees until it was too late.

He wrapped his arms around Sam's legs and yanked him down, Sam's Colt flying out of his hands and beyond reach.

From the bowels of the shrine, Jade heard the same low throaty chuckle that she'd heard earlier.

Only louder.

Sounds, like scents, have a primal effect. The maleficent tones gurgled up like toxic fumes burbling from a stagnant bog. Jade felt the sounds course through her sinews, weakening them till she felt as weak as a sick child. Her gaze was riveted on the hole, waiting with horrified fascination. She wouldn't have been surprised if that statue emerged.

"Jade!" shouted Sam. "I could use some help here."

He'd rolled over to a half-sitting position and kicked hard with his prosthetic leg. The heavy oak hit Mahir's jaw with shattering force. Jade heard the man's jaw crack, saw the teeth fly. Still the man kept coming after Sam as one possessed. With every wheezing breath, blood trickled from his wounds and out of his mouth. But the man was sustained by a power that seemed to make all pain vanish.

"Shoot him, Jade. Shoot him!"

Jade forced herself to block out Hazar's screams, Teasdale's shouts, and that hideous laughter and raised Allenby's pistol, a Webley revolver, .455 caliber. Her upper arm muscles quivered as she tried to draw a bead on Mahir who'd already gathered himself for another lunge at Sam. Mahir's bloodied lips curled back in a feral snarl, his eyes glowing in the moonlight.

Jade fired.

The gun "clicked" on an empty chamber.

She fired six times in succession, each with the same result.

Empty?

She opened the barrel chamber, expecting to see empty slots. All but three were full with rounds.

"Nasur," she shouted, "Nasur, help the girl. Get her away from here now."

Nasur, who'd stood riveted to one spot as the surroundings dissolved into horror all around them, blinked twice and, after a brief hesitation, lumbered towards Musa and Teasdale.

Jade stuck the Webley in her side pocket and ran towards Sam, scooping up a burning branch from the small fire as she did so.

She swung hard and slammed the wood into Mahir's side, knocking him away from Sam. The fire immediately caught on his cotton robe, licking up the sleeve of his upraised arm. Still the man kept coming, but by now Sam was up and ready to meet him.

Jade looked to see if Nasur had gotten away with Hazar but within seconds of stepping clear of Sam's pounding fist-fight, she heard the pack returning. Two hunched shapes leaped into the cemetery, charging her.

She went down under their combined force as two new barking voices joined in.

CHAPTER 32

Full membership in the Guild requires a tremendous sacrifice; the murder of a spouse, child, parent or other close family member. It must be done by the applicant's own hands.
- - The Traveler

Time suspended itself until Jade believed she's entered into Hell in a never-ending, living nightmare. Two bodies collided atop her, both growling, both snapping for her jugular. They fought against each other as much as against her, each trying to push the other aside in an attempt to rip her throat. It was all that saved her.

She held her left arm arced over her neck for protection and, with her right, punched and shoved each of the attackers. Once she was able to shove her right knee up into an exposed stomach, temporarily winding one.

But the respite was short, too short to reach around for the Webley. Not that it had worked before, but Jade prayed that this pair of lesser practitioners had less power and would be more vulnerable. The idea would have seemed ludicrous a day ago, but by now, Jade believed it.

The creature on the left - Jade had a hard time thinking of them as people - snapped at the raggedly dressed female on Jade's right. In a flash of inspiration, she decided to use that against them and play the pair off of each other. Instead of pushing her assailants off on their respective sides, she again jammed her knee into the female but this time shoved her hard into the male. As she hoped, the pair spent more time snapping and clawing at each other. It gave her just enough time to draw the revolver and fire point blank into the female's hip.

The revolver went off like a thunderclap and the female writhed, screaming in pain on top of the male.

Jade rolled away and scrambled to her feet as the two tore into each other. To her left, Nasur, Teasdale, and Musa struggled as one mass until Jade couldn't tell who was fighting whom. Poor Hazar had once again fallen in a heap at their feet, her legs dangling into the pit's stairwell. To her right, Sam grappled with Mahir, alight like a living torch. Before she could react and go to anyone's aid, four more howling practitioners raced into the cemetery.

The fire's glare made it difficult to discern much more than shapes but they ran hunched as on all fours. They split; one of the frontrunners racing towards Nasur, Teasdale, and Musa, a second towards Sam and Mahir, and the other two towards her.

The male on the ground had nearly ripped open the female's neck. Jade aimed and shot him in the chest, then turned the revolver on the creatures rapidly advancing towards her. The one running slightly to the rear was gaining, and Jade took a split second to decide which one to shoot first.

Two more barking voices joined the fray, these figures running upright. They separated, the larger one racing towards Sam, the other towards her.

Then she heard the newest attacker bark again and recognized the voice.

"Mother, get back!" Jade ordered.

"I have the one on my right, Jade." Inez held up a stout branch and swung hard.

Jade didn't wait to see what happened as the other howling body leaped towards her. The person, for it was human, made a horrid spectacle, jaws open, eyes wild and dilated, claw-like fingernails reaching, scrabbling for her skin. She fired just as the creature's arm reached her, the shot going wild. An empty click answered the next attempt.

Jade kicked, her foot striking a hard, muscular stomach. At the same time she flipped the Webley to her left hand, holding it by the warm barrel, and pulled the knife from her boot sheath. To the side, she saw that her mother had felled the other Pemban with a blow to his head, adding another to his legs for good measure.

Her attacker, a female, lunged again, and she saw that the woman's teeth were filed to points. Jade wielded the Webley like a club and struck the woman in the mouth, shattering several of her teeth as she sliced at the witch's outstretched palms. Another kick and the woman fell backwards. In an instant, Inez was there, her branch slamming down on the woman's chest.

"Hamstring her, Jade. And the other one, too."

Jade did without hesitation, rendering both of the monsters helpless.

When Jade looked up, it was to see her father pulling a large male away from Sam's back, Richard's muscular left arm wrapped in a chokehold around the witch's neck. Sam, free for the moment, went after Mahir with his bare fists, pelting the man's jaw, throat and chest in a relentless barrage.

Someone screamed and Jade saw Nasur try to crawl away from the last of the four newcomers. This witch was also on the ground and bleeding from his mouth, but he had one claw in a tight grip around Nasur's ankle.

"I have him," shouted Inez. "Get Hazar."

Jade spun around to face the monuments where Musa, Nasur, and Teasdale had been wrestling moments before. They were still there, minus Nasur. Now the muscular Musa had the advantage despite Teasdale's ferocious attempts to batter the man.

But where was Hazar? Jade had last seen her lying across the stone base, her legs dangling into the pit. *Did she slip inside?*

Had they pushed her in by accident?

Then Jade saw one frail little hand draped across the top of the entrance. She had slipped inside while Musa struggled to protect her. There was no way to reach her now, not without colliding with the two men. But the battle was nearing its end. Musa gripped Teasdale by his throat and, shaking him like a dog would shake a rat, hurled him aside. Without looking to see where he fell, Musa turned and went down the stairs, towards Hazar.

She must have come to for a moment, for her hand flailed in the air then gripped the stonework as though it were a lifeline. Musa scooped her up, cradling her for a moment. Then, to Jade's surprise and horror, he handed her down to someone or something waiting below.

Hazar's terrified scream cut the night air and was echoed by a low, cackling laugh from somewhere in the pit as Musa slowly descended out of sight.

Suddenly Jade understood. When Musa killed Darshash, he'd said, *"Al mawtu alaikum, Akhee."*

Death be upon you, my brother.

Musa had sacrificed his own brother.

But it wasn't enough!

CHAPTER 33

*But to turn back from the task once the choice has been made is to
risk a horrible death.*
- - The Traveler

Jade handed the Webley to her mother. "There's a round
left in there. Whatever happens, don't let them close the pit on
us."

"We won't."

Jade spared a loving glance at her father, busily binding the
hands and feet of the injured practitioners with vines. "Take
care of each other, Mother."

She grabbed a burning branch from the fire's remains,
turned and ran towards the pit, hot on Sam's heels. Sam, she
noted, had scooped up his Colt. Perhaps if he didn't yet believe
in his own power then it would work against Musa.

But Musa isn't the only monster in that pit.

The laugh bubbling up from below shook Jade to the
marrow.

*And that's the idea. He wants to weaken us before we enter the
shrine.*

She transferred the brand to her left hand and gripped her
knife in her right.

Witches burn.

227

The hidden witch's voice drifted up from the shrine as Jade and Sam's feet touched the first step.

"You have chosen a second sacrifice?" It sounded distant, inhuman, as though the shrine spoke, the words coming from the demonic mouths.

"Yes. The other, my brother, was not enough," said Musa. "I am not yet a man. You told me it would be enough."

Sam held out his left arm, cautioning Jade to slow down, to step softly.

"I know you let him take the girl so that you could meet him here and slay him," said the other disembodied voice. "But you hated your brother. What sacrifice was that to kill him? And yet, I do not think that this one is blood to you, is she?"

"She is as dear as my own."

"Yeeeesssss." The words hissed and sizzled. Fat in a fire.

Jade reached the bottom. Musa stood with his back to them in front of the altar, arranging Hazar on it as one might straighten a tablecloth and centerpiece. His gentle, loving movements as he straightened her robe made his plans more horrific. At his feet lay his brother's body.

"Then kill her now!" commanded the shrine. "Regain your manhood and take your power as a birthright."

Musa pulled the knife from his brother's corpse and raised his right arm.

In that instant, Sam took aim at the broad back and squeezed the trigger. Again, nothing.

"To hesitate is your own death!" screamed the other voice. "Do the deed!"

Sam and Jade didn't wait for Musa to make his decision. As one, they leapt forward.

Musa looked around, his face a contorted mask of pain and anguish. It quickly morphed into one of fury as he spun about to meet them. Sam dove for the big man's midsection, ramming his head into Musa's stomach.

"Ooof!" Musa grunted.

Unfortunately, Sam's force made little impact on the man's bulk and Musa's resulting loss of breath was as brief as their element of surprise.

Jade rushed in with her fire band and jabbed at Musa's right hand. The knife dropped, clanging first on the edge of the low altar and then onto the stone floor below.

She jumped back out of his reach, and Musa swung a beefy fist at Sam instead.

Jade flung the burning wood to the side and grabbed Hazar, dragging her off the altar. She hefted her, lifting with her knees and carried her towards the steps. But at every step the girl's weight seemed to increase until Jade staggered under the load.

The shrine laughed again, rejoicing in her difficulty.

Jade lowered Hazar to the floor near the steps and stood, breathing hard, striving to gain control of her quivering arm and leg muscles.

On the opposite side of the room, the malignant statue quivered as though it shrugged off its lifelessness and became animated. A shadowy figure emerged from in front of it or from inside of it. Jade couldn't tell and, by now, nothing would have surprised her.

"Lord God, come to my aid," she prayed. "Holy saints protect us."

The shape held the height and form of a human, twitching in the dim flickering fire light. It stooped, then raised again, the sacrificial knife in his hand.

My knife.

The figure stepped forward, letting the firelight illuminate his features.

"Jabu! YOU!"

Jade nearly didn't recognize the village elder for the chalky grey paint on his face streaked with red smears that appeared to wriggle across his brow and down his cheeks.

He grinned, his teeth flashing red in the light.

Sam continued his battle of feints and punches with Musa, striving to stay out of the eunuch's fists while driving home his own.

"Jade," he shouted. "Get away from here. Just go."

"You will not escape our reach," said Jabu in English. "We

have long arms for those that mock our rituals."

Jabu stepped to the side to circumvent the altar. As he did, his shoulder brushed the statue behind him. It quivered as though it anticipated the bloodbath to come.

It's wobbly!

"Sam, get ready to fire."

Sam landed an uppercut on Musa's chin and followed it with a left hook to the nose. "It doesn't work on them, remember?"

"You're not going to shoot them."

She retrieved her firebrand and raced forward to Sam's side, using the flame to drive Musa back as Jabu came around the altar. She jabbed the burning branch into Musa's face. He fell back against Jabu and the two tumbled onto the low altar.

"Aim for the base, Sam. Shoot!"

Sam fired his remaining shots into the base of the shrine as Jade ran around the back of it. Shards of coral limestone flew as the carved feet shattered. The sound hammered her ears as she ran to the back of the shrine and pushed with all her might.

The shrine teetered for a moment on its ancient base, resisting. Jade gave another heave. It made the decision. The shrine collapsed forward onto the altar, smashing itself onto the two witches.

Their screams echoed through the vault, dying out as low gurgles under the heavy stone blocks.

"Sacrifice yourselves!" Jade yelled.

She felt a pair of strong arms surround her and she let herself fall into Sam's embrace. "It's over. Right, Sam?"

He stroked her hair as he held her. "It's over. Let's get Hazar out of this pit."

"And close it back up," said Jade.

"Not yet. Not until we drag Allenby and all those other witches up top down here and lock them in that slave pen."

Jade pulled back to study Sam's face. "You're not thinking of leaving them to die in there, are you?"

"No. We'll tell the inspector in Mombasa about them. It may take him a while to get here or to send someone after them, but it will serve them right to have to face the same treatment they gave to so many others. Now let's get out of this hell hole and find your parents."

Sam kissed her lightly and led her by the hand away from the chalky cloud of rubble. When he reached Hazar, he stooped and picked up the girl, cradling her carefully up the steps and into the clear night air.

Jade's parents stood guard over the prisoners, some unconscious, others starting to rouse themselves.

"I've had enough of this dreadful island, Jade," said Inez. "If we're through here, I would like to go back to Zanzibar. I still haven't purchased any lace for your dress and--"

"Hang the lace, Mother. But yes, once we lock these people and Allenby in the slave pit, we should see about going home."

"We could wire the Sultan for his yacht," suggested Inez. "I'm sure poor Nasur would enjoy the privilege."

Nasur, having been saved a second time by Inez, knelt at her feet. "Honored lady. I owe you my life and my love. I will go with you anywhere and--"

"And that's *my* wife you are addressing, sir," interjected Richard. "If anyone is going to follow her around pledging life and love, that will be me."

Nasur sat down on a rock a few feet away, head on his hands.

"We should see if our Mombasa fisherman friends are still waiting for us. They've probably given us up for dead by now," said Sam, still holding Hazar in his arms. He set her gently on a patch of green, and stood behind Jade, his arms encircling her waist. "I'd rather us all go back together. I don't dare let you out of my sight again and I'm anxious to see how Gilbert and Robert are doing on my new plane."

Jade tried to turn to face Sam but he tightened his grip. "You know about the plane? Sam! That was supposed to be a surprise. Dad! How could you tell him."

Richard shrugged and grinned. "So are we agreed? Let's lock these prisoners in the slave pit and give them all a taste of their own medicine. Allenby, too. Then we'll all head for Chake

Chake, find a boat of some sort to get to Zanzibar, collect your things," He turned to his wife. "No lace, Inez, and get ourselves to Nairobi as soon as possible."

One of the witches roused herself and seeing Inez, bared her teeth and lunged, attempting to bite. Inez stepped neatly out of the way then clobbered the woman aside the head with the Webley's butt.

"Behave yourself!" Inez snapped.

Richard pulled his wife aside before she could deliver another blow. "Inez, what in the world am I going to do with you?"

Jade grinned and winked at her mother. "I wasn't aware, Dad, that anything needed to be done."

CHAPTER 34

There should be another word for those rites rather than "sacrifice."
True sacrifice gives of self rather than takes of others. Perhaps there is
another, more accurate term: murder.
- - The Traveler

Madeline Thompson stuck one last pin in Jade's wedding dress, securing the last bit of handmade lace to the hem. In the end, Inez had her way, but Jade didn't fight it. As long as the lace was limited to the bottom of her dress, she didn't mind. She knew that it could have been much worse. Her mother might have insisted in swathing her in yards of it over her head in some elaborate veil. Instead, Inez surprised her with her own wedding veil, a simple, but elegant fall of ethereal tulle held in place with a wreath of tiny, silk ribbon roses.

"This is so lovely, Mrs. del Cameron," said Maddy. "You have such exquisite taste. I'll have the lace sewn on by this evening, Jade," she added. "Oh, Jade, you look so beautiful. Sam is a very lucky man."

"Speaking of Sam," said Beverly Dunbury, "where is he?"

Jade stepped down from the foot stool.

"He went with Dad, Avery and Neville back out to Neville and Maddy's farm. They are all working on that plane. I'll be surprised if we see any of them for the wedding tomorrow."

A pitiful chirp sounded outside of Beverly's bedroom door.

"Biscuit's still calling for you. He isn't going to hold out much longer," said Maddy. "You'd better change out of your dress and go to him before he wakes the children."

"Since I came back he hasn't let me out of his sight," said Jade. She slipped off the gown and pulled on her usual trousers and shirt. Then taking hold of her boots, she motioned to her mother. "Come, Mother, let's take the old boy outside."

"We'll join you in a moment," said Beverly.

Jade and Inez opened the door and collided immediately with a majestic cheetah whose throat erupted in a deep rumbling purr. Jade led the way out onto the Dunbury's spacious and shady veranda and sat down to pull on her boots while her mother took a chair. Biscuit kept butting his head against Jade's chin and shoulders, making it impossible for her to don her boots.

"I missed you, too, Biscuit." She scratched his broad head and soft, rounded ears. "Now go say hi to Mother and let me finish getting dressed."

Biscuit gave a quick rub against Inez's legs, brushing her split skirt.

"Hello, Biscuit. What a lovely cat you are. Are you going to behave when Jade goes on her honeymoon?" She looked up as Maddy and Beverly came out and joined them. "Is Biscuit going back to your farm, Madeline, while Jade and Sam travel?"

"He's going with us," said Jade.

"What?" asked Inez. "But, Jade."

"There's room in that new plane for a third person. He'll fly with us."

"Should be a most interesting honeymoon," said Beverly with a melodious laugh. "A ménage a trios of a different sort."

"Jade," said Maddy, "I didn't hear your entire story last evening. I missed some parts when I went to tend to little Cyril." She pulled a notebook and pencil from her pocket.

"Maddy, you're not planning on using this in another book, are you?"

"Why not, Jade. They sell so well. And this one is deliciously twisted. Now explain to me about Musa and Darshash being brothers"

"Twins, actually," said Jade. "A situation that is not always welcome. It seems on Pemba that one of the twins is usually not left to live. Musa's mother must have tried to keep them both, but at some point, she had to make a choice. So, she sold Musa as a slave to be made a eunuch and kept his brother intact. Musa saw his brother often in later years and hated him for his situation and full manhood."

"They did resemble each other," added Inez. "Jade, do you remember the questionable ladies of Chake Chake? They had seen Musa and thought he was Darshash at first."

"Do you suppose he would have really sacrificed that girl, Hazar?" asked Beverly.

"We'll never know, but I would guess, yes," said Jade.

Beverly adjusted the skirt of her pale yellow dress. "But your friend Teasdale found his treasure so I should imagine he'll marry his Hazar soon and she'll have all the pretty gowns that her spoiled little heart desired."

"No," said Inez.

"No?" asked Beverly and Maddy at once.

"No," repeated Jade. "The last we heard, Hazar ran off with a wealthy German merchant."

"Poor Mr. Teasdale," said Maddy. "I suppose he's better off, though."

"Poor Tisha," said Jade. "She was the one sunny soul in all of this and she's gone now."

Inez stood and walked over to Jade. She kissed her daughter atop her head. "Tisha is at peace in heaven now, Jade. And you brought her killer to justice. I am proud of you."

"So Musa killed her?" asked Beverly. "Not Darshash?"

"I believe so," said Jade. "She must have overheard Musa tell Darshash that he would come to Pemba with them and help him sacrifice Hazar. From what the head witch said, it was all a ruse to put Musa in the position to kill his brother. Maybe Tisha didn't know that, or maybe she suspected that Musa himself might kill Hazar. Either way, Tisha must have worn the kanga to warn Hazar, but Hazar didn't understand the language of the kangas. So she ran to Teasdale for help.

Jade sighed. "Even when Tisha had her freedom, she still thought about Hazar and gave her life trying to warn her. But Musa *did* understand. He must have followed and killed her. I can still remember his fury when he learned that Hazar had been taken away while he was out; that they didn't wait for him."

"And then, knowing that we might follow, he had our boat weakened to drown us," added Inez. "An evil man. At least Allenby told the authorities how to stop the slavers. All to reduce his own punishment, I'm sure."

"A lot of evil, selfish people," murmured Jade. "And one brave little girl." She leaned over and buried her face in Biscuit's golden fur.

***

The Nairobi newspapers described the wedding in as brief of terms as possible, the Standard simply stating: *American photographer Jade del Cameron wed American pilot and filmmaker Sam Featherstone at the French Catholic mission, Father Jacquinet officiating.* The Leader chose to focus on Lady Avery Dunbury's private reception at Madeline and Neville Thompson's coffee farm.

With so few people receiving invitations, and so little information posted in the papers, speculations ran wild.

They had no idea that a gorgeous cheetah insisted on striding down the aisle with Jade and her father and lounged beside Jade and Sam as they knelt before the altar.

And though it was spoken of by house servants and Kikuyu farm hands, no one reported that the young Kikuyu shaman, Jelani, blessed the marriage before the huge ngoma on the Thompson's farm, a celebration that lasted well into the night.

Several outlying farmers reported seeing a new, larger aeroplane fly north east from the Thompson's farm, but no one remarked on the frantic, rasping yelps of the nervous cheetah riding in the front seat.

AUTHOR'S NOTES

Witchcraft is real as are underground slave pits. Slavery
continued illegally for years after it was "officially" stopped.

Some cemeteries are purported to have underground
shrines, but not to evil. I invented this shrine and the statue,
but the sacrifices of family members for full membership in the
Pemba Island witchcraft guild has been documented by several
people.

For those wishing to read more about early Zanzibar and
Pemba, they might try the following:

*From Slaves to Squatters: Plantation Labor and Agriculture in
Zanzibar and Coastal Kenya, 1890-1925* by Frederick Cooper,
1997.

*Pastimes & Politics, Culture, Community, and Identity in Post-
Abolition Urban Zanzibar, 1890-1945* by Laura Fair, 2001.

Pemba, The Spice Island of Zanzibar by John Evelyn Edmund,
1913.

Zanzibar, Its History and Its People by W. H. Ingrams, 1931.

Zanzibar The Island Metropolis of Eastern Africa by Major F.B.
Pearce, C.M.G., 1920.

Lastly, thanks to all the faithful readers that waited patiently
for another Jade mystery.

ABOUT THE AUTHOR

Suzanne Arruda, a zookeeper turned science teacher and freelance writer, is also the author of several biographies for young adults as well as science and nature articles for adults and children. An avid hiker, outdoorswomen, she lives in Kansas with her husband. You can reach her on Facebook (Suzanne Arruda, Mystery Writer) and at www.suzannearruda.com.